Harmon Creek

By

Thomas Fenske

Harmon Creek

The Model A's door opened and Earl emerged with one hand tightly pressed against his shoulder. He recognized the man as the same fellow who was reading the newspaper at the café.

"You! You're her partner in all of this?"

"Hey, mister, I just stopped to help, that's all." Fred approached the passenger side of the car, keeping the auto between the two of them. Earl began to maneuver toward the rear so Fred quickly ducked his head into the car, spied the ice pick and grabbed it. By the time Fred emerged, Earl had closed the distance and grabbed him by the lapels. Fred reacted against this onslaught with one swift, practiced motion. Earl released the smaller man and clutched at the center of his chest, then gasped and started to speak but dropped to his knees, and fell to his side.

"Oh, geez, Freddy," Betty said, as Fred stepped back, still holding the bloody ice pick in his hand.

"He put his hands on me. It was just instinct, like I was back in the pen."

"What do we do now? This ain't what McIntyre wanted. I have a feeling he ain't going to like this at all."

Fred wiped at his hands with a handkerchief, then wrapped it around the ice pick and stuck it in his pocket. "Like it or not, he's as deep in this as we are now, but we gotta figure a way to fix it."

He hesitated and looked up at the moon, then turned to Betty. "I followed you the whole way out the café and down the road, so I don't think nobody saw any of us. It was dark. That means they got nothing on us except at that café and that was all innocent-like. I'll go down tomorrow and slip the waitress a Jackson. After that, I'm sure she'll keep her mouth shut."

Earl moaned and they both stared wide-eyed.

"Oh, geez, Freddy. He's still alive."

"I've got me an idea, but I'll need your help. Let's put him back in the car."

What They Are Saying About
Harmon Creek

"Well-written…The writing perfectly evokes the 1930s rural Texas setting. The characters' situations, Claude's troubles and Earl's election, are compelling.

This is a solid historical crime novel."

—Black Rose Writing

Harmon Creek

By

Thomas Fenske

Crime Novel

Copyright © 2022 by: Thomas Fenske
ISBN: 979-8-9928799-5-7

Originally published by Wings ePress, Inc.

Edited by: Jeanne Smith
Copy Edited by: Linda Rettstatt
Executive Editor: Jeanne Smith
Cover Artist: Trisha FitzGerald-Jung

Published In the United States Of America

Dedication

I dedicate this book to all of my grandchildren: Justin, Alex, Travis, Griffin, London and Tierney Pearl Sweet.

***

The following fictional tale is based on a true story.

One

Tuesday, July 1, 1930

Huntsville, Texas—9:55 a.m.

Claude fidgeted in the freshly laundered clothes Evie had brought him to wear in court. He ran clammy fingers between his neck and the starchy collar that bit into his skin like a convention of ticks. The stiff pant legs in his overalls crinkled whenever he readjusted his ample frame on the hard bench. He looked around, but no one seemed aware of the racket except for him. The relentless rhythmic tapping from the clock in the corner reminded him of the weeks he'd wasted in jail and every click represented another second away from his life.

Claude knew deep inside he had always tried to be a good man, but he wished he had paid attention to Evie's warning last May, the night before he'd ventured onto the roadway near Harmon Creek.

"I seen something awful out there by that creek," she had told him. "There was blood and a car wreck and I seen you there too, tending to a dying man. But what hurt him the most wasn't from no accident."

1

That was all he could get out of her, except for her beseeching him not to go. Her visions always scared the dickens out of him, but he had business to conduct that night and they needed the money, so he had gone anyway.

He'd put in ten long, hard years at the Laidlaw Sawmill before it went out of business the last week of December. Jobs were hard enough to find for a white man, but for Claude, it was almost impossible, even though he had a reputation for dependability and a knack for fixing things. He sometimes played dominoes with a few fellows down the road, and shortly after the layoff, one of them suggested he could possibly pick up a few bucks making hooch.

"The money's good and I knows your daddy taught you how to do it," JoJo had told him. "Just don't run up against the big boys. Keep it small. If they find out about you, they'll lean on you hard." JoJo was a good domino player so Claude figured at the time he must know a thing or two about getting by.

Claude set up shop on a flat area in the bottomland close to Harmon Creek, near his secret hunting and fishing spot, a location he'd known since childhood. He remembered the first time he'd seen the odd, tiny clearing next to the large, bent pine tree. His granddaddy had told him the ground was permanently bare because it was a place where the devil did his dirty work. Since that day, he'd avoided it for years, silently passing by while in pursuit of food for the table.

"Maybe it's as it should be," he said when he surveyed it for his new enterprise. He deemed the flat and secluded location perfect for the task. "Preacher Davis calls alcohol 'the Devil's elixir,' so maybe this *is* a fitting place."

He began to assemble what he needed just as soon as it was spring enough to work outside. Beulah, his mule, had done the heavy hauling for him, at least until she died. He hated to lose her, but she was old when he got her and he knew she'd had a rough life.

He learned something of the basics when he was ten. Like JoJo had reminded him, his daddy dabbled in the distilled arts, and he'd helped when he could. Making hooch wasn't totally against the law back then, but it was, as his daddy had said, "a way of grabbing some liquid refreshment on the cheap." Claude was sure the fact the old man could pick up some gaming money on the side was an added benefit. His daddy worked hard, drank hard, and played hard, the very recipe that led to his early passing.

He remembered the old man whittling kindling strips off dried oak branches with his oversized ivory-handled pocket knife, then starting a fire under the boiler. The knife had intricate carvings in the handle and Claude would marvel at them whenever his father let him hold it for even a little while.

"Scrimshaw," the old man had said, although the word meant nothing to the boy.

He'd slice thick, even curls of wood and add them under piles of larger branches. The crisp splinters crackled like his great-grandmother's knees as they sparked to life and began the process of turning the mash into a brew.

Claude pulled again at his collar, rousted out of his daydream momentarily as more people filed into the cavernous chamber. The courtroom in July was almost as hot as it had been that late May night weeks earlier when he'd been arrested. He had carried a box of six mason jars full of his moonshine up to the turnoff for the new bridge over Harmon Creek, where he had arranged a sale. His hidden still was within walking distance to the bridge. Without Beulah, he had to hoof it everywhere and could only sell as much as he could carry, but that was a lot. Years of wrestling log carcasses into the big spinning sawmill blade had tempered his muscles and tendons into bands of steel. A car appeared and he was happy they were on time because he needed the money.

"I got my eye on a new mule," he had told Evie a week or so earlier. She'd been dead set against the idea of bootlegging from the start. He was headstrong and had won the argument that one

3

time and that night he had ignored her vision as well. As it turned out, she had been right all along and he wished he had listened to her.

The car slowed and three white men got out. They were definitely not the college boys he had talked to the previous day in town.

Then he heard, "You in a heap 'o trouble, boy," before he saw the flash of a badge on the coat of the driver and realized someone had squealed on him.

The two others rushed him and one hit him in the head with a two-foot length of thick dowel, knocking him to the ground where another man kicked him once in the ribs. He knew he could have likely held his own, but a black man just didn't raise a fist to a white man in this state, especially white lawmen. Not fighting back was risky...he knew many who would have tried, but he figured he had a better chance of living if he just took it. He was glad he had forgotten his daddy's knife, or he might have entertained more of an inclination to put up a fight. He'd sure hate to lose that knife; it was the only thing of his daddy's he still owned.

They put heavy manacles on his wrists, and it took all three of them to lift him to his feet. "You're lucky we're with the county. The G-men would have been rough with you," one of them quipped.

After a week in jail, the white man sitting next to him in court sent for him. Claude had liked the man from the start because he got right down to business.

"My name is Earl Swanger. I'm not about to let you go to trial without a good lawyer," he had told him. "Reverend Erasmus Davis has arranged for me to take the case. I've done some work for him in the past and he assures me you deserve a fair shake."

"I don't have no money to pay you," Claude protested.

"We'll worry about that later. Now let me see what I can do to work something out with the court, okay?"

Claude's daydream was again cut short when a burly bailiff stood and cast a stern gaze across the courtroom. He could see the judge adjusting a black cloak over in a doorway to one side. The people sprinkled around the room fell silent at the bailiff's next words.

"All rise."

Claude Davidson assumed the judge's apparent mean stare was directed at him, so he leaned over and whispered to attorney Swanger who stood next to him, "Is he or ain't he?"

"Shhh, Claude," he whispered. "I did everything I could. We'll just have to wait and see if the judge is going to be lenient." The dapper gentleman adjusted his tie.

The bailiff glared at Claude, who stiffened and leveled his head to face his judgment.

"Be seated."

Claude stooped to sit but Earl Swanger put a hand on his elbow and whispered, "Not you. We both keep standing."

The judge shuffled some papers from his high perch, and two stern blue eyes twinkled like fireflies as he fixed a bespectacled gaze right at Claude, who instantly felt his frame wither several inches. Claude's forehead glistened as beads of sweat formed a wide arc from temple to temple.

The judge said, "I've considered the matter carefully. You, Claude Davidson," he paused and again directed his steady glare at the defendant, "have been accused of the manufacture and sale of alcohol in Walker County, Texas. Are you ready to hear the court's judgment?"

Claude cleared his throat. "Yes."

"Your Honor," Earl murmured from the side of his mouth.

"Uh, Your Honor. Yes, Your Honor."

The judge frowned and continued. "Your attorney, Mr. Swanger..."

Claude could almost feel Earl wince at the mispronunciation. He had heard the name corrected more than once, his attorney saying it was like 'swan' and not like 'sang,' and he wondered how on earth anyone could fight the impulse to correct the judge because Claude struggled to keep his own mouth closed.

"...has argued that you have fallen on hard times and were trying to support your family. He reminded the court that the amount of alcohol was small and of limited consequence and has changed your plea to guilty, mentioning these extenuating circumstances. Yet making whiskey is against the laws of both the State of Texas and of the United States of America. You do love your country, don't you, boy?"

Claude hated that word and took in a deep breath but fought down his disgust and meekly answered, "Yes, Your Honor."

"You've had no other arrests and were gainfully employed until the Laidlaw sawmill went out of business. Oh, and Reverend Davis of the Antioch Episcopal Methodist Church has also sent me a note on your behalf. Both he and your attorney assure me that you plan to get out of the illegal enterprises you have been arrested for and that you'll stay in church and will continue to lead a good law-abiding life. Because of this, the court will accept your guilty plea and sentence you to time served." The wood-on-wood sound of the gavel hitting the sound block echoed from the walls.

Claude's eyes widened. "Uh, thank you, Your Honor."

"You can thank Mr. Swanger. He presented a very good case on your behalf."

At the next table, a balding Alvin R. McIntyre, the district attorney, slammed a book closed and shoved it into a battered briefcase. He looked over at Claude and Earl and sighed. "I don't like losing to you, Earl."

Swanger smiled. "Now, Alvin, I suspect it's something you're going to have to get used to in a few weeks. Besides, it wasn't a loss. My client pled guilty and was convicted. You've just lost him to your road gangs."

"Two weeks is a long time before an election, Swanger," he said, pointedly mimicking the judge's mispronunciation.

"It's SWAN-GER, as you well know. I think you had better get used to it. Come on, Claude, let's finish your paperwork and get you back home to your wife."

As they made their way to the back of the courtroom, Claude said, "That district attorney don't like you too much, do he? I reckon he don't like me too much either."

"I'm running against him in the primary election in two weeks. Sorry to say this was a felony, Claude. You can't vote now. What about your wife? Have you paid her poll tax?"

"I don't reckon I have. Money too hard to come by." Claude grinned. "You said so yourself."

Earl sighed. "That's another thing I wish I could change. No one should have to pay to vote. It just isn't right."

"I don't know much about voting and such, but I hope you win."

"You and me both, Claude," he said as he disappeared into an office and quickly emerged, tucking some papers into his briefcase. "That about takes care of you. You're free to go. Now, about my fee."

"You told me you'd be needing some work around your place. I can do most anything I set my mind to."

"Yes, I need help preparing a little garden area that came with our house. It's been neglected for a while, but I suspect we will all be needing bigger gardens soon. That and perhaps just a little more work around my place should be fee enough."

"I heard Mr. Hoover said things is going to be all right if we just sits tight."

"Yes, he does, but I have a feeling he's wrong. I think things are going to get much worse."

"Well, you're a good man, Mister Earl. I wouldn't have a good lawyer like you if you weren't willing to work with me some."

"You just be sure you stay in church and keep out of trouble, like I promised you would. There's a big criminal organization trying to control all the alcohol in the area. You can't compete with them and it's dangerous—for you and your family."

"I know them big boys is the ones who turned me in. Plenty of business in this prohibition stuff for everybody, but they greedy."

"Just steer clear. I want you to get rid of that still. How soon can you take care of it?"

Claude looked down and shuffled his feet. "Nobody but me knows where it is. I'll make my way out into the woods as soon as I can and bust it up. I promised my Evie I'd spend some time with her after I got out of jail, then there's the work I promised to do for you."

"You need a little something to help you get by?" Earl held out his hand with a bit of folded green paper showing.

"Mister Earl...I'm the one who's beholden to you."

"I promise, you'll be paying me back this and more, but I worry about your family. And, Claude, you can call me Buddie. My friends all call me Buddie."

"Mister Buddie, me and Evie are grateful for all your help. I'll keep on the straight and narrow, I promise. And you can keep your dollars. She still house cleaning for the Liebermans, so we getting by. And as soon as I can, I'll go out there and wreck that still."

Earl put the money back in his pocket. "Bye, Claude. I'll see you up at my place in a couple of days and show you what I need you to do."

Huntsville, Texas—11:15 a.m.

Earl watched Claude make his way down the street and turned toward his office two blocks away. He paused beside the entrance and dusted off the small sign beside the door that said, Swanger and Bryant. His wife, Lily May, had painted it for them when they first set up shop in Huntsville. They'd recently moved to this smaller office and had brought the sign with them. He never failed to admire the stylish flourishes she had added to the lettering.

He smiled at the blond man sitting behind a mound of papers and books just inside the doorway. The office was cramped, with barely enough room for the two desks. To one side there was a tiny alcove with a table and several chairs.

"Hello, Jimmy."

The man looked up. "Oh, I didn't expect you this soon. How'd it go?"

"Just about as I expected. Time served."

"How'd Claude take it?"

"He's happy to be out of jail."

"Do you think he'll get out of the business now?"

"I hope so. He can't compete against the other operations in this area. McIntyre was fit to be tied. He tried the case himself."

"Really? Why? Do you think he was behind it, the arrest, I mean?"

"I think his people pressured Claude to join with the organization. From what I've heard around the jail, Claude made some of the best stuff in the county."

"So you still think McIntyre is involved in the local booze business? I mean, you really think a district attorney could run that big of an operation?"

"It's what I'm running against. And, yes, I am sure he's connected with everything troubling our area. The people paying off McIntyre are the ones I want to get, and he knows that. It's one reason he pushed so hard against poor Claude. The man was making a few gallons at a time. I don't agree with what he was doing, but he was trying to provide for his family. For heaven's sake, he told me he was going to use the money from *that* sale to buy a new mule. I don't even think he drinks the stuff he makes. At least not much."

"Well, just be careful. If you're right about McIntyre's involvement, going head to head against him in court could impact your campaign."

"They wouldn't dare push too hard against me, in court or during the campaign."

"Don't be too sure. McIntyre has run unopposed since the war. So has Sheriff Steele. I overheard McIntyre a few days ago at the luncheonette bad-mouthing you something awful. I know he took great offense when you grabbed Claude's case."

Earl sat at the empty desk and opened his briefcase. "Every man has the right to an attorney, even the coloreds. I've helped that Preacher Davis out a couple of times and he came to me on Claude's behalf. How could I say no?"

Jimmy smirked. "You're right, but I wish you'd make more of a strong stand with paying clients."

"I'll get my fee out of him in bartered work. And he'll be a resource for more business, paying business. I know most Negro clients don't have a lot of money, but they usually pay in cash."

"Eventually." Jimmy shook his head and turned his attention to his small mountain of papers. "I wish we hadn't over-extended our credit with our last office. Bad advice on my part."

"We're just fine in these cozy digs and things will pick up. We both have enough small cases to pay the rent."

"And the lawsuit?"

"I hope to settle that out of court. They should never have sued us for such a small amount. And besides, Jimmy, no one knew the stocks would take such a beating. It's my fault for borrowing and investing so much—it took most of our capital when things crashed."

Jimmy laughed. "I thought it was a good idea, too. Everybody we know was investing. Anyhow, Hoover says it will soon bounce back."

"I'm not too sure about that. And we aren't the only ones that Lone Star Finance outfit is going after. They're pulling in almost all of their late accounts. The docket is full of them. That's a panic move."

"I know it doesn't look good. But how bad could it get for us? Won't people always need lawyers?"

Earl set his mouth in a grimace. "Not as much as you might think they do. If things get rough, folks just won't have the cash. Anyway, I need some work done around my place, so Claude Davidson will at least save me some time and money."

"Well, I have the Peterson divorce on tap. He's loaded and I've got her set to take him to the cleaners, what with his wife-beating charge on top of his philandering ways. That should give us a leg up. He should have kept his hands to himself."

"In more ways than one," Earl quipped.

"Still, I wonder what a nationwide financial crisis will do to the divorce rate."

"I suspect it will soar." Earl as he began to work.

After several hours he checked his watch. "Oh, my. I promised Lily May I'd be home early. We've got some people coming over after dinner. How late are you staying?"

Jimmy was hammering away at a typewriter with his index fingers. "I've got to finish this brief. I wish we could afford to get a girl in here."

Earl waved his arm around the room. "And where do you propose we put her?"

"You've got a point. Maybe if business picks up..."

"If I'm elected, you'll soon have the place all to yourself."

"That's right. I can keep doing my own typing until then."

Earl snapped his briefcase closed and flipped the clasp. "I better get a move on."

"Give Lily May my regards."

"I will. I'll see you, Jimmy."

Earl left the office and walked the half block to his green Ford Model-A four door sedan, and then drove the short distance to his house.

He opened the door and sneaked a peek at his wife who was rushing around the kitchen. He stood in the entryway and watched her as she scurried back and forth, almost in a blur, intent on her preparations. He smiled. No one had embraced his candidacy as intensely as she had. She'd supported him when he ran for county attorney in Leon County and stood by him after he decided to skip reelection and move to Huntsville. For him, it was the next logical step. First, move to the bigger area, get well-known, and then try for district attorney of the Twelfth Judicial District. He purposely scuffed a sole on the wood floor to attract her attention.

"Buddie! You nearly scared me to death!"

"I'm sorry, dear, I was transfixed by your loveliness as you darted around the kitchen."

"Oh, you hush. But you're sweet. Now we have the officers of the Elks Lodge coming after dinner, so tonight will be a sandwich night. I have so much to do before they get here. Come in and help me so we can eat."

In the kitchen he spied a variety of platters on one counter, each full of either small sandwiches, crackers, or spreads. Sliced tomatoes covered another platter. Their huge punch bowl sat on another counter, full of a pinkish liquid.

"It looks lovely, Lily May. I don't deserve you."

"You probably don't, but now that I've got you all trained, you're stuck with me."

Earl stopped her in mid-stride and hugged her, following with a kiss.

"Now you've messed up my lipstick and got a smudge of it on your cheek. Grab that napkin and wipe your face, then cut us four slices of bread and don't forget to put the loaf with the cut side down on the breadboard after you're finished. There's just enough of my special mayonnaise left for our sandwiches, so after you finish slicing, spread some of it on the bread."

Earl did as he was instructed and handed Lily May the plate. She proceeded to layer cheese, sliced corned beef, lettuce, and tomato on one slice of the bread, added the second slice of bread and placed one of the completed sandwiches on another plate. She then deftly sliced them both in half and handed Earl the plates.

"You take these into the other room, and I'll bring us some water."

Earl sat at the dining room table and was soon joined by his bride, who brought two glasses of water along with two napkins.

"Now, Earl Swanger, you eat your sandwich, and don't you drop any crumbs on my clean floor or you'll be mopping it."

He laughed at her and they quickly ate their sandwiches.

"I got that Negro out of jail today with time served," he said.

"Oh, the one who made moonshine? What was his name?

"Claude Davidson. He's going to do some work around here to pay me off. Fix up the garden."

"I hope he can fix that porch, too. I swear I'm fearful of breaking a leg bone every time I step outside."

"Yes, dear. I'll also ask him to look at the porch. Preacher Davis assures me Claude is quite the handyman."

"Now you brush those crumbs off your lip and put the plates in the sink. I've still got a lot to do before those Elks get here. And don't eat any of those other sandwiches!"

"I guess this goes with seeking political office," he joked as he stood, but paused to reach out and squeeze Lily May's hand.

She clasped his hand in return and said, "Now, get a move on. The Elks will be here in twenty minutes, and I need to wash these dishes. If you would, lay out the tablecloth and bring in the refreshments. Hurry! How will you ever be elected if you dawdle about?"

Two

Thursday, July 3, 1930

Huntsville, Texas—1:30 p.m.

A grizzled man with the makings of a salt and pepper beard almost dislodged the tattered hat he wore as he vigorously shook Earl Swanger's hand.

"Mr. Swanger, I want you to know I appreciate you running against that Alvin McIntyre. He's the crookedest district attorney we've ever had in these parts," then added with a twinkle in his eye, "...and that's saying something."

The speaker had leaned forward as he emphasized every word and when Earl bent his head to listen to this enthusiastic voter, he noted the knee patches on the man's tattered overalls and the ragged shoes he wore. It was the type of hardscrabble groundswell of support he enjoyed the most. He was thankful to hear similar testimonials almost every time he walked down the street. He expected to encounter such talk at scheduled events, but as the primary grew near, he was often cornered by voters. It happened to him after church, in the café or barber shop, and even when he simply shopped in stores. It told him people were ready for a change.

14

"I'll do my best," he always responded, with a practiced reply. "I appreciate your support."

Returning from the courthouse, the brutal July sun wore him down a bit as he made his way to his small office. He met his partner, Jimmy Bryant, walking in the opposite direction.

"Buddie, are you going to the July Fourth shindig tomorrow?"

"How could I miss that? With the primary looming on the twenty-sixth, it should be a real boost to my campaign. It'll be a long weekend for me. Well, for both of us, if you're still interested in helping out."

"Of course I am." Jimmy removed his bowler and wiped his wet brow with his wrinkled handkerchief. "That's the right thing to do, spend a lot of time speaking. I heard you really impressed the Elks the other night."

"That was just the officers. I think they were more interested in Lily May's refreshments than they were in anything I had to say."

"Don't sell yourself short, Buddie. McIntyre has held the courts of this district tight in his hands for long enough. Other lawyers tell me he is really worried about you. You heading to the office?"

Earl nodded. "Need to finish up some papers before the holiday."

"Yeah," Jimmy added. "It's always nice when a holiday falls on a Friday. Gives us a long weekend. What papers?"

"I just finalized that Lambert case. It's worked out mighty nice for us. We'll get enough to clear out some debts and give us a tidy cushion."

"That's great. I'll sure hate to lose you as a partner, Buddie. You carry us both sometimes."

"I haven't won the primary yet, Jimmy. And even if I do, there's the general election to worry about."

"The Republicans haven't even put up a candidate, so if you win the primary, you're in. Hey, if you lose the primary, you could…"

Earl laughed. "Hold on there. Let's not get too far ahead of ourselves."

Three

Friday, July 4, 1930

Huntsville, Texas—10:00 a.m.

A hot and dry Friday bloomed over the small Independence Day crowd forming near the courthouse, but the throng grew by the minute. July Fourth was generally a good campaign opportunity since so many people were off work for the holiday. Sporadic firecrackers popped in the distance, adding a festive mood to the gathering. Many candidates were milling about, some cordial and some made dour by a perceived lack of voter enthusiasm.

Over to one side of the courthouse, Lily May straightened Earl's collar and dusted off his shoulders. "Now, Buddie, do you know what you're going to say?"

"This is not my first speech. I've run for office before, dearest."

"I know, but Lordy, I get butterflies in my stomach just thinking about it."

"Don't worry, this is just another election."

"But when you ran before, it was for county attorney. The twelfth district covers a lot of counties. Of course, they know you in Leon County, so that should be easy, and that's why I'm going up there to visit my aunt in Marquez. She's already been setting up opportunities for me to go speak for you."

"And I appreciate it. You've always been my best advocate with those folks."

Lily May blushed. "How could I be anything else? I love you, Buddie. And I know you'll make a fine district attorney. Now you just go on up and tell everybody else that same thing."

Earl took a deep breath and ascended the courthouse steps. At the top, he slowly exhaled and turned to face the crowd.

"Friends of Walker County. I wish you a hearty welcome on this July Fourth as we celebrate the founding of our grand republic, the United States of America."

He waited for a flurry of applause. The small crowd began to grow as people who had been loitering on the surrounding sidewalks approached.

"My name is Earl R. Swanger, and I'm a candidate for district attorney of the Twelfth Judicial District of Texas. Many of you know that I relocated here from Leon County where I was formerly county attorney. In my time in that post, I became dismayed at some of the practices of the current district attorney. I believe Mr. McIntyre serves the interests of Mr. McIntyre more than he serves the good citizens of the Twelfth Judicial District. I promise you here and now that, if elected, I will restore honesty and decency to the office. I'm asking for your support and urge you to vote for me in the primary election on July twenty-sixth. Good citizens, can I count on your support?"

Someone spoke up. "Sure, he's a crook, everybody in politics is a crook, but he puts the bad guys away too, don't he? How do we know you're not a crook, too?"

Earl chuckled. "Friend, let me introduce my darling wife, Lily May, who teaches school to many of your children." He held out a hand and urged her to stand beside him. "Would anyone as pretty and talented as she is have a crook for a husband?"

Lily May blushed slightly and pushed him away, calling out to the laughing crowd, "Just please vote for Earl, you hear?"

"There you have it, ladies and gentleman. I *am* the right man for the job. As I said before, I promise to expose myself only to truth and justice and will steer my office away from crime and corruption. I, Earl Swanger, will faithfully serve the citizens of this district. Vote Earl R. Swanger!"

A smattering of applause followed, and another speaker nodded to Earl as he left his lofty perch to make room for the newcomer.

Lily May beamed. "That was good, Buddie. Short and to the point."

They made their way down a second set of steps and, as they turned at the sidewalk, a balding figure approached them.

"You scoundrel! Corrupt, am I?"

Earl stepped in front of Lily May to shield her from the onslaught. "Come now, Alvin, everyone knows you and all the sheriffs of the district look the other way on half the bootleggers in the county." Several spectators turned to witness the impromptu debate.

McIntyre's face turned crimson. "How dare you."

"Oh, I dare. I don't have the goods on you yet, but with your reputation, I assure you that your days are numbered. I hear you've been bad-mouthing me all over town. If you were on the up-and-up, you'd leave the campaign talk to events like this. All any candidate can ask is for the opponents to run a clean campaign. That's what I'm doing. We'll see who wins."

Sweat streamed off McIntyre's scalp and a vein loomed large on his neck. "I knew I should have pressed harder on the judge to send that Davidson boy away for a good long time."

"Oh, that? It was a little thing called justice, something you seem to have forgotten since you read for the bar. Claude Davidson is a grown man, not a boy, and he was a small operator, yet you wanted to prosecute him like he was making barrels of the stuff."

"Let me tell you something, you little upstart. You obviously don't know who you're dealing with. I promise you this, the day will come when you regret you ever tried to run for my office. I suggest you withdraw now, while you still have your reputation intact."

Earl smirked as he replied, "*Your* office?" He moved his arm in a wide arc. "Let me remind you, you work for these fine people. You can't intimidate me here on the sidewalk any more than you can in the courtroom, Alvin. I plan on surprising you on the twenty-sixth. Get ready for it." He nodded toward the onlookers before adding, "Threats are unnecessary, let's let the voters decide."

Several of them laughed as he pushed past McIntyre with Lily May glaring at the bald man as she followed. They could hear McIntyre breathing hard through his teeth as they left him seething behind them.

They drove to several other small holiday gatherings in town and in the surrounding communities. Earl gave similar speeches at each stop, and politely sampled modest examples of the finest local cooking. At one point, a small thundershower slightly cooled the July day, but soon steam rose from the hot streets, making the thick air stick to their skin like swamp muck. When they finally returned to Huntsville, Earl turned the car toward the train depot where he parked. He retrieved a large suitcase as Lily May exited the car.

"Are you sure you want to do this?" he asked.

"Of course, dear. I'm way overdue visiting my Aunt Laura at the old conservatory and she's already lined up several rides to help me meet with church groups and various ladies' functions throughout the county. People still love you there, you know. I'm simply going to remind them of your honesty and integrity. If I have anything to say about it, Leon County will be firmly behind you."

"I just worry about you when you're away."

19

"Don't be silly. You don't have to worry about me one bit. It is I who'll worry about you. You need me around to make sure you eat and don't work too hard. Now, you be careful with that fried chicken people always seem to throw at politicians...you know how the grease upsets your stomach. I bought an extra box of bicarbonate powder for this campaign. It's in the cupboard." Earl stifled a laugh as she continued, "Where are you going tomorrow?"

"I'm driving up to Madisonville first. I've got a full afternoon of stops planned. I'll make the rounds of local church groups on Sunday, then I'm off to Crockett on Monday. Tuesday evening I've got two meetings scheduled in Trinity. After that, I'll have to settle down and do some work to help pay for this campaign."

Lily May put a soft hand to the side of his face. "Just be careful, dear. There are a lot worse things in this world than losing a silly election."

He smiled and said, "I know. I'll be careful. And I've got Jimmy running shotgun for me tomorrow and Sunday. But for my stops on Monday and Tuesday, I'll be on my own."

A train whistle sounded and Lily May looked down the row of cars toward the steaming and hissing engine. "Dear me, I better go get to my seat." She kissed him. "I so love you, dear. I'll see you soon."

"You're the love of my life. I'll love you always, Lily May. Give your Aunt Laura my love and tell everyone back home I appreciate their support."

"I will," she said as she managed one last wave from the top step of the car as it lurched forward. She held fast to her suitcase and had to steady herself by latching onto the handrail. She continued to look back at him until she was out of his sight.

Earl took a deep breath and sighed. He hated being apart from his wife, but he knew he never would have been elected county attorney without her help. For him, she was the queen of Leon County, and she'd be the key to that section of the district this time around as well. Besides, he knew he couldn't deny her some family time. Lily May's Aunt Laura had practically raised her after her mother died and her father became an inconsolable wanderer.

He retreated to their house where he made a small cold meal with some of the prepared food Lily May had left in the icebox for him. He checked and emptied the drip pan before retiring to the cooler shade on the front porch to eat.

"I'm a lucky man," he decided as he munched and worked on speech preparations. He absent-mindedly listened to the rattling oscillations of the fan he'd turned toward the open window behind him. It reminded him of a Model T about to throw a rod.

~ * ~

The next day he and Jimmy loaded up his Ford and made a few campaign stops in Madison County, concentrating on the county seat in Madisonville.

Along the way Jimmy commented, "I heard about your confrontation with Alvin McIntyre."

"How'd you hear about that?"

"Seems you attracted a little crowd. It was all over town."

"He's worried I'll break up his little empire. I guess I gave him both barrels in my speech, so I don't blame him for speaking up. He *should* be worried."

"Just be careful, Buddie. It's well known he's got a lot of friends on both sides of the law, and some of the friends on his payroll don't want to lose the good deal they've worked out with him. You could bring yourself a whole mess of trouble if you antagonize him too much."

"I know, Jimmy, I'll be careful, but that's the kind of foolishness I'm trying to stop."

"Well, in just a little over two weeks, we'll know who the people want for the job."

"That's right, there's no one else on the ballot, so there will be no need for a runoff."

Jimmy sighed. "I can't help but worry for you. McIntyre doesn't like to lose, in court or at the ballot box."

"I'll be careful, I promise. I can't imagine him being able to do much of anything to me other than words, and I've never been one to be afraid of words. Now, what churches should we try tomorrow?"

"I've made a list for you, and I think several are having picnics, too. Do you know where you're going in Crockett and Trinity?"

"Yes, I have Monday and Tuesday all planned out."

Four

Sunday, July 6, 1930

Huntsville, Texas—12:45 PM

Alvin McIntyre stopped chewing the worn and soggy end of his cigar, relit it and blew a cloud of smoke that settled around the room like a fall morning fog along the Trinity River bottomland.

"We can't have this," he said.

Dub Jenkins coughed and waved a hand in front of his face to clear the hazy, acrid wisps before responding, "What do you mean?"

"What do you think I mean? I'm talking about Earl Swanger. I've been district attorney for ten years and have things set pretty much the way I like them. I don't need an upstart like him making waves and messing everything up."

Dub rose and paced for a minute. "You've had challengers before. What's different this time?" He paused at the window before returning to stand in front of his chair.

McIntyre rolled the cigar between his thumb and index finger. "You fool. He's young, he's got spirit, and he has the political knack that gets people to believe in him. He makes sense."

McIntyre paused to knock an inch long cylinder of ash from the end of the cigar before resuming his smoke. "This man has a serious chance of beating me."

Dub sat and crossed his right leg over his left knee. He examined the sole of his boot before responding. "You have all the sheriffs, most of the judges, and the local police in your corner. Heck, half the district is obligated to you in one way or another. Ain't hardly nobody gets a drop to drink here, runs a gaming house, or buys the services of a young lady unless you've got your cut from it. You are well aware who has seen to that."

"It's not enough. Look at that case with that danged colored, what was his name? Davidson? Cut and dried. He should be on the road gang for at least a year, but Swanger swayed the judge, who should have been *my* judge. He got that boy just a slap on the wrist. Now he's out, probably making more hooch that will cut into the syndicate's profits."

"Want me and my men to go out and persuade him to play for our team? I hear he makes the best stuff for miles around."

"I don't want the coloreds making booze, not in my district. I agree with the Maceos...it's a white man's business."

Dub turned toward the open window, attracted by the sputtering sound of a passing truck's motor. "Sounds like a bad cylinder," he muttered. He turned back to McIntyre. "But, boss, we sell to coloreds."

"Sure, we *sell* to them so we can keep them drunk and happy, but selling and making are two different things. The people who pay us want to control the production. After that, all I want is everybody satisfied and quiet while I get rich. It keeps you employed, too."

"So's maybe I go lean on him and convince him to get out of the business."

McIntyre stood and bent forward, placing two fists on the desk. "You tried that how many times? He never budged an inch."

Dub continued to pick at the sole of his boot. "I poked around but couldn't find his still. Most of the time he keeps to himself out in that shack of his with his wife. Somebody told me he's going to do some work for Swanger to pay off his legal fees."

"We're getting off the subject. Let's forget about Davidson for the time being. He's small potatoes. We need to concentrate on Swanger."

Dub lit a cigarette. "I heard his missus went off to Leon County to campaign for him. That's where she's from. She's a real mixer and knows pretty near everybody out there."

"Dub, he was county attorney, and everybody there already knows him and plenty voted for him. Leon County is a bust for us, you know that."

"Yeah, but my point is, she's away. He'll be here alone for a few days. Primary's in two weeks, and I reckon he's going to take a couple of days after this long weekend to campaign some more."

McIntyre intertwined his fingers in front of his face and stared blankly. "Dig into recent cases and find a woman who can help us out."

Dub scratched his chin then answered, "You mean..."

"Find somebody who knows how to use her womanly ways. Nothing turns a campaign on its ear more than a good old-fashioned scandal."

"That could work." Dub's smile slowly turned down. "But Swanger is honest, he's not likely to fall for any advances. I've seen him and that wife of his, they're solid."

"He's a man, isn't he? And remember, we only need the *appearance* of impropriety."

A knock on the door interrupted them, and the sweaty head of another assistant appeared. "Boss, I just got word that Swanger is over at the First Baptist."

"Oh, Lord, churches will be getting out, and he's got the drop on me," McIntyre said with a start. He turned to Dub and whispered, "See if you can come up with a plan to somehow generate the kind of scandal we want."

"Will do, boss."

"Now, I've got to hurry if I want to beat Swanger to the Methodist congregation!"

Huntsville, Texas—1:20 p.m.

"That was one fine talk, Mr. Swanger." A red-faced man was enthusiastically shaking Earl's hand. Streams of sweat ran down his face as he spoke. "It's high time we had somebody honest in that office. Bootleggers have run amok ever since McIntyre has been in charge."

"With the support of people like you, I'll do my best."

This scene was repeated for the duration of the after-services Baptist picnic. The heat and humidity stuck to his skin like a rash, but Earl strove to keep smiling and continued shaking every hand that was extended. He'd seen one of McIntyre's men lurking about when he first arrived, which didn't surprise him, but he was disappointed McIntyre didn't show up to counter his short speech. He was ready for another confrontation.

Earl looked at his watch. "Oh, I guess I should be moving along now." He raised his voice, "I want to thank all you fine people for allowing me to interrupt your meal."

The pastor approached. "Thank you, Mr. Swanger, and God bless you."

Earl made the short drive to the Methodist church, where a similar gathering was still in progress. He winced when he recognized McIntyre's Cadillac. He parked and approached the crowd, where he saw McIntyre mopping his face with a damp handkerchief.

McIntyre noticed Earl and spoke up, "Ah, here's the challenger now. A little late on the case, aren't you, counselor?"

"We're not in court today, Mr. District Attorney. I just dropped by to share a few friendly words with these fine people."

"Mr. McIntyre was just telling us he plans to continue his work keeping crime in check. I must say that was a good message to hear in these unsettling times." Earl recognized the speaker as Barney Simpson, a local shop keeper and well-known small-time gambler who was no doubt quite familiar with McIntyre's surreptitious dealings.

"Indeed, it is. It's a pity he does not extend that vision to the entire populace."

McIntyre flushed. "Why, you...what are you accusing me of? How dare y—"

"Calm down, Alvin, that's just some friendly campaign banter. I'm sure you've already done your best to cut me down a few notches, but of course that's easier with me not here to defend myself."

Simpson chortled. "He's got you dead to rights there, Alvin." He patted McIntyre on the shoulder. "Come on, now, let's see if there is any of that fried chicken left." He winked at Earl as he led McIntyre away.

Earl recognized Pastor McClinton approaching, who paused between nibbles of the drumstick he was holding. "We didn't see you at service today, Earl."

"Sorry, Pastor. I'm afraid I'm busy these last weekends before the primary. I need to browse as many other congregations as I can."

The pastor chuckled. "Well, I guess that's to be expected. Where is Miss Lily May?"

"She's gone to see her Aunt Laura in Marquez."

"I expect she's doing her own fair share of electioneering while she's up there as well."

"She is indeed."

"Well, I'm certain you have more friends in this congregation than Mr. McIntyre does."

"I hope so."

"Just trust in God, my boy. Stay honest and true according to His word, and you'll do fine."

Earl made the rounds, making sure to steer clear of McIntyre, who soon left. "Probably on his way to First Baptist," he muttered to himself.

"Buddie?"

It was Lily May's friend Mary Margaret Alcorn. "Oh, hello, Mary Margaret. What can I do for you?"

"Lily May asked me to make sure you ate something. I'm going to box up some of the leftovers here and have Vern drop it off for you later, so you can have at least the makings of a good home cooked meal to eat."

"Thank you ever so much. That is very kind of you. I expect I'll be home about three-thirty or four o'clock," he said with a smile, before continuing to talk to others who were scattered about under various shade trees on the church grounds.

Huntsville, Texas—4:00 PM

Vern showed up on schedule just after Earl arrived at the house and left a picnic basket of food on the front porch. The inside of the house was quite hot because it had been closed up all day, so Earl opted to leave the basket outside and eat on the porch.

"The best thing about Methodism is the food," he whispered to himself as he nibbled on a drumstick. "Although I think the Pentecostals have cornered the market on peanut brittle."

A voice from around the side of the house startled him. "Mister Buddie?"

Earl looked up as Claude Davidson's large frame filled his field of vision.

"Oh, you gave me quite a fright, Claude. Come on over. You want a piece of fried chicken?"

"No, sir, I ate my fill over at my mama's house today. I'm full as a tick."

"What can I do for you? You haven't got yourself in any more trouble, have you?"

"No, sir. I promise you that. I just checking in with you to see what I can do to pay off your fee." He fidgeted with a weathered straw hat as he talked. "I been waiting in the woods," he said, motioning with a jerk of his chin. "I guess I figured you was out grabbing some of them votes you was talking about."

"Of course." Earl wiped his hands on the edge of the cloth lining the basket and stood. "The main thing I'm interested in is my garden. I never had time to get it going this year and I'd love to get it ready for a fall planting."

"Yes, sir. It's time to get them pumpkins and root vegetables going, cabbage and collards, too. I can fix you up."

They walked around back and approached the overgrown garden patch. "I'm sorry, it's quite a mess. I just didn't have time to work it up this spring."

"Give me a day and a good spade and shovel and I'll get this ready for planting." Claude knelt and cupped some of the soil in his hands. "This dirt is good, just needs a bit of turning and weeding, maybe a little coaxing. You get the seeds and such, and I'll do your planting for you, too." He looked toward the side of the house and pointed at a hose attached to a spigot. "That work?"

"Yes, it does."

"Good. I'll water it down some before I leave. It'll make it easier for me when I come back." Claude looked up at the sky. "That summer sun can bake the ground like a kiln. What else you got what needs doing?"

Earl led Claude to the back porch, and the big man bent over for a better look before Earl even had a chance to point at the warped and worn boards.

"Ah, those bad boards need replacing. Somebody going to break a leg-bone on that."

29

Earl laughed. "My missus just told me that exact same thing."

"You get me the lumber and I'll do the fixing. I'll look around and see what else needs mending. I owe you big time, Mister Buddie."

"Well, I appreciate the help. I suspect you'll pay off your legal debt in no time and then after that, I'll pay you for your work."

Claude straightened and smiled with a full set of teeth. "I reckon I better get started on watering that garden. Pumpkins almost too late, but I think we can squeak them in."

Earl showed him the small shed where the garden implements and other tools were kept and shook his hand. "Thank you, Claude."

"No, sir, thank *you*," he answered as he began to unravel the hose.

Once Claude was busy with the garden, Earl walked back to the front porch and continued his meal. As he finished the third piece of chicken, he heard the rattled approach of a dusty Ford two-seat roadster. The driver straightened his trousers as he walked up to the porch.

"Hello, Jimmy."

As Jimmy Bryant approached, Earl could tell he had noticed the basket of food.

"There's one more piece of chicken here. It's good *Methodist* chicken, too."

Jimmy reached into the basket. "Don't mind if I do. I've been around to several of the smaller congregations, except the colored ones, of course."

The sound of a soulful gospel hymn reached their ears as if on cue, and Jimmy looked up at Earl.

"Claude Davidson is clearing my garden for fall planting. Paying off his legal fee."

"So he's already making good on your barter. Good for you."

"You've got plenty of divorces to keep you fed. I've been thinking about our speculations on the number of failed marriages that might be caused by the October crash. I think it will ultimately be good for business, and that's your bread and butter."

Jimmy smirked then said, "Anyway, McIntyre was hitting a lot of the same places I visited, along with the VFW."

"I planned on attending a VFW meeting next week but forgot they had a picnic today."

"It was a small affair, but thought I'd give you fair warning. He's still criticizing you with some awful things any chance he gets. I heard about it every place I stopped and did my best to set the record straight. At the VFW it certainly helped that you served and he didn't."

"I was mostly just a cook."

"They say an army marches on its stomach," Jimmy kidded.

"Well, I always knew the campaign would turn dirty. I don't like to go that way, but if I knew what he was saying, I could counter it better."

"That's the thing," Jimmy said between bites, "he's got nothing concrete on you. My pal at the VFW said McIntyre was making insinuations about you...hinting at some sort of impropriety."

"What? That's preposterous."

"Like you said, it's turning dirty. Be careful, Buddie."

"I will, indeed. Thank you for the information."

Five

Monday, July 7, 1930

Marquez, Texas—9:00 a.m.

Laura Carrington stood at the bottom of the long stairwell, hesitated a moment, then called up, "Lily May! Jeff Dinkins is here."

"There's no need to holler up the stairs, Aunt Laura, I'm coming. I'm coming."

Lily May paused for a moment in front of a hallway mirror and admired her smartly dressed reflection. She knew she looked a bit fancy for the small farming communities of Leon County, especially on a Tuesday, but she wanted to make a good impression for her husband. She had helped him get elected county attorney, and she was bound to do the same thing in the upcoming primary. She straightened her collar, smoothed her skirt, and took one last look. Satisfied, she descended to the first floor.

At the bottom of the staircase, Laura said, "My, don't you look nice?" as she brushed imagined fluffs of lint from the shoulders of the dress.

Lily May blushed. "Thank you."

"Now hurry out there. Jeff is using his day off at the gin to haul you up to Centerville. Do you have those leaflets you brought with you?"

Lily May lifted her oversized pocketbook. "Of course."

Marquez was little more than a whistle stop on the railroad, but that had been enough for the small town to take hold, and it was now home to seven hundred souls. She had already met with some of the local church women's associations for afternoon refreshments. In past elections, she'd found wives to be her most valuable resource. The vote of women was important, and she well-remembered her excitement when the country had finally awakened to the reality that women should have a voice in the selection of leaders. And she also knew that women had a knack of manipulating the votes of their husbands.

"'Morning, Miss Lily May." Jeff Dinkins was behind the wheel of a black Model T. The engine was sputtering as it idled.

"Lordy, are you still driving this rattletrap?" she asked as she stepped up into the seat beside him.

"Oh, she's noisy, but she'll get us there all right. I got her serviced up as soon as I heared you'd be needing me."

"Well, I surely appreciate it."

"Proud to be of service. It's high time Mr. Swanger started moving up in politics. I expect one of these days he'll be running for governor."

Lily May chortled. "Listen to you. Let's not count our chickens." She wrapped a thin scarf over her head to protect her hair from the onslaught of breeze from the moving car.

They were soon off the dusty streets and proceeding down the paved highway to Centerville, seventeen miles away.

Jeff Dinkins dropped her off outside the courthouse. "I've got some business to attend to, but I'll be by the café about two o'clock. Do you think you'll be done by then?"

"I'll be mostly passing out leaflets and talking to everyone I see. I don't need to hard sell anybody on Buddie's merits, folks around here already know him pretty well, but they may not know he's running for district attorney. That's the word I have to get out."

"Practically anybody you meet ends up loving you, Lily May. If you tell them, they'll listen. See you later."

"Thank you, Jeff." After the car clattered its way down the street, Lily May removed the scarf, put on her hat and tugged at her gloves. Her purse had a long strap that allowed it to hang from her shoulder. She reached inside and extracted a small number of leaflets, holding one up to check for errors. It read, Vote for Earl R. Swanger for District Attorney of the Twelfth Judicial District. At the bottom it reminded, "The Primary is July 26!"

She made her way down the sidewalk and started offering them to everyone she encountered. Lily May was well-known in Leon County, and most of the people she bumped into graciously accepted the papers, although many returned them.

"I know these things cost good money and I'm already supporting Earl, so there's no need to waste one on a sure vote," was a common refrain.

She was thankful for the sentiment because they were running the campaign on a shoestring. She wouldn't have admitted the truth of it out loud, but the move to Huntsville had not been as lucrative as they had hoped. She secretly wished he would win because it would mean a steady paycheck in these hard times. Earl, she knew, had started accepting barter for his services, like he did with Claude, and she'd even started to see a drop in the music lessons she offered.

She heard similar tales of hardship as she caught up with old friends. The stock market had hurt a lot of people the previous October. She and Earl had lost a bit of money, but many people had lost much more and were just beginning to deeply feel the effects. As she walked around the downtown area, she noticed a solemnity in many people's faces, a look she hadn't seen since the first casualties returned from the war with Germany more than ten years earlier. But that time the somberness was tempered with a wave of patriotic feelings. Now, it seemed more like a deep, dark cloud of despair had settled over folks and threatened their souls.

"Good morning, Miss Lily May." A tall man with a thick shock of white hair and a bristly white mustache smiled at her.

"Land sakes, Darius Martin! I haven't seen you since we moved to Huntsville."

Lily May and Earl had known Darius Martin for years. He was an attorney in Centerville and had served at the opposite table from Earl on many cases during his term as county attorney, but their professional relationship was completely separate from their friendship.

"I've been meaning to drive down there and speak with Buddie ever since I heard he had thrown his hat into the ring." He deftly grabbed Lily May's sleeve and pulled her into a doorway and lowered his voice to a whisper. "I've heard a few things about McIntyre that Buddie needs to know."

Lily May looked deep into Darius' blue eyes and knew immediately this was important. "What on earth is it?"

"I don't want to burden you with it. I'll try to get down there as soon as I can and talk with him directly."

"Darius, if it's that important, you can tell me."

He looked down at his feet and said, "All right. I'll tell you this. McIntyre is worried about running against Buddie. I know the man. He's on the take and he and the people he works for will stop at almost nothing to get Buddie out of the way."

"You mean he may be in danger?"

"Don't rightly know, but I do know that when folks like McIntyre are feeling threatened, they're as dangerous as a cornered bobcat. Buddie just needs to watch his back."

"I know he's going to Crockett today, and Trinity tomorrow. I'm afraid I won't be home for several days. I planned on spending the entire week in Marquez."

"Please tell him to be careful. The best thing for this district would be for Earl Swanger to win this election."

"I will. Thank you, Darius."

After this meeting, Lily May wondered if she should send Buddie a telegram, or possibly cut her trip short. She had a ride arranged to take her to Normangee on Tuesday, and on Wednesday two churchwomen had agreed to take her on the grand tour of Buffalo, Jewett, and Leona. She planned to spend Thursday helping her Aunt Laura air out the old dormitory room upstairs. Although Laura still made money giving music lessons, the old place tended to get a bit stuffy since it no longer housed conservatory students like it had when Lily May was younger. Aunt Laura had been so good to her, and Laura was, after all, her father's sister, so she felt obligated to lend a hand when she was in town. It was a big job.

A brief thunderstorm managed to temporarily cool things off and when it first started raining, she managed to find refuge in the beauty parlor where she handed out a few more leaflets. It also gave her a chance to catch up on some of the gossip. The things she heard in Huntsville never seemed quite as juicy because she was still getting to know people, but here she was immersed in an onslaught of local information. It was better than reading a newspaper.

She said her farewells and departed, only to confront a thick humidity that felt like a sticky curtain she needed to push through to get down the sidewalk. She noticed steam rising from the streets and fanned herself with a short stack of leaflets as if that would help ward off the effects. She noticed a clock through a store window and saw it was one-thirty, so she stopped by the café and squandered some of her money on a cheese sandwich and a Dr. Pepper. The sweating, ice cold bottle was refreshing after walking in the sweltering July downtown heat, and she pressed the bottle's thick glass to her cheek for added relief.

Jeff entered the café at two o'clock, just as he had promised. Lily May was dabbing the crumbs away from the sides of her mouth when he entered and stood in the doorway, scanning the interior. He smiled and approached when he saw her.

"You ready?"

"Don't you want to eat? I'd gladly buy you something."

"No need, I grabbed a hamburger a while ago. I've been talking up Buddie to everybody I've seen."

"I appreciate the help."

The engine was warm and its electric starter kicked it to life with minimal effort, but as they moved down the road the old car seemed to strain against the heat of the day, and the warm breeze did little to cool them.

"Tires seem a bit gummy in this heat, but I reckon she'll be okay."

Lily May simply managed a, "Mmm, hmm," as her thoughts turned to Darius Martin's warning.

Trinity, Texas—11:00 a.m.

Dub Jenkins parked outside a dingy bungalow and adjusted his tie. A speckled mongrel watched him from a corner as he approached the door, and he shooed it away with a wave of his hand. Ragged, overgrown weeds, wilted by the summer heat, sprawled against the weathered siding. His knock elicited a faint response beyond the closed door, which had a conspicuous hole in the center, shielded on the opposite side.

A woman's voice uttered a questioning, "Yes?"

"Are you Miss Johnston?"

The cover moved away from the hole and a bloodshot blue eye peered at him, then disappeared as the cover slid back in place.

"Who wants to know? I don't open my door to anybody I ain't expecting or don't recognize."

"My name is Jenkins. Mr. McIntyre sent me to talk to you."

The cover beyond the hole again slid aside and the blue eye squinted at him, then the door cracked open. "McIntyre? That man from court?"

"Yes. It is important that I speak with you right away."

The door opened, revealing an attractive, although slightly disheveled young woman. She clutched a small pocketbook as she stepped back. It attracted his attention because when he had read her file, he noticed Betty Johnston was known to carry an ice pick in her purse for protection. The top button of her blouse hung loose because she had missed a hole while hurriedly dressing. "Have I done anything wrong?"

"May I?" Jenkins pointed toward the interior.

She sighed and stepped back. "Come on in." She shuffled her bare feet, rustling the folds of a wrinkled skirt as she walked. The wrinkles provided more evidence of a rushed attempt at dressing.

The interior room was small, but the furnishings were stylishly arrayed in a welcoming, yet sparse manner. A simple upholstered chair flanked the pink settee and she pointed to it.

"Please sit down. I'd offer you some refreshment, but I'm afraid I don't have anything at the moment."

Dub stood by the chair and waited for her to sit. "That's quite all right." He extended a palm toward the settee. "Please." He looked at the floor so he could avoid the gap in her blouse, and noticed her toenails were freshly painted bright red. She sat and crossed her legs, again drawing his eye to the floor to avoid staring at the beginnings of thigh just above the bare knee.

"Well, at least you're a gentleman, I'll give you that, Mr. Jenkins." After Jenkins sat, she added, "What is this all about?"

"Mr. McIntyre sent me to ask if you would do him a little favor."

Her mouth set itself tight, and she gathered the collars of her blouse before she answered curtly, "What kind of favor?"

"As you may know, he is up for reelection soon, and it would benefit his campaign if he could cast some doubt onto his opponent, Mr. Swanger."

"I'm afraid I don't know this Swanger. Someone of that name has never made my acquaintance. I don't do business with anyone unless I know them. It's too dangerous. A lady has to protect herself."

Jenkins chuckled. "Yes, of course. It will be quite easy to arrange an introduction. We believe he'll be coming to Trinity to campaign tomorrow. All you have to do is speak with him, closely, some place where you will be seen together. Of course, we don't expect you to do anything that might be considered inappropriate, but as for the *appearance* of impropriety, well that is quite another matter."

"So you want me to be seen with him and make it look like we're—"

"In a nutshell, Miss Johnston. How you achieve that is entirely up to you."

"Look here, I know I'm no angel, but you can't come in here and insist I do nasty things to help a man get some silly votes. Oh, and considering what you're asking, he's probably married. What if his wife is with him?"

"She is out of town for the week, so I assure you he'll be alone."

"Well, at least that's something, but I don't even know this Swanger. I have nothing against him."

"Ah, but of course, Mr. McIntyre knows you quite well. You'd be in prison right now if he hadn't helped you. And, I might add, you could *still* go to prison. You have one remaining charge he hasn't prosecuted."

"I thought he dropped that!"

"Not yet."

She moved her right hand to open the pocketbook she still clutched tightly with the left. "Mister, you best not be making any threats."

Dub grabbed her wrist. "I know girls like you often keep a weapon handy. Don't make me break your arm. I'm sorry, but I need you to please listen to me. We will pay you handsomely for your help. Much more than you might imagine."

"What do you mean girls like me?" she said, pulling her arm away from his grip with a twist of her torso. She dropped the purse and rubbed her wrist. "I don't know, Mr. Jenkins, I can imagine an awful lot."

Jenkins smiled. "Will you help us out?"

She inhaled deeply. "I just need to figure a way to do what you want. I don't know this man, but that means he likely don't know me either. You say he's coming out here tomorrow to do some campaigning?"

"Someone told me he's going to Crockett today, and he'll be coming here to Trinity tomorrow. I'm fairly certain he'll be by himself."

"I need to figure out a way to get us seen together for whatever reason."

"Yes. I'll leave that up to you."

"I don't want my name spread all over the newspapers."

"Of course not. Such matters are generally kept quite discreet. We'll do our best to keep it that way. It's the implication we are after, and we will strive to protect the delicate flower of your virtue."

Betty Johnston let out a deep belly laugh. "Ha! My virtue. Okay, I like the sound of that." She chuckled to herself again. "Well, for the sake of my virtue, how much are we talking about?"

"How does three hundred dollars sound?"

"Five hundred sounds a lot better to me."

"I might be able to go four."

She spat in her palm and extended it. "Done."

Jenkins shook the hand and stood. He reached into his coat pocket, withdrew an envelope and extracted four hundred dollars in twenty-dollar bills.

"It's pretty strange that is exactly what you had in your pocket."

"Well, it was the maximum authorized by Mr. McIntyre," Jenkins lied. He had much more in his back pocket.

She took the bills and placed them on the small table between the settee and the chair. "I'll do my best. I need to figure an angle, but I'm good at that."

"Just make sure you take care of this tomorrow, as it gives Mr. McIntyre ample time to take advantage of the situation. Thank you, Miss Johnston, I'll see myself out."

Jenkins stuck his head out of the door and looked both ways, but the only witness was the dog, watching him as it vigorously scratched. Assured of his privacy, he quickly left the bungalow and drove away.

Betty Johnston sat on her pink settee and picked up the crisp twenty-dollar bills. She spread them out in her hand, kissed them, and fanned herself. "Four hundred! That's a lot of cabbage for next to nothing. Well, unless this yokel is good-looking, then maybe I can get even a little more scratch from him." She added, "Now I better call Freddy."

Huntsville, Texas—3:00 p.m.

Earl worked at his office for a few hours Monday morning before heading to Crockett, where he planned several stops. His first destination was the Monday Afternoon Society, a group of church women Lily May had some previous involvement with. Then it was the local Grange, the Elks, and the Masonic Lodge. He planned a short stump speech in front of the courthouse, too.

He received a warm reception every place he stopped, where he shared the same prepared message: "I will strive to remove the taint of corruption from the office of district attorney."

After each speech, people approached him to share some of their own stories of how McIntyre manipulated prosecution for his personal benefit, particularly involving the sale and manufacture of alcohol, but Earl also heard stories about prostitution and gambling.

"We look forward to a return of honesty and integrity to the office," was a repetitive refrain.

He opened a small box he kept under the seat of his car and added the few folds of cash earnest voters had slipped into his palm. These were some of the sparse campaign donations he received at the end of every one of his talks, and for the most part served to buy gasoline for these visits. "My support is growing," he mused, "slowly, but steadily."

Earl made his way home to Huntsville after an extended visit with the Masons. They'd thrown a dinner in his honor. He'd picked sparingly at the wieners and beans they had served but had relished a refreshing serving of the ice cream they had churned for the occasion. He loosened his tie as he drove, and inwardly contemplated, "I wish the state would relegate primaries to a cooler month."

Trinity, Texas—3:00 p.m.

Fred Darby loosened his tie and smoothed the end of his waxed moustache with his finger. He took a long swig from a jar, swishing the clear liquid in his mouth to mellow it before he swallowed with a gulp. He coughed as his throat and stomach rebelled slightly to the biting warmth of the hooch as it made its way down.

"Where'd you get this batch, darling? It's a might harsh."

Betty sat demurely on her settee. "Same place I always get it, Freddy."

He sniffed at the contents and said, "Smells like I'm driving past a refinery over Beaumont way," then put the jar on the small table. He burped again. "But the aftertaste reminds me more of Texas City."

She made a face at him and reached past him to grab the jar and, after first taking a deep drink, put it on a nearby doily.

"How many times do I gotta tell ya, not on the table, put it on the doily. I swear, were you raised in a barn?" She daintily wiped at the corner of her mouth with the back of her hand.

He burped. "Sorry, baby. What can I do for you?"

"I got a special deal, a sort of blackmail deal."

"Branching out, are you?"

"McIntyre wants me to frame a john."

"Not me, I hope," he quipped.

Betty laughed deeply. "I've already got the goods on *you*."

"So let me see if I can guess. He wants a Sheba who's known to skate around to be seen in public with some weak sister."

"That's the crop. I've got the goods to play the end game, but I'm not much with the planning."

"Which is why you want me in on the deal. What's my end?"

"I figure maybe a yard, but I might be needing more help than just a plan."

"A cool C note? Tell me more."

"The mark is a candidate running against McIntyre."

"Oh, that Swanger fella."

Betty seemed surprised. "Yeah, that's the name."

"I know some fellas who had run-ins with him when he was county attorney up in Leon. He's about as straight as they come. One guy got an attempted bribery rap added to his sentence. The guy can't be bought."

"I don't care about that, we ain't trying to buy him."

"It's a tricky business, though. I mean, if it goes south..."

"Listen, Freddy, McIntyre never dropped all the charges from last time. His man says they'll prosecute me if I don't help him."

Fred brushed a hand against her knee, "We can't have that, can we."

She leaned and playfully slapped his hand away. "Business, Freddy, I'm trying to talk business. McIntyre's jobbie says this Swanger fella's coming here to Trinity tomorrow evening to shake the trees for some votes."

"Tomorrow evening." Fred rubbed his chin. "He coming alone? I heard he's married."

"McIntyre's man was pretty sure he'd be alone. He said the wife is out of town, and he's coming up here from Huntsville to campaign."

"That's good. What I am thinking about won't work unless he's alone. It'll play like the old cat's away joke."

"Tell me more, Freddy."

"It's a pretty standard scam. We find where he is down in Huntsville. You know, like you go up and see him at his office or maybe even some other place. He's got to eat, right? I mean, with his wife off visiting, I'm thinking maybe when he gets dinner. Wherever you waylay him, you strike up a conversation and tell him you've got the goods on McIntyre. If he's like any politician I've ever seen, he'll bite, but you'll have to convince him that the proof is back here in Trinity."

"Oh, and he's coming to Trinity anyway."

"Right. Then you tell him you're stuck without a ride, which should make it easy for you to play the damsel in distress routine. That puts you both together in his car all the way to Trinity. I'll follow you, just to keep tabs and make sure everything is okay."

"And once we get back here to Trinity, I'll make sure he's seen with me, then a hug, maybe a smudge of lipstick. Word will spread like wildfire and his reputation will be shot."

Fred chuckled. "What about your reputation, Betty?"

They exchanged glances and then both burst out in laughter that rattled the windows. A moment later, Betty jumped when a sharp thunderclap shook the entire house, interrupting their laughter.

She put a hand to the base of her throat and gulped a deep breath. "I hope that—"

"It ain't no omen, sweetheart, it's just a summer thunderstorm and believe me, that's a good thing. It will cool things down for a while. Trust me, if the good Lord was gunning for the likes of us, we'd have been picked up by the grim reaper long ago. I'll come get you tomorrow afternoon. Put on your finest and get ready to vamp."

"I'll be glad when this is all over."

"Me too, baby." Fred reached for her knee again. "Now that the business part is over, maybe we can get on with something else."

Huntsville, Texas—3:00 p.m.

Claude slammed the garden spade into the ground and followed up by jumping on it, using his weight to drive the blade deep into the soil. He then pushed down hard, using the handle as a lever to release another clod from its captivity. The baked earth did not give up its treasures easily as he broke through the crusty topsoil, but he hefted each mound of dirt and twisted his hands to release it over the divot created by his previous effort. He finished every chunk by chopping at it with the shovel point to break it into smaller pieces.

"Hello, little worm" he said to a wiggling blush in the dark background of dirt. He gingerly chopped around the writhing figure and added, "You go along now, do your worm business," before gently placing the clod in a spot of freshly turned soil.

He continued digging down one narrow row and back up another. It was a hot day and the work was hard, but he knew he owed a debt and was thankful for the miracle of his freedom.

"Mister Buddie did his job, and now I'm bound to make it right with him," he said to himself. "But I sure wish Beulah was still alive. With her and a small plow, I could turn this garden in minutes instead of hours."

As the afternoon wore on, he was thankful for the bit of shade a grove of nearby trees provided when the sun dipped lower in the western sky. He paused again and surveyed his handiwork, proud that he had already turned three-quarters of the garden, then returned to his toil until the entire garden plot was a finished rectangle of darker, freshened soil. He lightly sprayed it with water from the nearby hose, then took a long drink directly from the hose before turning the water off.

"There. Gonna let that sit while I go look at that rotten place on Mister Buddie's porch."

As he walked toward the porch, he spied a man coming around the side of the house closest to the street. He squinted through the sweat in his eyes and remembered seeing that same man around town. He drove a fancy roadster and was easy on the horn when a pretty girl was passing by. Claude knew the type, a man who fancies himself something special but needs to put on a show to prove it. His spotted bow tie was an example.

"What you doing over here, boy? Does Mr. Swanger know you're prowling around his house?

"Yes, sir. I doing some work for him. He knows I'm here."

The man chuckled. "You're the one I was looking for anyway. You Claude Davidson?"

"That's my name. I don't rightly know who you is, though."

"Name's Jenkins. I represent certain parties who have an interest in your still."

Claude took a deep breath and held it a second before slowly releasing it. "Mr. Swanger told me to bust it up."

"That's just the thing, boy. *We'll* bust it up for you. We just want to know where it is."

Claude fought an intense spark of antagonism that began to kindle inside of him. "I told you, Mr. Jenkins, I aims to bust it up myself. That way I knows it's done and gone."

"I'll be honest with you, boy. You've been making some of the best booze in the county. We want to see how you did it."

"That still won't do you any good. That's all right up here," Claude tapped his temple. "You see, a still is just a still, like a hammer is just a hammer. You got to know how to use things like that if you want to make anything right. No thank you, sir, my hooching days is over."

"So that's your final answer?"

Claude took another deep breath and stiffened his frame, towering over the smaller man. "Yes, sir, it is. I am done with breaking the law. There's plenty of bootleggers around that will show you how to make better stuff. If you think I'm the best, just go and ask around and find the second best. I reckon that will have to do for you. I just want to get back to my work here," he said, pointing toward the back porch.

He stood staring at Jenkins until the smaller man lowered his eyes and left. He called back over his shoulder, "This may not be the last word you hear on this subject."

"Last word or no, I'm not changing my mind."

Claude followed to the corner of the house and watched the man drive away, although the engine sputtered a bit as the driver tried to coax it harder than it wanted to go. He spied a lone mangy yellow dog watching him as it panted from just beyond the tree line. He sighed deeply as he turned back to the house. "I sure don't needs no more trouble. Now, let's go see what's up with them boards."

He returned to the porch and saw two fresh planks leaning against the clapboard siding, along with a saw, a hammer, and a paper bag with nails.

"I'll have to pull the old boards out real careful, so I can use them to measure, but this should do the job." He got on his hands and knees and started working at the nails holding the damaged boards to the frame with his knee.

An hour later, he stood back to admire his work. The bright yellow pine replacements stood in sharp contrast to their weathered counterparts, but Claude smiled broadly and then tested them with his full weight. "I think Mister Buddie will be satisfied with that." He glanced around the porch. "If he could get me a splash of paint, I could make this porch look real nice."

He returned to the garden and proceeded to chop and hoe the still-moistened clods until the entire plot had a uniform texture, then he used the hoe to form long furrows of soil running down the length of the parcel. Satisfied with his achievement, he put all of the tools in the small shed and made his way home. He preferred walking circuitous trails in the woods, following first one creek then another. It took him a mile or so out of his way, but it reduced the chance of meeting any other disagreeable individuals like Jenkins. The thick vegetation seemed to trap the heat and any puff of breeze felt like he'd just opened an oven door. Every step produced more sweat, and he imagined he was leaving a wet trail as he walked. He could not wait to wash away the grimy remains of the day with the makeshift shower he'd set up in his side yard.

"Hope Evie has my spare overalls all washed and dried," he said as he walked, before adding, "...and something good on the table."

His home was little more than a shack, set away from the road a few miles on the northeast side of Huntsville, outside the city limits. As he approached, he saw his hound dog Jack sleeping in the dust in front of the weathered wooden steps. "I swear Jack, you ain't much of a watchdog." he said as he stepped over the prone figure and onto the porch with a creak. "Sounds like I need me some new boards on this porch, too," he said.

He and Evie had been married for a year. Things had seemed better then, when he was still working, but she'd stuck by him when he lost his job and then stuck even tighter by him when he got arrested, even though she had been dead set against his bootlegging from the start. He figured he'd chosen well, although deep inside he knew their marriage had been more of her choosing than his and it warmed his heart to hear her voice as she greeted him with a hearty, "Did you wipe those big feet of yours, Claude?"

"Yes'm, I did."

"You got all squared away with that nice Mr. Swanger?"

"I reckon I am, but need to show him what all I done, and there'll still be a little planting, if he wants it. He out politicking today, so I never saw him."

Evie emerged from the kitchen. Claude still couldn't believe she had agreed to marry him. She was petite, but very pretty. She smiled broadly, showing her gleaming white teeth with only one gap along the side she said had been caused by the knuckle bone of a ham hock she'd bitten down on while eating some black-eyed peas. He reached out as she approached him with open arms, and they embraced with a tight hug.

She pulled back and looked him in the eyes. "Don't you ever do that bad stuff again, you hear me?"

"We needed the money."

"I'm working for the Liebermans now, we'll do okay. You find something honest. You're a good man, Claude, that's why I married you. No more making moonshine." She shook a finger in his face. "You hear me?"

"I do. I heard you the first time. But I do need to go out to Harmon Creek and bust that still up before somebody finds my spot. I promised Mister Buddie I'd do that. I reckon I'll go on up there tomorrow night and get that done. I'm supposed to see him the day after tomorrow, and I want to tell him it's gone." He began to wonder if he should tell her about Jenkins but reconsidered.

"I'll be glad when you're finished with that nasty business. Ain't no place in the Lord's world for it. Preacher Davis speaks on its evils almost every Sunday. Grief and wickedness is the only thing it sows."

"Easy money is all it was for me."

"The devil's pay and look what came of it—you got yourself arrested and dang near put away for a long time."

"It was other folks who turned me in, jealous of how good my daddy taught me to make it. Fella came up to me today wanting the still." Claude paused, realizing he had said more than he wanted to, but now the cat was out of the bag.

"Say what?" Evie had placed one fist on each hip.

"Yeah, he said they wanted to see how I made such good stuff. I reckon that's why they turned me in, to force my hand."

"Don't be prideful over ill-gotten praise. That's like trying to single out a good man in a lynch mob. I hope you told them no."

"I sure did. I want out of that world as much as you want me out of it. That's why I got to head out there and bust it into pieces. I want to be done with it."

"If that's so, why don't you go on out tonight and do it?"

"I been working in the hot sun all day—I'm tired and hungry and I need a wash. I'm thinking tomorrow night will be fine. Ain't nobody going to find it before then."

She wrinkled her nose. "Yeah, a bath will do you good, but you'll have to pump the water and load it yourself. I'm trying to finish mixing up a batch of cornbread to go with your ham hocks and beans. If I had been thinking, I'd have done that so it would be ready for you. The water would have warmed a bit in this heat."

Claude sniffed and said, "Shore smells inviting. I guess I could have thought of the water too, before I even left, but a good shower will cool me off. It was powerful hot today." He headed out the back door and started pumping water into a small tub. He then lifted it to another rusted container located above a wooden framework. After several loads of water, he noticed Evie had brought out some clean, folded overalls and skivvies and placed them on the back porch along with a towel.

He undressed and opened the creaky gate to the enclosure, then pulled a chain hanging in front of him, releasing a thick spray of ice-cold water. He gasped in response, then recovered and stooped to pick up a bar of lye soap. Claude lathered his head and body, then released another spray. He shook against the chill and ran his hands down and around to squeeze off the soapy droplets that remained. He then doused himself a couple of more times until he was sure all the suds had washed away, along with the sweat and grime of the day's toil. He pulled the chain one last time to make sure he had used all the water.

He grabbed at the towel, which felt warm after the repeated splashes of cold water. He dressed and went into the house for his dinner, first wiping his wet, bare feet on the mat.

Huntsville, Texas—8:30 p.m.

Earl returned from Crockett a little after dark. The house was quiet and lonely. He missed the comforting sight of Lily May's smile welcoming him when he got home, and most days he looked forward to smelling good things to eat as he entered.

He felt good about the way this day had gone. The citizens of Crocket had welcomed him with open arms. He hoped Tuesday would be just as productive. He had eaten sparingly at the Masons and was famished.

He dropped the bag of seeds he had bought onto the counter and wondered about what he might eat. The ice man had come early that morning before he left, so he knew the icebox had preserved the remains of some ham and beans Lily May had left, so he pulled out the bowl. He thought about firing the stove to heat his dinner, but he was hungry, and the house was very warm, so he decided to just eat them cold. Lily May had also left a large section of leftover cornbread. It was a little stale but once he'd eaten the beans and ham, it sopped up the cold liquid quite nicely when he crumbled it and stirred the pieces into a mush. He had just finished his feast when there was a knock at the door.

He cracked it open and saw a familiar face. "Jimmy?"

"Buddie, I think I've got the dirt on McIntyre you need."

"It's hot in here, let's sit on the porch. What did you find out?"

"A fellow found *me*! He said he can give us information about McIntyre's whole graft operation. It's a lot worse than we ever imagined. The DA's on the take, and he's got his fingers into just about everything in all the surrounding counties. That Claude Davidson you just represented? It was one of the syndicate's men who turned him in because he was cutting into business."

"Well, we always figured it was something like that. Who is this fellow?"

"His name is Thornton."

"Oh, yes, Bill Thornton. He's worked for McIntyre for a while now. I heard him being cursed out just this morning outside the courthouse square. McIntyre was obviously mad about something."

"Yeah, he told me he's on the outs with McIntyre and is afraid for his life. Buddie, whoever McIntyre works for is dangerous. We need to be very careful."

"When can I meet Thornton?"

"Soon, if I can set up a safe place."

"I'm going to Trinity early tomorrow evening to do a little campaigning."

"I'll try to contact him and see if I can set something up. This may be just what you need to turn this election on its ear."

"We'll have to be discreet. I don't want McIntyre or anybody he works for finding out what we know."

Jimmy wiped his brow. "I'll be careful."

"If what you say turns out to be true, once elected I should be able to prosecute him and do a lot to reduce crime in this area, crime he's obviously allowed to flourish with such foolishness."

After Jimmy left, Earl went out to the back porch to smoke a cigarette. When he lit the match, he noticed the two new boards he had bought were firmly in place.

"Well, I'll be. I guess Claude was busy while I was out today."

He lit another match and examined the work. "Looks like a good job." The match burned his fingers and he waved his hands to extinguish it before dropping it in the dirt just off the stoop. He looked out toward the garden area. "I'm betting he's got that all squared away as well. I'll have to give him a little something extra for this added effort. A good, honest, hard day's work is worth more than my paltry legal manipulations."

He finished his cigarette, grabbed the bag of seeds from the kitchen and took them out to the tool shed. It was quite dark, but he felt around and deposited the seeds on a crossbeam near the leaning hoe. He was sure Claude would see them when he returned. Back inside the house, he said his evening prayers and prepared for bed.

"I will be glad when Lily May is home," he said to himself. "I sure do miss her when she's away."

Six

Tuesday, July 8, 1930

Huntsville, Texas—8:00 a.m.

Claude returned to the Swanger home early Tuesday just as Earl was leaving the house.

"Good morning, Claude. I was just admiring your handiwork. The porch steps look perfect. Good job."

"If you can find some paint, I could match the new boards up with the old. I've gots your garden in pretty good shape, too, Mister Buddie."

"I took a look at it this morning. It looks all set. I bought some seeds yesterday and they're in the shed. The bag is on a crossbeam just inside."

"I'll get you a good garden all planted and watered, then you'll be ready for the fall. Is you working on your election again today?"

"Yes, indeed. I have some lawyer work to do first, but I plan on heading to Trinity this evening. I have a couple of meetings with some groups of people there."

Claude considered telling Earl about the encounter with Jenkins but decided to keep it to himself. "Well, you drive careful out on that road. They're building that new bridge over Harmon

Creek, but the way the road curves around to the old rickety one, well, it ain't something you can take too fast, especially as it gets along dark."

"The new one will be an improvement, that's for sure. But I know what you mean. I drive that way a lot, so I know to slow down and be cautious. Oh, and Claude?"

"Yes sir?"

Earl reached into his coat pocket and pulled out his billfold. "You've done such a good job, really, it looks like you've done a lot more than I asked you to do, let me give you a little something to make up the difference."

Claude held up a palm and said, "No sir, I told you what I'd do to pay you back, and the job ain't complete. You can just put that billfold away, I ain't taking your money. I appreciates the sentiment, but this is the way it is."

As Earl put his wallet into a pocket, Claude reconsidered his misgivings about Jenkins and took a deep breath. "They is something you needs to know, Mister Buddie."

"What?"

"Fella name of Jenkins came calling yesterday just as I was finishing up. Squirmy kind a guy."

Earl knew exactly who Claude was talking about and his heart began to race. "He wanted me?"

Claude shook his head. "Said he wanted *me*. Said his people wants my still."

Earl reset his feet. "You haven't gotten rid of it yet?"

"No, sir, I've been fixing to take care of it, but been working a lot here, and we had the holiday, and then it was Sunday and all, you know?"

"Ah."

"I had already planned on knocking it apart tonight. I appreciate all you done for me. Evie too. Even if I ever had any second thoughts, she'd push me out the door and tell me not to come back until it was gone. She always hated the fact that I built that thing. Ain't nobody but me knows where it is, and to tell the truth, I likes that spot. It's kind of a private secret place I don't want nobody to know about— good trapping there. Thanksgiving's right around the corner, a lot of turkeys be lurking nearby in the fall."

Earl chuckled. "Well thank you for everything. You be sure to take care of that still, you hear?"

"It's as good as done, but now I better get to the seeds. I'll water it all down real good when I'm done planting."

Claude watched Earl drive off then retrieved the bag of seeds and read the packets. "Pumpkins, collards, carrots, radishes, cucumbers, squash—gonna be a nice garden."

He stood in the center of the plot and looked at the sky, trying to anticipate the expected late summer and fall tracks the sun might take so he could plant the garden in a way he judged would best take advantage of it. After he was finished planting, he found a few fallen sticks under a couple of the shade trees and fashioned crude markers with empty seed packets, then liberally watered the entire plot, again running fast streams of water down the furrows.

"That should fix them up for a couple of days." He looked at the sky. "We're about due for some short rainstorms, too. That will help get everything started before things begin to dry out in August." Claude wiped his brow. "Yes, sir, gonna be a fine garden for them."

Huntsville, Texas—8:15 a.m.

Alvin McIntyre fixed a blank stare at Dub Jenkins, and he inwardly cringed with each loud masticating crunch on the crusty bits of bacon his assistant was devouring. The stench of the scorched fat on the bits of meat, fried almost black, made the balding man gag.

"How can you eat it that way? Burning it like that makes it really hard. Your teeth must be capable of grinding pebbles."

"It's how my momma fried bacon. My people have always had good choppers. Grandma Winnie died way up in her eighties and still had a full set of teeth."

"Well good for her." McIntyre turned his gaze away from the spectacle as he continued. "So you contacted this Betty Johnston. How'd it go?"

Jenkins interrupted his chewing. "You let her off on a whoring rap a while back. She's perfect for this. Pretty, lives in Trinity, and she was easy to coerce 'cause one charge is still pending."

"So she'll do what we need her to do?"

"I explained it real nice and simple—made sure she knows she could still be prosecuted if she doesn't. I think she knows what's good for her in the long run."

"And you paid her four hundred?"

"She wanted five but she took four."

"For that kind of money, she had better deliver. I'm hearing from all over that Swanger, his partner, and that wife of his have been canvassing the entire twelfth district. He *has* to be knocked down a peg or two."

Jenkins leaned forward and whispered, "Yeah, losing this primary will not be welcome news to certain folks."

McIntyre glanced around the café, then glared at Jenkins. "You fool, not another word about that. Not here, not anywhere."

"I held it down, boss. Nobody heard."

McIntyre scoffed, then asked, "What exactly is she going to do?"

"Who?"

"Betty Johnston, you ignoramus."

"Oh." Jenkins continued his incessant chewing. "I don't know for sure. I left it up to her. I gave her the basics of what we needed. She was upset to find out she could still be charged. She thought she was in the clear."

"They always do—but can she be trusted to keep her mouth shut?"

"She's a regular 'do anything for a buck' girl, so I'm sure she'll do what we want *and* keep quiet. I gave her the lowdown on Swanger's plans in Trinity, so I reckon she'll figure a way to meet up with him. A working girl like her knows how to be devious in the course of her trade, so I'm sure she's quite capable of coming up with something."

"As long as her ruse is convincing. We can't afford any slip-ups."

"Calm down, boss, it's in the bag. I mean, I can't very well instruct the likes of her on how to go after a man, can I? Oh, and by the way, there's one other thing I wanted to ask you about."

"What now?"

"It's Bill Thornton. I needed to talk to him, but nobody's seen him since yesterday morning. I asked at his rooming house, and the lady said she hadn't seen him since late yesterday."

"Yes, I was wondering where he was."

"I know he rubbed a few people the wrong way, but he knows a lot, boss. Too much."

"Well, if he was smart enough to leave, he's smart enough to know he needs to stay gone." McIntyre looked away as he nervously tapped the table with his thumb.

Huntsville, Texas—10:45 a.m.

Earl opened the office door, took off his hat, and wiped his brow. In the corner, an oscillating fan squeaked from side to side as it struggled to move molasses-like molecules of humid air.

He fanned himself with his hat momentarily before hanging it. "Already a scorcher out there today."

Jimmy Bryant looked up from his perpetual mound of paperwork and swiped at a bead of sweat trickling toward the end of his nose. "Yeah, well, it's summer and we've still got a long, hot spell of it ahead of us. How'd court go this morning?"

"Fairly routine. Delbert London is sorry for his fifth bout of public drunkenness and will spend a week on the road gang, probably working around that new bridge out highway 19." Earl reached into his coat. "Paid me ten dollars." He handed the bill to Jimmy, who deftly grabbed the cash and spirited it into a strongbox in his desk drawer.

"Every little bit helps."

"Talked to a couple of people who didn't have a lawyer yet. I proselytized them pretty good, I think."

"Well, it sounds like you did as well as you could with that Delbert fellow, and people sitting in the courtroom notice that sort of stuff. Courtroom talk is boring, and they've got nothing else to do. I'm sure at least one of them will look us up. You're a good lawyer, Buddie, and it will just take a while for people around here to realize that."

"I always try to do my best. You're a good lawyer too, Jimmy."

"Not as good as you, but that's why you'd make a good district attorney. I mean, I hate to lose to you as a partner, but I'd much rather be sitting opposite from you than that crook McIntyre or his toadies."

"Well, I still have to win that primary first. What about that contact you told me about? Did you set up a meeting?"

"I'm afraid that's a dead end. I went by where he lives this morning to see if I could get up with him, but he wasn't there."

"He probably got cold feet. I tell you, if I worked for McIntyre, I'd be afraid to say anything for fear of what might happen to me. Well, it's just another indication of how dangerous McIntyre's connections are. This fellow is probably in Mexico by now." Earl chuckled before adding, "Or Oklahoma."

"Everywhere I go, folks tell me they're tired of his nonsense, and it's not just the people working for him who are afraid. If this groundswell of support continues, I think you've got a good chance of winning. I think old McIntyre must be running scared."

"I hope you're right, but I've got a strong feeling he's working for somebody else. Here, he's just a big fish in a small pond."

"You still going to Trinity tonight?"

"I'm heading over there this evening after an early dinner. I'm going to hit the Tuesday night meeting of the Woodsmen of the World and then talk at the Masonic lodge. Going to try to get to the Woodsmen somewhere around eight-thirty. I think they're almost done about then. The Masons run longer, so I can catch up with them after that."

"Just keep doing what you're doing. People like you, Buddie. You've got a better chance than anybody else to beat him."

"In the meantime, I guess I had better hunker down to see what I can do to help keep the lights burning around here."

At five, Jimmy and Earl locked up the office, and Earl drove to his house. After parking, he walked around the back to see if Claude was still there. The garden area was deserted but Earl could see that the entire plot was well-watered. He bent over to inspect the seed packet markers that identified different sections of the plot.

"That Claude is a hard worker," he said to himself. "I'll have to see what else I can have him do around the house, but after this I'll insist that he let me pay him. I know he can use the money."

Earl entered the house, put on a clean suit, and made a mental note to take a bundle of the last several days' clothes to the laundry because he knew Lily May would not return until Friday. "She must have gone to Normangee today," he said to himself.

Earl looked over at a small photo of his sister Pearl on top of his dresser. "I wish she still lived in Normangee. I know Will lost almost everything in the crash when his bank failed. I hated that they had to move to Austin to find work. It was comforting to know they were still fairly close."

Earl had exhausted his food reserves at the house, so he drove downtown, where he stopped for dinner before continuing on to Trinity.

The café was deserted when he arrived, but shortly after he sat down, a pretty, smartly dressed woman entered and took a seat alone along the opposite wall. Earl enjoyed his privacy when he ate on his own, so he was glad there was a bit of space between them. After he ordered, a short man with a waxed mustache entered and sat at another table in the center, several paces behind him. The newcomer was facing Earl's table, but the man opened a newspaper and hid behind it. Earl sipped his coffee, and in a few minutes the waitress delivered his food.

He had about two bites left on his plate when the woman rose as if to leave, then hesitated, turned around, and approached his table.

Earl looked up and could see her face sported an abundance of makeup, something that always gave him the impression that a woman perhaps felt she was not as pretty as she wanted to appear. He'd done some drama work in college and knew that on stage one had to use a lot of makeup to project a false sense of normalcy to the audience, because the actors' features would otherwise be washed out by the bright stage lights. As he watched her approach, he thought to himself that she would do her features more justice if she used a lighter touch.

Then she spoke, and her words managed to surprise him.

"You're Mr. Swanger, aren't you?"

Earl began to rise.

"Oh, that's all right. My, you're such a gentleman, but you don't need to get up."

He was already standing. "What can I do for you, miss...?"

She interrupted, "Johnston. My name is Elizabeth Johnston. Do you mind if I sit?"

Earl glanced at the other patron in the café, who was trying hard not to notice what was going on, but one eye was evident at the edge of the newspaper. "If you know my name, you must know I'm an attorney. Do you need a lawyer?"

When she sat, she quickly examined her makeup with the mirror in her compact, then replaced it in her purse. "You're the man who's running for district attorney."

"Yes, I am. Well, one of them."

"I have some information about Mr. McIntyre that might help you."

Earl adjusted himself in his seat. "What might that be?"

"Something about his other interests in this area. He's a bad man, Mister Swanger, and I can help you prove it."

"The election is in a little over two weeks. There's not much time to validate any information like that."

"Oh, this is pretty solid proof. But I didn't bring it here—it's at my place in Trinity."

"I'll be busy in court tomorrow. Perhaps my partner could come retrieve whatever it is during business hours."

"Well, I imagine that *could* work," she said, lazily shifting her gaze around the room before locking eyes with Earl. "But I have another idea. You see, I'm stuck here without a ride home. I heard somebody say you were going to campaign in Trinity this evening. Maybe you could give me a ride, then I could just give you what I have."

She batted her eyes at him in a way that made Earl uncomfortable. He asked, "Who could have told you I was going to Trinity?"

She giggled and said, "You know there aren't many secrets in a small town. Anyway, it's no surprise that you're going all over the place with your campaign. You were in Crockett yesterday, right?"

Earl took a deep breath and nodded. "Look, Miss Johnston, I am interested in seeing what you might have, but I think it would be quite inappropriate for me to give you a ride. I'm a married man, and my wife is out of town."

"If that's true, even talking to me here could be seen as a problem for you." She pointed with her chin at the other diner, who again tried to give every appearance of not watching them by adjusting his position and quickly turning pages. "Please, I really need a ride home. And I think what I have can help you win your election. I don't like McIntyre. A lot of people don't like him." She tilted her head and raised one eyebrow. "Everybody speaks very highly of you."

"I'm still not interested, not under these circumstances. Perhaps tomorrow or the next day. If I could come see you with my partner, I'd be willing to take a look at what information you have."

She leaned forward and whispered, "Listen, I'm on the level, and I really am stuck here and desperately need a ride. What I've got is good stuff, and it will help you, but it's now or never."

"Again, it's simply not appropriate."

She pouted and stood. "Well, if that's your answer, then it's your loss. I guess I'll just start walking." She stood and turned toward the door.

Earl glanced at the clock and could see he'd have to be leaving soon in order to catch the Woodsmen meeting. He sighed and rose.

"Miss..."

She stopped with her hand on the knob and crooked an eye in his direction. "Yes?"

"I suppose I can't have a lady out walking that road in the dark. Parts of it are dangerous."

She smiled and turned to face him, again batting her eyes. "Glad you came to your senses, sweetie."

Her tone grated on Earl's nerves. He returned to the table and left money to cover his tab and came back to her. She patiently waited for him to open the door. A lone stray dog watched them from the shadows next to a nearby storefront.

"Well, I'm in a bit of a hurry to catch a meeting, so I don't know if I'll have time to see what you might have."

She clutched her purse close to her body and walked through the doorway. "You're going to be glad when I show you what I've got."

She paused on the sidewalk until he pointed to his car. He reached down to open the passenger side door and she remarked, "It is such a pleasure to meet a gentleman for a change. Any woman's bound to love a man like that."

The comment made Earl feel uneasy, but he proceeded to the driver's side door. Before he got in, he could see that the woman had inched over to the center of the seat.

"I'm not having that," he said and pointed, waving his finger toward the passenger door. "You need to move over."

She pouted again and moved her body an inch or two right of center. "I just don't like it to seem like I'm being chauffeured around."

Fading streaks of dusk were already beginning to darken on the horizon as Earl slowly moved the car down the street. Grave concerns weighed heavily on his mind, and his heart raced. On one hand, he felt like he should insist she exit his vehicle immediately, but on the other hand he was concerned about leaving a seemingly defenseless woman stranded miles from her home. Any possible information about his political opponent was secondary to these considerations. He simply wanted to get this woman to her destination as quickly as possible and get her out of his car so he could continue with his planned activities. He remained confident in his ability to control any situation. He navigated the dusty streets of Huntsville and turned left on Highway 19, the road to Trinity. The road was deserted except for a lonely pair of headlights far behind him.

Huntsville, Texas—7:15 p.m.

Claude ducked under a low branch only to trip over a protruding root as he made his way along the meandering path through the thick woods, hoping he wouldn't miss one of the turns as he struggled to follow the faint traces of trail in the moonlight. The overgrown bottom land near Harmon Creek was especially hard to navigate at night, even on a route he had followed for years. He occasionally lost his way and had to backtrack. He looked up at the nearly full moon as it dodged between assortments of clouds and was thankful for its help.

"Bright night for it, at least. I'll be able to see what I'm doing when I get there," he muttered to himself.

When he was preparing to leave, Evie asked him not to go because she'd had another one of her peculiar dreams the previous night. She woke up in a cold sweat, and Claude knew exactly what it was. He consoled her, even though she didn't tell him any particulars at the time, but this evening after dinner she related a few details about her nightmare.

"It was just like the last one. I seen something bad happen up near Harmon Creek. Something fearful. You know me and my dreams, so you know I'm right. I'm begging you, stay home tonight, Claude."

"But, honey, I promised Mister Buddie I'd bust it up tonight. I need to get rid of it so we can put all this nasty business behind us. I wants us to be free and clear of everything."

With tears in her eyes, Evie shared more. "I knows one thing. If you go out there, I know that we'll be free and clear of nothing. Just leave it be."

"You saying something going to happen to me if I goes out there?"

"That ain't rightly clear—but something evil is at work, something horrible. And it gonna affect you and me both in some awful way. I can still feel it right now, deep in my bones. I don't want you to go."

But the big man had remained adamant about his intention. Now, he replayed the conversation in his head as he continued through the thicket.

"Now you listen, I respects your visions. Lord knows they is usually right, but if I know to be wary, I know I'll be all right—ain't nobody can sneak up on me out there without me hearing them. I promised Mister Buddie and that's that."

An image of Evie's tearful expression haunted his mind as he continued to break branches and walk through wisps of fog gathering in shallow depressions along his path.

He knew he was close because he could see the bowing tree that was his best landmark. It had been bent into an arc by some long forgotten blue 'norther's ice storm. It stood along one side of the clearing, and his granddaddy always joked that the tree was bent so the Devil himself could sit there and rest a spell. The devil's perch was what he always called it because it stood guard over the bald patch of land the old man had also associated with Satan's work.

Claude paused and twisted his head to glance all around. Bullfrogs sang from the nearby creek and a symphony of crickets made a joyful noise. He sniffed and could detect the faint aroma of damp ashes, even though his last fire out here had been two months earlier. He entered the clearing and could see his still was just as he had left it. He usually draped it in a cover of branches but when he was arrested, he hadn't had the chance. The clearing, surrounded by thick underbrush, served him well as a blind. That was one reason he had chosen this spot. If it was good enough to hide him from deer and turkeys, it was good enough to hide his still from prying eyes.

He always came in the long way, hiking a circuitous path from his home, but in truth, it was not that far from the Trinity Highway. He'd often hear traffic rumbling down the road and clickety-clacking over the old bridge as he was working, making his moonshine. But if you didn't know how to find the trail, the thicket on this side of the water made these woods almost impenetrable. The ancient, weathered span over Harmon Creek would soon be replaced. It had been built primarily for horse and wagon traffic, and as motorized vehicles had become bigger and heavier, the highway department decided it had outlived its usefulness and began work on a new bridge over the creek. He listened as a car passed over it in the distance and thought to himself that he'd miss the rhythmic ticking sound when the new bridge was finished.

Claude used the creek as a water source for his operation and at his usual fishing spot along the creek he could easily see the outlines of the new bridge downstream. He remembered being afraid the new bridge would make his operation more difficult when construction began but he also appreciated the fact that these woods were thick enough to conceal his special spot.

As he cautiously crept into the clearing and eased alongside the shadowy mass in the center, a segment of the copper coil gleamed at him in the bright moonlight. He remembered the day he had filled the copper tube with sand, the way his daddy had showed him, and heated it over a fire in the back yard to make it soft enough to bend around a section of old stovepipe like a spring.

"The sand will keep that tube from kinking," the old man had told him.

The contraption wasn't big, as stills go, but it provided a couple of gallons of hooch in a batch. It had been enough to give him and Evie a few extra dollars after he'd lost his job. He never touched the stuff he made except for a taste as it came out of the coil, when he'd swish about a tablespoon's worth around in his mouth, judging the purity and strength by the sting on his tongue and gums before spitting it out. It always reminded him of the one time he'd gotten himself drunk when he was much younger and got sick as a dog.

He tapped the boiler. "Got arrested afore I had time to clean it out. Mash in there has most likely gone sour."

He hummed gospel hymns as he worked. The dismantling process was fairly simple and soon he had the several components arrayed around him. He cracked the top of the boiler drum open and a sour, yeasty odor of spoiled mash slammed into his nose like an invisible sledgehammer, making his eyes water.

"Hoo-wee! Better let that set a while to air out." He pulled out half a cigar he had secreted in his top pocket. Evie didn't like him smoking, but she knew he puffed a stogie from time to time. She had to know, because he'd make one last a couple of days and would stash it in that pocket between puffs, and the opening now sported a brown badge of shame etched into the fabric. A match illuminated his workspace momentarily, and he puffed at the tobacco cylinder until the end glowed crimson and a swirl of smoke rose into the patchwork of clouds above him. He studied the rising plume for a second or two but spun his head toward the highway when an odd series of noises caught his attention. He tamped the cigar end on a rock, and carefully perched it on another, then lumbered through the thick woods in the direction of the highway without bothering to find the trail first.

Between Huntsville and Trinity—8:30 p.m.

The Model A's tail lights were barely visible to Fred Darby as he followed at a distance. He was proud of the way the woman had played on Swanger's manhood, just as he'd taught her.

"That damsel in distress routine works every time," he remarked.

Betty's instructions had been to stay far enough back to keep Swanger from getting suspicious, but to be ready. If something went wrong on the trip, she was going to make Swanger stop, and she'd get out of the car so he could pick her up.

Their plan beyond that was simple. Once they got to Trinity, she'd noisily make a scene and get out of the car. She'd time it for maximum effect, expecting to put on a show for several onlookers. She wasn't worried about her reputation—that was long since established—but she'd say enough in public to make sure Earl Swanger's character would be irreparably harmed. For all of her faults, Betty was intent on earning her wages as best as she could, no matter if it was whoring or blackmailing.

Fred couldn't help but feel sorry for the sap. Everything he'd heard about Swanger indicated he was a good egg. But, on the other hand, a diligent district attorney wasn't much good for his usual business dealings either. Even though they were being paid for this little affair, Fred assumed Betty would also earn some manner of additional protection from McIntyre, and he was sure she'd extend some of that good will his way if need be. In all likelihood they wouldn't need any protection for this caper because he was confident their plan was solid.

He struggled to keep up and was glad Swanger was driving slowly. Some lead foot might lose him because his car couldn't make speed for long. Despite the occasional bright moon, at dusk this road was devious, and he was sure this was part of the reason Swanger was being cautious.

"Got to watch for that new bridge," Fred said to himself. "That construction around there is tricky. Hope Swanger knows it's coming up."

As if on cue, there was a sudden flicker and flash of the Model A's tiny brake lights. Fred instinctively took his foot off the gas and coasted for a second as he watched the tail lights move in an odd fashion, momentarily disappearing from view then reappearing in a different spot as if by magic.

He pressed the gas and aimed for the red points of light. The car was askew, down the cutoff to the new bridge and stretched diagonally across the roadway. Fred slowed and saw two partially broken sawhorses and a splintered plank pushed to the side of the opening. He'd seen them before, serving as a crude barricade to dissuade people from crossing the incomplete bridge.

Betty stood next to the Model A, waving both arms frantically.

Between Huntsville and Trinity—8:35 p.m.

At the same moment Earl noticed the headlights behind him, Betty Johnston reached out and stroked the side of his face and said, "You know you're a nice looking man. I'm wondering if maybe this little trip might include some added benefits, you know? Like for both of us."

He immediately realized he had been played for a fool and fallen for one of the oldest cons in the world. He lamented the way he had stifled his initial misgivings and surrendered himself to her seemingly innocent demeanor. He realized in that instant that he had fallen for her guile, hook, line, and sinker, but now he was ready to put a stop to it.

He recoiled from her touch and glared at her in furtive jerks of his head, making sure to keep his car pointed straight down the road. He knew the split to the new bridge was coming up and didn't want to miss it because it afforded a safe opportunity for him to stop the car.

She nonchalantly began to freshen her lipstick and he exclaimed, "You can stop this act right now. McIntyre must have put you up to this. What are you, some harlot on his payroll?"

The accusation caught her off-guard and she fumbled for words in an attempt to defend herself from this truth. "Wh— what? How dare you? You, you, lowlife. Are you calling me some chippy? We'll see what your wife has to say when I tell her you lured me into your car."

Earl took his foot off the gas. "I'm going to let you out right here. I'm sure your partner in the car behind us will pick you up."

"Listen buster, you just keep driving." She shook her head with rage and mumbled, "And to think I was maybe gonna to let you sample the goods, and for free, too. You're just a good-looking, goody two-shoes shyster that's what you are."

The car lurched as Earl downshifted and began to quickly brake. The motion pushed her forward in a jerk and she dropped her lipstick as she reached into her bag with her other hand.

"I said, don't stop this car!" She withdrew her hand from the bag, and a blurred object lurched toward him.

Earl winced at a fierce pain in his right shoulder and jammed on the brakes. A squeal of tires accompanied the swaying motion of the car as it spun on the roadway, knocking aside a plank and two sawhorses stretched across the newer section of pavement. The car skidded to a stop, stretched diagonally across the road, and Earl noticed a guardrail made of fresh new planks illuminated in his headlights. He clasped his shoulder with his other hand and turned toward Betty. She raised her hand again and he saw the ice pick clenched in her fist coming down hard toward his chest. He twisted and the implement glanced off his collarbone, but it still hurt.

"Ow," she said, dropping the ice pick, which had stung her hand when the tip hit hard bone. She clenched her other hand into a fist and slugged him in the chin then opened the car door and retreated.

The shock of the sudden attack and the subsequent near accident had unnerved him. He panted against the pain as he watched her get out of the car. He looked to his right as he became aware of headlights slowly approaching and saw a car inching toward them from the highway.

He heard the other car's door open, followed by Betty Johnston's shrieking voice. "Dammit, he made me stab him."

"What? You stuck the guy?"

"The jig was up, and he was going to stop."

"Nobody was supposed to get hurt, doll. Did you kill him?"

She rubbed her hand. "No, but I jabbed him pretty good. I tried to gig him another time but hit bone and dropped my shiv." She rubbed at one wrist. "I hurt my hand something awful."

The Model A's door opened and Earl emerged with one hand tightly pressed against his shoulder. He recognized the man as the same fellow who was reading the newspaper at the café.

"You! You're her partner in all of this?"

"Hey, mister, I just stopped to help, that's all." Fred approached the passenger side of the car, keeping the auto between the two of them. Earl began to maneuver toward the rear, so Fred quickly ducked his head into the car, spied the ice pick and grabbed it. By the time Fred emerged, Earl had closed the distance and grabbed him by the lapels. Fred reacted against this onslaught with one swift, practiced motion. Earl released the smaller man and clutched at the center of his chest, then gasped and started to speak but dropped to his knees and fell to his side.

"Oh, geez, Freddy," Betty said, as Fred stepped back, still holding the bloody ice pick in his hand.

"He put his hands on me. It was just instinct, like I was back in the pen."

"What do we do now? This ain't what McIntyre wanted. I have a feeling he ain't going to like this at all."

Fred wiped at his hands with a handkerchief, then wrapped it around the ice pick and stuck it in his pocket. "Like it or not, he's as deep in this as we are now, but we gotta figure a way to fix it." He hesitated and looked up at the moon, then turned to Betty. "I followed you the whole way out the café and down the road, so I don't think nobody saw any of us. It was dark. That means they got nothing on us except at that café, and that was all innocent-like. I'll go down tomorrow and slip the waitress a Jackson. After that, I'm sure she'll keep her mouth shut."

Earl moaned and they both stared wide-eyed.

"Oh, geez, Freddy. He's still alive."

"I've got me an idea, but I'll need your help. Let's put him back in the car."

Between Huntsville and Trinity—8:45 p.m.

Claude made his way to the edge of the woods that bordered the bridge site. He could see two cars and two people standing, excitedly talking. He deftly made his way a little closer and strained his ears to make out their words.

"Let's put him back in the car."

He squinted in the moonlight and could tell one car was at an angle.

"Looks like a Model A," he whispered to himself. He thought back to Evie's premonition and had a bad feeling. "Mister Buddie, he drive a Model A."

The two figures crouched and lifted something. Claude rose slightly to see more. The man and woman struggled with what looked like a dead weight. Then he saw what they were doing. It was a body, and they were trying to place it behind the wheel of the car. The second car sputtered intermittently, idling behind the first.

The man spoke. "Got to hurry it up. If my car dies on us out here, we're done for."

"Let me push his legs in place." The woman was crying as she crouched and struggled and began a shoving motion toward the floorboard.

Claude watched the man reach into the car and set the motionless figure upright behind the wheel. He then ran back to the second car before returning.

Claude heard, "Got to pull some nails from the railing."

Then the woman said, "He's still moaning, Freddy," then added, "What nails? Why?"

He pointed to the rail. "This is all new construction so it will be really tough. I want to nudge the car through the rail and if I pull some nails, it will go through easier. Believe me, Betty, I've worked enough road gangs while in the can, I know what I'm talking about."

Claude heard the creaking sound of long nails being extracted. The man, who the woman had called Freddy, handed them to the woman as each one was removed. He struggled to make note of the names. Her name was Betty, he remembered, Freddy had called her Betty.

Freddy returned to the Model A after extracting several nails and leaned into the passenger side momentarily before returning to Betty.

"Now what?" she asked.

"I'm going to shove it through the rail with my car so it will go down the embankment. The cops will think he ran off the road."

"He's stabbed, Freddy."

"I smeared blood on the nails and dropped them inside. They're almost as long as that ice pick. The cops are stupid, they'll see those and maybe figure the nails did it."

"You think so?"

"A man alone on this highway at night? He fell asleep, missed the curve, and busted through the barricade in a wreck."

"I hope you're right."

"Get back in my car. We need to finish shoving his heap and then hightail it back to Trinity. We'll both need to clean up and get rid of these clothes and then all we gotta do is sit tight."

Icy fingers of fear held Claude motionless. He dreaded any prospect of dealing with these evil people and again thought of Evie's prophetic dream. He was afraid for his own life and for Evie's as well. With widened eyes, he watched the two get into the second car, and then the driver pulled around and matched bumpers with the Model A. After he shunted it forward about two feet, he repositioned his car to get more directly behind the first and touched bumpers again. His car strained as he gunned the engine and Claude heard the sound of splintering wood, followed by a creak and crunch of metal as the Model A disappeared from sight.

The driver got out and looked over the edge then removed his coat and used it to wipe at something on the pavement. A sand pile stood nearby and he scooped a handful of sand and added that to the spot, spreading it around with his foot, before returning to his car. The smaller roadster backed up then drove past the tumbled sawhorses and turned left, proceeding down the highway via the old bridge, its staccato clatter fading as it moved away from him.

When he was sure the second car was gone, Claude emerged from his hiding place and made his way up his side of the embankment, which wasn't as high as the other side. He paused at the last spot where he saw the man working but couldn't really make out anything in the moonlight. He then proceeded to the gaping cavity in the railing and looked down toward the creek. He saw the Model A sitting on its roof.

"Must've rolled when it went over," he muttered as he made his way down to the car. A body had been partially thrown from the car and was wedged under a portion of the car. When he got close enough to see the face, his initial fear was realized.

"Mister Buddie! I was afraid it was you!" Claude said as he reached out and shook a shoulder with one hand.

Earl moaned and cracked one eye open. "C-C-C-Claude?"

Earl's head and face were battered from the impact, but he managed to keep the one eye open.

"Gonna run get you some help, boss. Gotta get somebody out here to help you. I was out here busting up my still just like I promised. I heard the tires and rushed over through the woods and seen it all, I knows the names, I heard them talking."

"Claude, I'm afraid I'm done for," Earl whispered, then coughed and something dark dribbled down his chin. "You can't do anything like that, they, they'll blame you. You know they will. Black man on the scene when a white man dies, they'll pin it all on you. McIntyre did this," he panted and struggled to continue through fits of coughing. "He'll put everything on you and hang a death penalty on you. You have to keep quiet, you hear? Protect yourself and your family or they'll kill all of them, too."

Deep inside, Claude knew Buddie was speaking an unwritten truth. The implications of a Black man found on the scene with a dying white man would come with dire consequences. He would be the first to admit he was not good at math, but he did know that two and two didn't necessarily add up to four under such circumstances.

Even in the shadows of the night, Claude could see the color had drained from Earl's face and every time he coughed more blood sputtered out of his mouth. "I'm dying, help would never get here in time, but I need a favor from you." He coughed again, "Can you do me one favor, Claude?"

"I'll do anything I can Mister Buddie, anything!"

"Take care of my wife. You know her, Lily May. Keep her safe from McIntyre. Keep her safe for me. You hear? I know her. She'll want to get mixed up in everything, she'll want to get to the truth but if they could kill me, they'll kill her, too, I know they will. Will you promise me that?"

"I will. With Jesus as my witness, Mister Buddie. I promise."

What followed was a deep gurgling groan and a faint gasp. In all of his life, Claude had seen four men die from various circumstances, so he knew his friend had passed from this earth. He bowed his head and shared a private prayer, then touched Earl's shoulder before scrambling back up the embankment.

He crossed into the woods and again struggled through the underbrush until he saw the bent tree.

"The devil's perch," he muttered. He reattached the top to the boiler and leaned everything down as low as he could. He remembered his cigar and picked it up from the rock, then found the trail to home on the other side of the clearing.

"Gotta get far away from here as fast as I can. I'll get back to this another time."

He lit the stogie as he walked, hopeful that smoking would help his frayed nerves.

The smoke stung his eyes as he wept. "I'm powerful sorry, Mister Buddie, I'll do what you asked if it's the last thing I do."

Between Huntsville and Trinity—9:00 p.m.

Fred clasped the steering wheel so tight the white of his knuckles almost glowed in the dark. He pressed down hard on the accelerator, sending waves of pain from the soles of his feet all the way up to his aching calf and thigh.

Betty dabbed at both eyes with her bloodied handkerchief. "Can't this car go any faster?"

"I'm trying, baby, I'm trying. We're way down the road already, we're in the clear, I promise. Nobody will find him in time to tie us to the wreck." Fred kept looking back but saw no headlights behind them. He fumbled with a cigarette. "Hey, light me a gasper, will ya?"

"You promised your plan would work," she said. She bent down to strike a match, then puffed lightly before handing the smoke to Fred.

He dangled it from his lips and said, "Damn it, Betty, *you* stabbed him first."

She sobbed. "I know, it was my fault. I started to go soft on the guy—he was good looking, ya know? When I touched his cheek, he went all sour on me. He was going to put me out of the car, Freddy. Our whole plan depended on people seeing Swanger and me together in Trinity. I panicked."

"The jig was up, so what? I would have come up with a new plan. I never figured we'd have to push a Harlem Sunset on the guy."

"*You* zotzed him, Freddy, I just stuck him in the shoulder." Betty rubbed her throbbing wrist. "I forgot how bad it hurts to hit bone."

"I croaked a guy in the joint one time. Had to shiv him twice because the first time I hit a rib. Hurt like hell."

"I feel real sorry for you, Fred, poor baby." She feigned a pout. "So what do we do now?"

Fred reset his cramping leg and again slammed his right foot on the pedal, as if it would somehow hasten their progress. "Got to get me a faster car for one thing. Okay, we need to change out of these rags and wash up, then I need to get rid of them."

"What about my ice pick?"

Fred shot her a quick glance. "I've got it in my pocket. Thanks for reminding me, doll. Need to toss it somewhere around the river. I'll look for a place when we get to the bridge near Riverside."

There were several cars on the road when they crossed the bridge so Fred didn't stop.

Betty asked, "What now?"

"I know a spot where me and a buddy used to fish when we was kids. It's not far, there's a small turnoff. The river's created a lot of forgotten lakes during floods. It would change course and lock off an old bend. That place will be perfect—quiet and hidden."

He slowed and found the turnoff. It was little more than a muddy trail off the highway.

"Do you know where you're going?"

He said, "Yeah, baby. It's not far." He then made a turn around a stand of trees. "There it is, see?"

They approached a clearing bordered by a small body of water shimmering in the sporadic moonlight. He parked the car but left the engine running and opened the door. He pulled the bloody rag from his pocket.

"I'll toss this thing and we'll get back on our way," he said, before walking to the bank. He threw it as hard as he could. A faint splash was his reward for the effort.

Back in the car, he winced as he ground the complaining transmission into reverse, then glanced at Betty as they moved forward again. "Getting rid of that goes a long way to making sure we're not tied to anything that happened."

"I hope so," she answered.

"I'll drop you off so you can strip outta those clothes and wash up. I'll do the same at my place. Double wrap them in a couple of sacks and I'll come back by later and get them, then take everything out to burn somewhere." He then added, "Shoes too."

"But I *like* these shoes."

"When I say everything, I mean everything. We don't want to leave a drop of blood anywhere." Fred thought for a moment. "Reminds me, I need to clean out this car real good, too."

Betty's voice wavered. "Wonder what McIntyre will do when he finds out about this?"

Fred laughed. "He wanted the guy out of the way, didn't he? It's probably not what he bargained for, but as far as things go, Swanger's off the ballot as of today."

"It ain't funny, Fred." Betty stifled a sob. "What if somebody else saw us, you know, besides the waitress. Don't forget you were going to go pay her off."

"We need to figure out our story real good just in case the cops come asking questions."

"I guess I'd just say he was giving me a ride back to Trinity because I thought I'd missed my other ride, then I noticed the car coming up behind us and figured it was my pal trying to catch up." She smiled. "That's it. I asked him to let me out so I could ride with my friend."

"What friend?"

"You, Freddy."

"Oh, right. I guess that will be all right as long as the waitress plays ball."

"What if she don't?"

"I can be very convincing when I want to be, sweetheart," he said, brushing her thigh.

"Oh, Fred," she giggled. "You are quite the charmer when you want to be."

He smiled and eyed her as he drove on toward Trinity.

Between Huntsville and Trinity—11:00 p.m.

Deputy Zeke Tannehill noticed something out of place on Highway 19 during a routine patrol and pulled over to investigate. He was only two hours into his shift and was grateful to finally have the possibility of some police work to do. As he stopped at the beginning of the turnoff to the new bridge over Harmon Creek, his headlights confirmed the initial observation.

"Danged barricade's been knocked over. Probably some fool kids have been messing around out here again." He got out of his patrol car and scanned the surroundings. "I get tired of this sort of silliness."

He walked over and examined the sawhorses and saw the plank that used to stretch between them sitting at an odd angle over to the side. He shined his light on it.

"Cracked," he said to himself, then shined his light down the path to the new bridge. "Hope nobody went off that danged thing."

He slowly made his way down toward the new construction. He kept one hand on the butt of his revolver as his eyes strained to see anything ahead of him in the moonlight. He got to the bridge and shined a beam all around. Another crude barricade at the bridge entrance was intact.

"Looks okay, I guess." He retraced his steps. Bullfrogs in the creek heralded his intrusion and crickets joined in with the reprise. "I'll just reset the plank across the road and report it when I get back to headquarters," he intoned to himself. On these lonely night patrols, he was the only person who would listen to his remarks.

As he made his way, a sparkle of moonlight reflecting just off the road caught his eye. He shined his flashlight over the area where he thought he had noticed the momentary glint. At first he saw nothing, but as his eyes adjusted to the shadows he caught a glimpse of an image looming in the darkness and trained his light on it. A form took shape, blacker than the shadows but barely perceptible in the moonlight.

He shook his flashlight in a futile attempt to make it shine brighter. "Danged light can't reach that far, gotta get closer."

Then Tannehill saw something else. He had been so intent on looking down the road toward the bridge, he had missed the narrow gap in the railing. He walked over to it and examined the splinters of wood, then noticed parallel tracks leading down the embankment toward the dark shape in the shadows. He made his way down the steep slope and pulled his pistol out as he inched forward. He could see a car sitting upside down on its roof. He'd seen enough wrecks in his five years as a deputy to know this one was probably fatal. He shined his light around the scene and saw a body partially trapped.

"Lordy," he blurted out.

He reached down and touched the side of the man's neck to see if he could find a pulse. He'd learned to do that in France during the war. He retracted his hand immediately because it spurred another memory of a reality he knew all too well, the cold and empty feeling of death. He'd learned that in France as well.

He gulped. "Gotta get back and report this."

He checked again for a pulse and brought his ear down close to the lips to listen for any hint of breath. He shook his head. "Can't help this fellow now, but the sheriff will want to know." He scribbled the plate number in his ticket book, scrambled up the embankment and ran to his patrol car. Along the way he stopped to reset the two sawhorses and replace the splintered plank between them. "Don't want nobody else wrecking tonight, we got enough trouble on our hands."

He thought about turning on his siren but decided against it. "There'll be enough sirens later on," he said to himself.

He pressed the pedal to the floorboard and raced back to Huntsville.

Huntsville, Texas—11:00 p.m.

Claude was furiously pumping water and splashing it on his face and arms. He shook the droplets off, then pumped again, repeating the action several times. Evie heard the commotion and hurried out, letting the wrinkled screen door crack loud against the frame like a gunshot.

When he looked up, he knew she could see the pitiful and mournful emotion in his eyes that is generally reserved for grief.

"Claude! What's wrong?"

"You was right, Evie. I should have listened to you. Something bad done happened out there, something evil. I'm afraid to even say it out loud."

She could see he was trembling. Her husband was a strong and proud man. She had never seen him tremble before.

"Did you see a ghost out there? Or did someone jump you? Tell me!"

Claude settled his large frame on the muddy ground and let out a deep sigh. "They're a ghost now, I reckon."

"Will you quit this nonsense and tell me what happened?"

"It's Mister Buddie."

"Your lawyer? *That* Mister Buddie?"

He nodded. "He done been killed out by Harmon Creek. Not far from my still. I was...I was..."

Evie knelt beside him and rubbed his shoulder as he sat and sobbed. "You're here, safe with me now. Tell me what happened."

He continued through stifled sobs, "I was busting up my still, just like I promised. My secret spot ain't far from the highway."

"I know, you've told me that before. You put it close to the creek so you could get fresh water."

"That's right. I heard a screeching of tires, then some shouting. I made my way through the woods, thinking maybe somebody was in trouble. Well, somebody was in trouble...Mister Buddie."

"He wrecked his car on the bridge?"

"No, he was hurt and there was two people intent on killing him. He was facing them off, holding one of his arms like he'd already been hurt some, but he was moving up on the other two. Then the other fella stepped up to him and stabbed him. Couldn't have been nothing else. Mister Buddie dropped like a sack of potatoes."

Evie gasped. "May God have mercy."

"I was afraid, Evie. At first, I didn't know it was Mister Buddie. Couldn't rightly see nothing much in the dark but their motions and some yelling, but I've seen enough fights to know that's what I was seeing. Then I heard them other two plotting what to do with the body.

"So it was two people."

"Yes, a man and a woman. They put Mister Buddie back in the car and shoved it through the railings off the embankment. Then they took off, high-tailing it down the highway."

"How could they push his car through a railing?"

"Used the other car to shove it until it broke through and rolled over."

"How'd they get him to stop?"

"I don't know, I didn't know anything was happening until I heard the tires screeching, but they did. Then those two drove off. When they was gone, I went across to the rail and made my way down to the car. It was sitting on its top and somebody was sticking out, trapped under it. That was when I found out it was Mister Buddie. He was still alive, but he was hurt bad. I've seen the face of death enough in this life, so I knowed he was fading fast."

"We should report this to the law."

"Too late for that. He said so himself before he died, he told me to keep quiet about being there—that everybody would most likely blame me."

"He got a point. With a white man dead and black man on the scene, you'd be the easiest one for the white folks to put the blame on. And worse, you wouldn't have Mister Buddie to help you none. These other people, you sure they didn't see you?"

"No, they didn't, but I think I recognized the man's voice. He's a two-bit hustler from up Trinity way. I sold to him once or twice."

"What kind of beef he have with Mister Buddie?"

Claude started to rise. "I don't rightly know, but I do know one thing."

"What's that?"

"Mister Buddie was fearful they'd go after his wife, made me promise to look after her."

"Miss Lily May? Why, she's one of God's own angels on this earth, who'd want to harm a hair on her head?"

"I reckon anybody willing to kill a man in cold blood out next to Harmon Creek would do just about anything."

"Let's dry you off. I've got some corn bread in here, and some food will warm your soul while we figure this out. We're okay as long as nobody knows you were out there, not the police or those two people you saw."

"What about Miss Lily May?"

"From what you said before, she's out of town. We'll figure out what to do about her when she gets back. Somebody will surely find that car and the law will contact her soon enough. Lord have mercy, she's going to be grieving something awful. Almost ain't nothing worse in this life that to be widowed at such a young age."

Seven

Wednesday, July 9, 1930

Between Huntsville and Trinity—12:15 a.m.

Several vehicles crowded the spur to the new Harmon Creek Bridge, and they parked to create a makeshift perimeter around the broken rail overlooking the small embankment with their headlights. Below them, a pack of uniformed men loitered around the wrecked car, illuminated by the ring of headlights from the roadway. Deputy Tannehill stood to one side with Walker County Sheriff Nathan Steele, as other deputies, a wrecker driver, and an ambulance driver worked to pull the body out. The victim had been thrown out and the car had rolled on top of his legs.

"We've got to get this car off of him," the ambulance driver observed.

"Yeah, maybe a bunch of us can lift it enough to pull him out from under it." The wrecker driver scratched his chin. "You sure he's dead?"

The ambulance driver looked back from the broken window. "I ain't got no medical training to speak of, but I know a dead guy when I see one."

The wrecker driver went to his rig and came back with a long pry bar and managed to lever the car up a few inches. Then he leaned in hard and coaxed it another inch and as he held it, a muster of several strong hands pushed and lifted the car enough to allow the ambulance driver to pull the body free. The car creaked ominously when they all released their hold on it.

The ambulance driver reached down to grab the shoulders. "Here we go. Somebody grab his legs. Let's move him farther from the car."

Two men complied and with a joint struggle the body was moved away from the car and placed on the moist ground.

"Why is it so wet down here?" came a question from the crowd surrounding the body.

"A small thunderstorm rolled through just after I started back to headquarters," Deputy Tannehill said.

The sheriff beamed a flashlight across the dead man's features. "Looks familiar." Then a wave of recognition flushed his face. "Oh my God, it's Earl Swanger."

"That lawyer fella? Why, he goes to my church. I didn't even recognize him."

Another voice in the crowd said, "Hey, isn't he running for district attorney?"

"Wonder how he ended up off the main road and over here?"

It was an anonymous question, but as they exchanged curious glances it was evident they were all inwardly asking themselves the same thing.

Another car's tires crunched on the gravel and Tannehill took several steps up the embankment for a look, then called out, "It's the county health officer."

A portly gentleman struggled down to the assemblage with Tannehill's help. "So what do have we here, Sheriff?"

"Thanks for coming out, Doctor Mendelson. We just pulled the body out of the wreck." Sheriff Steele shined his light up the embankment. "Went through that railing, rolled, and he ended up under part of the car here. Not sure how long it was before Deputy Tannehill found him. We just pulled him out."

The doctor huffed slightly as he knelt beside the body. He pulled a stethoscope out of his bag and listened at the chest and shook his head. Without looking up, he checked the eyes and tested the arms and legs of the victim. "No rigor as yet," he muttered, more to himself than anybody listening.

The sheriff commented, "Yeah, they had a hard enough time getting him out from under that car. Rigor mortis would have made it a damned sight harder. I hate it when we have to break a leg or an arm to just get somebody away from a wreck."

Mendelson glanced up at the sheriff with his mouth set at stern angle. "Yes." He struggled to get up and the sheriff lent a helping hand. "Thank you. Now I'd like to have a look inside this car if I can."

The doctor got on his hands and knees and peered into the passenger compartment, shining a flashlight around the steering wheel, the seat, and the floor. He emerged and returned to Sheriff Steele. "I need this body transported to my office immediately for a thorough examination."

"Why, Doctor? Seems pretty open and shut to me."

"I've seen many accidents of this type in my career and never want to draw immediate conclusions. I will perform an autopsy and make a detailed determination of the cause of death."

"Waste of the county's money," the sheriff observed, "but we'll bring him on over, if that's what you want." He waved to some of the men, who were standing together, talking and smoking a few feet away. "Gather him up, boys, and haul him up to that ambulance." He spoke to the driver. "Doctor Mendelson here will tell you where to take him."

"Strap the body securely to the stretcher, please," the doctor instructed, "or you'll never get it up that embankment. I don't want him knocked around more than he already has been. Please. My work is hard enough without additional bruising."

87

It took four men to haul the body up to the waiting vehicle. It was hard going, and they slipped more than once on the wet ground, but they never let go of their burden. Once they reached the broken railing, it was smooth going and the body was deposited in the ambulance. One of the deputies helped the doctor back up to his car, and the ambulance soon followed the doctor's sedan down Highway 19 back to Huntsville.

While this was going on, Sheriff Steele was busy examining the car. He studied each dent, first pushing at the metal, then rubbing his fingers along the paint. He spent a long time on the ground, shining his light around the passenger compartment. "Think you can get this thing back up the embankment?" the sheriff asked the wrecker driver.

"My winch will pull just about anything out of just about anywhere, but I might need a few more hands to help me right it and guide it out. Can it wait until morning?" The driver spit a brown glob to the side. "It will shore be easier in the light."

"I reckon," Sheriff Steele said. "You got room for it in your garage? I'd like to keep it out of the weather until we have a chance to look at it more thoroughly."

"We can store it for you, Sheriff. Regular county rate."

Sheriff Steele smirked. "I'll be by later with a couple of detectives. Call my office when you have it over there."

"Will do, Sheriff."

"And don't mess with anything inside.

"You got it, Sheriff."

Steele put his hands on his hips and sighed as he surveyed the scene one last time. He shook his head and made his way back up to his waiting car.

Trinity, Texas—2:30 a.m.

Betty Johnston was brushing her damp hair when a gentle rapping at the door made her heart skip a beat. The knock repeated.

88

A whispered message followed the second tap. "It's me! Open up."

She gathered the front of her robe and peeked out the curtains to make sure it was Fred. He widened his eyes and crooked his head at her with a questioning smirk. She opened the door and let him in.

"What's the holdup? You knew I was coming. The longer you make me wait, the better chance somebody might see me," he said when he was finally inside. She could see he had changed his clothes.

"I'm sorry. I'm spooked, Freddy, that's all."

"You got the bundle ready?" he asked.

She pointed at a small pile of clothes on the bathroom floor. "I'm just barely out of the shower. I'll get them."

Fred walked over to the kitchenette and poked around until he found two paper bags, "Never mind, I've got it." He returned to the bathroom where he gingerly picked up each article of clothing and carefully placed it in the bag. He picked up the shoes last and put them on top of the clothes.

"My favorite shoes!" she said.

"They got splashes of blood on them so they go," he said.

When he was finished, he rolled the top of the bag down haphazardly, then placed this bag into the second one and folded it down neatly. He rose to his feet and observed, "Couple of spots of blood there." He pointed at the floor. "You best clean those up right away before they dry. A little Clorox helps."

Betty's eyes welled up. "I'm sorry I panicked and messed everything up, Freddy."

"I know, honey, but what's done is done. Listen, I gotta go someplace quiet and burn these clothes, you know? Let's cool it for today. Just do what you'd normally do. Business as usual."

"I don't feel like any business right now."

Fred gently stroked her shoulder. "Aw, baby, I didn't mean like that. Just stick to routine stuff. You got a radio? Listen to some shows, it'll help pass the time. Right now you should maybe get a little shut-eye."

"All I can see in my mind is the look that fella gave me when I first stabbed him. I'm not sure I'll ever be able to sleep again."

"It gets better, Betty, I promise. Just give it some time."

"You know, it ain't the first time I poked a guy, but all the other times they was roughing me up or stiffing me for the money they owed me. This was different."

"Yeah, I kind of feel the same way. I just sort of lost it when he lunged at me, well, you know, the ice pick was already in my hand. It was just like getting jumped in the big house. I just reacted, you know? I didn't have time to think."

Betty nodded, sobbing.

Fred started toward the door, carrying the bag. "I'll be in touch. Maybe we can just blow this joint, get a change of scenery for a while until things cool off."

"Don't forget the waitress. You said you were going to pay her off."

Fred inhaled through his teeth. "Right. She was working in the afternoon, so she probably won't be there until later on. I'll do it right after I burn this stuff and maybe grab a few z's myself."

"You sure we're going to be okay, Freddy?"

"We're a cinch, sweetie, it's in the bag," he said, patting the bundle as he laughed to himself. "Get it?" He laughed again.

"It ain't funny, Freddy," she said as she slammed the door.

Betty watched through the curtains as Fred tossed the bag to the floorboard of his red two-seater and drove off. She began to cry again. "It's not funny at all."

Marquez, Texas—7:05 a.m.

Laura Carrington busied herself in the kitchen and looked up as Lily May entered the room and sat at the table where she sighed deeply. Laura got a cup and saucer, poured her niece a cup of coffee and sat next to her. Commodore the cat followed and curled at Lily May's feet and began to purr.

"You just don't seem yourself this morning, dear. What's wrong, are you coming down with something?"

Lily May sighed again. "I didn't sleep well last night."

"It must have been this awful humidity. That thunderstorm really steamed up the air."

"It wasn't that, Aunt Laura. It's a feeling deep inside me. I swear, I've never felt anything quite like this before, well, at least not since Mama died. It's like I'm expecting the sword of Damocles to fall right on my head."

Laura put a consoling hand on Lily May's arm. "My goodness, you were all of ten years old then. I have a great respect for feelings of dread like this, but in my experience they usually end up being nothing. Nothing at all."

She was interrupted by the telephone ringing in three short bursts and one long burst.

"Oh, my, three short and one long, that's me," Laura said, rising to rush down the hallway. "Probably about your ride today. Those ladies can never do anything according to plan."

A few seconds later, a scream pierced the stillness and Commodore jumped to his feet, arching his back with ruffled fur.

"Lily May!"

Commodore lifted his head and quizzically gazed toward Lily May as she ran past him. He tilted his head, momentarily confused by the wailing sounds that followed behind hallway door. Then he placed his chin back on his folded paws and resumed his nap.

Huntsville, Texas—7:40 a.m.

"Morning, Sheriff. Coffee?"

"Please, Miss Sue," he said, flipping the upside-down cup and nestling its base into the depression in the saucer.

"Rough night?" she asked as she was pouring the steaming liquid into his cup. She placed a tiny bottle of cream next to it.

"Car wreck, northeast of town, next to Harmon Creek."

"Anybody hurt?"

"One dead. Can't say who, the office is in the process of tracking down next of kin, but he's well-known."

Sue sat down. "I'm no gossip, Sheriff. You can tell me. Look, I'm tired too, I had to work a double yesterday. I was here all danged day long. Come on."

"Can't do it, honey, sorry."

The door opened and another officer entered. He looked around and spotted Sheriff Steele at a table and came over. He smiled at Sue, who the sheriff waved away. She took the pot back behind the counter.

"Can't you leave me alone long enough to eat my breakfast in peace?"

Mike Adams stopped in his tracks, melting under the older man's withering stare. Steele liked the kid, but he was young and new to the department.

"I'm sorry, Sheriff, but I figured you'd want to know right away. I found her...neighbor lady said she went visiting in Leon County, said she stays with her aunt in Marquez. I just got off the phone with Mrs. Swanger. She took it pretty hard."

The sheriff gasped. "Over the phone? What is wrong with you?"

"Wh-what was I supposed to do?"

Steele almost growled. "You call Leon County and they go out there in person, usually with a parson who knows her. Oh, Lordy, can this day get any worse? If you are going to be in law enforcement, you have to think. You get shot out in the field one day, do you want me to *call* your mama, or you want me to go over there and hold her hand when I break the news to her?"

The deputy's head dropped. "I-I-I...no, you're right. I'm sorry, Sheriff."

He drained about half the cup of coffee in one gulp and winced as the heat made his teeth ache and his gums sting. "Can't even take time for breakfast."

"Where you going?"

"Got to go call the Leon County sheriff and get somebody over there with the preacher and console that widow. I hope to God you haven't outright killed her." He rushed out the door, muttering under his breath, "...on the phone!"

The deputy started for the door as well, but Sue approached him. "Did I hear you say Swanger? Was it Earl Swanger, the lawyer?"

The deputy turned white. "Can't say. I'm in enough trouble already." He knew his own day had just gotten worse.

"I know what I heard. Listen. He was just in here last night. I saw him talking to some floozy. Didn't know the girl but overheard them talking—something about going to Trinity. There was one other odd thing, though."

"What's that?"

"There was another guy in here. I'd swear he was paying way too much attention to them. You know. He was trying not to show it, but he was eavesdropping on them two."

"What do you mean?"

"We get used to the way people act in here. Most keep to themselves. Some conduct business. You might see a man notice a pretty girl. I tell you, I swat away enough wandering hands myself to know that. But this guy was locked on those two. Oh, not in an obvious way, but he was watching them. He caught my eye because he had a tight waxed mustache. Funny little guy, maybe five-six. He left right after they did. No tip, either. I always remember the fellas who stiff me."

"Did you see anything else?"

"The guy was fishy, so I went to the window to watch him and saw Swanger and the woman getting into a green Ford. I know it because my daddy has the exact same car."

"And the other guy?"

"He got into a red two-seater. A bit beat up. He seemed to be struggling to keep up with the other car after they all took off."

"You may have just saved my bacon, Sue. Listen, don't say anything to anybody else about this." He placed a silver dollar in her hand. "Please?"

She smiled. "Sure, for a tip like this I'd say the moon was made of cheese."

Marquez, Texas—9:45 a.m.

Laura Carrington clutched a handkerchief to her quivering lower lip and stared out the window as she watched the Leon County sheriff and Reverend Tomkins trudge down the steps and return to a patrol car. She heard Lily May sobbing behind her. An intense wave of grief had swept through the house after the phone call from Huntsville, but this latest visit served to renew the shock when the visitors verified the tragic news. Laura closed the curtain before returning to the drawing room to sit next to her niece.

Lily May dabbed at her eyes with a wet handkerchief. "How could this have happened?"

"Now, now, the sheriff didn't know, did he? And like Reverend Tomkins said, we can never truly know the workings of the Lord, can we?"

"And to first get the news on the telephone. Who ever heard of such a thing?"

Laura put an arm around her. "He told me the Walker County sheriff was livid and asked him to personally come here to help make things right. Apparently, it was a very young deputy who called. His mama didn't teach him any common sense, did she?"

"It's all so sudden. I don't know what to think. I need to get back there and find out things for myself. Oh, my, what about Buddie's mother?"

"The sheriff said he was going to Normangee next, so he could express his condolences to Eugenia in person. I've also called several friends. Is there anyone else you want me to call?"

"Buddie's sister."

"Oh, that's right, Pearl moved to Austin. I'll make the long-distance call."

"It's so expensive."

"Never mind that, dear, we do what's right in this house, you know that. If we can think of anyone else out of town, I'll send some telegrams."

"I need to pack."

"Lily May, there isn't anything you can do and in the state you're in, you need to stay right here and let me take care of you. The sheriff over in Walker County is doing everything he can, and I'm sure when he knows something, he'll be sure to tell us."

Between Huntsville and Trinity—9:15 a.m.

Fred gathered a pile of sticks and arranged half of them in a crude crisscross shape. He doused them with kerosene, pouring from a can he brought in his car. The oily odor of the fluid burned into the membranes of his nose and he sneezed.

"I'm glad the can was half full, hopefully it will be enough."

He put one of the bags on top of the sticks and poured more liquid.

He struck a match and stood transfixed as the reddened globule at the end flashed to life. It never ceased to amaze him, the way a flame magically appeared at the end of a match, like something alive, its only purpose to destroy something else with its fire. He knelt down to one of the protruding sticks, touched the flame to it and again marveled as one twig after another burst into flame. As the fire began to grow, the bag caught fire and smoke billowed off the pile. He added a few larger broken branches he had found, breaking them in half and sometimes smaller. When he judged the fire was big enough, he added the second bag of clothes. Some of the wood was still damp from the recent storm and he was sure that added to the smoke, but he splashed more kerosene from a few feet away and the fire flared again, and the wood began to burn with more intensity. He added several more branch scraps then scrambled around in the underbrush to find more because the bundles were smoldering again.

"Taking more than I thought," he mumbled.

He jabbed at the flames with one large branch, stirring more fuel into the center of the inferno then he scurried off just beyond the tree line and returned with another armload of sticks and placed them on top of the smoldering ruins. He poured the remainder of the can onto the fire and stepped back as it reawakened the blaze. His face flushed from the heat and he broke into a cold sweat.

"It's really too hot to be burning stuff like this." He surveyed the surroundings in the dim light of the dawn. He had returned to the same secret spot of his youth, hoping the small secluded clearing in the forgotten patch of woods next to the little lake would give him the privacy he needed.

"It's finally burning down to nothing," he said, shaking his head. "Good clothes, gas, kerosene, this caper has ended up costing me a lot. Plus, now I got to drive back to Huntsville and find that waitress to pay her off." He lifted the empty can. "Guess I should get rid of this, too."

After removing his boots and socks, he rolled up his pants legs and walked into the water a few steps and made a face as the muck on the bottom squished through his toes. He took the top off the can and placed it on its side in the water, pushing it down so it would begin to fill. An oily film exited as the water rushed in, and he was momentarily transfixed by the swirls of rainbow sheen that formed on the surface of the small lake. He felt the can begin to sink of its own accord and he gently shoved it away from the shore where it slipped beneath the surface like the *Lusitania*.

He swished his feet before exiting the lake to clean them as much as he could, then returned with his boots and socks to the fire. He poked at it with a long stick, stirring it to momentarily enhance the flames and took turns extending each foot to more quickly dry them. In all of his many experiences, this was his first attempt to burn clothes. He silently wished his old friend Squint was with him to give him another one of his lessons.

"...but Squint's a lifer, still in the joint," he mumbled.

In the endless prison nights, his cellmate would regale him with stories of past crimes. Fred looked up to Squint, regarding him almost as the big brother he'd never had. To Fred, Squint was an experienced and successful crook who knew the ins and outs of the business and freely passed along his trade secrets. But, of course, like everybody else in the big house, he got caught.

"Ratted out," as Squint had told him.

Fred laughed out loud. "It always seemed like everybody in the joint was ratted out." He stirred at the fire again. "But good old Squint, he would have known how to get rid of this stuff a lot easier. He had the knowing of a lot of things."

Fred pulled a watch out of his pocket, frowned, and then poked at the fire again. "How much is enough?" he wondered. "It's mostly ashes but some of it is still smoldering."

By stirring and prodding he eventually got the flames going again for a minute, but they died down. Fred walked back and forth in frustration, and as he paced, he swatted at the wisps of smoke that followed him like a little puppy dog yapping at his heels. He put the last few pieces of wood on the smoking embers and got on his hands and knees to blow into the ashes. Each breath resulted in an intense glow, sometimes erupting in a flame or two, then it died back down to a smoking mass. He prowled the nearby underbrush but found he had exhausted the easy supply of sticks, but a lingering lifelong fear prevented him from venturing deeper into the woods.

"I hate the thought of running into a snake out there," he said to himself as he peered deeper into the thick brush surrounding him. "Geez, I need to get going. I've been up all night and I've still got things to do."

He returned to the smoking rubble and determined the fire had done a good enough job. "Nothing much is left. It looks like somebody was camping and burned up their trash. Don't much like leaving it smoldering like this, but didn't think I'd need something to fetch water," he said. "I'm sure Squint would have known to bring along a bucket." He looked out at the lake, silently wishing he'd kept the kerosene can.

He impulsively looked around, then relieved himself on the remains of the fire. It popped and sputtered, releasing more smoke, but he could tell his minimal effort had diminished it. He scraped up dirt and spread double handfuls over the smoke. After several applications it was reduced to sparse wisps that disappeared a few feet above the blackened pile.

"Gonna have to do," he remarked, brushing his palms against each other, then he bent down and brushed dirt from his pant legs. "Hopefully I can snooze a little before that waitress gets on duty." He struggled with his memory, trying to conjure an image of her name tag as he drove and finally exclaimed, "Sue! That was her name."

Huntsville, Texas—9:45 a.m.

The sheriff stood in a corner as Doctor Mendelson completed his examination of the body. Eventually he pulled a sheet over the dead man's head and turned to Sheriff Steele.

"Although he was found in a wrecked car, it's mighty suspicious." The doctor removed his spectacles and wiped them with a handkerchief.

"What do you mean, Doc?"

He pulled the sheet down again to reveal the upper body. "Stab wounds, here, here, and over here," he said, pointing to the center of the chest, at the right collar bone area, and on the right arm just below the shoulder."

"Those little dots?"

"My educated guess would be an ice pick. A most effective weapon in certain circumstances. Deep enough to do some serious damage to tissue, but it doesn't outwardly bleed as much as say, a knife wound."

The sheriff bent forward and looked closely. "So, if an ice pick bleeds less than a knife wound, that would account for the lack of a large amount of blood."

"Yes, but he suffered an extraordinary amount of internal bleeding. I'd say the stabbing did not cause instantaneous death. He most likely lingered for a short while before the bleeding essentially caused heart failure. The technical term would be exsanguination."

The sheriff knew the term. "He bled to death?"

"Precisely. From internal bleeding, like I said. It makes the time of death much more difficult to determine. Mr. Swanger likely passed away some time after the apparent accident."

"Can anything else cause wounds like this?"

"Anything long and pointed can do it, but a wound from an ice pick is certainly more common."

"But it could have been something else?"

"It's possible...but—"

The sheriff interrupted, "But without the actual weapon we don't know for sure, correct?"

"I suppose, but Sheriff..."

Steele again interrupted. "Listen, Doc, we've got a political candidate dead two weeks before an election. There's already too many people who know about this so word is going to get out. This will cause attention, and attention is one thing we don't need right now, not this kind of attention."

"I have an official capacity in this county, I have to uphold the sanctity of my office and the medical profession."

"Doctor Mendelson, you are just as dirty as most of the rest of us in the county. You're in up to your eyeballs."

"I liked Earl Swanger."

"Who you like or who you don't like doesn't enter into the equation. You have to remember which side your bread is buttered on, if you catch my drift. I'm going to check in with the county attorney and the district attorney. Don't share *any* of this until we can convene and agree on an acceptable cause of death."

Mendelson blinked. Beads of sweat were rolling down his forehead into his eyes. He rubbed away the droplets and replaced his glasses before he lowered his head and managed a weak, "Of course.

Trinity, Texas—10:00 a.m.

Betty Johnston lifted a jar and took another long drink, but it didn't help at all. Even in her drunken stupor her mind replayed the look on Swanger's face when she first stabbed him.

"The jig was up, and he knew exactly why I'd insisted he give me a ride," she said, and took another nip. "But I didn't mean to poke him, I was just trying to make him keep going, afraid what Jenkins would do if I failed," she slurred. "It was Freddy's fault. We could have left him there, but it was Freddy who finished him, and it was Freddy's idea to push the car."

She realized she was still holding the jar. She sniffed at it and gagged, then reached out to put it on the table beside the settee, which was further away than it seemed, but the room was spinning. She missed the table and tumbled off to the floor as the jar rolled across the rug, spilling the contents. She tried to get up but passed out and rolled her head into the wet stain on the rug.

The sound of chirping birds caught her attention and she cracked her eyes open. The room smelled of cheap booze.

"Stupid birds," she slurred, still harboring the after-effects of the early morning binge. "Why is my hair wet?" she said as she felt around her head, then she raised herself and assessed the situation. She realized it wasn't just the room that smelled of booze. She saw the jar on the floor and the wet stain, then ran her fingers through her hair and smelled her hand.

"Drank myself into a pile of trash on the floor," she said. Her eyes began to tear. "Is this what I've come to?"

The night's events came flooding back to her, and Earl Swanger's blue eyes burned out at her from somewhere deep in her soul. It was a reflection she couldn't shake and it roused a wave of anger, remorse, and revulsion.

She stood, wavered a moment to regain her balance, then stumbled to the kitchenette to set up her percolator to make coffee.

"I need to make some changes. Maybe I'll get a real job. I need to clean up. No more hooch, no more lowlifes like Fred. I gotta get out of here."

The aroma from the coffee pot brightened her spirits. "There's something about that smell," she softly murmured, sitting at the small kitchen table. "It reminds me of cold winter mornings at my grandma's house. It warms my soul." She sobbed gently. "And my soul needs some serious warming."

After several minutes of intense bubbling, she turned the heat down and poured a cup. Her hands were shaking and some of the coffee sloshed into the saucer as she walked the three steps to the table. She poured the coffee out of the saucer into the cup, then sipped at it, almost burning her lips and tongue. "I need to figure out a way to get far away from here."

She looked at her pocketbook and remembered the three hundred dollars and wished she hadn't already paid Fred the other hundred. "Mr. McIntyre will be none too pleased with the way this turned out."

She took another sip.

"That's another reason to take a powder."

Huntsville, Texas—10:15 AM

McIntyre rose from his chair and leaned his watermelon crimson face forward as he screamed, "What do you mean he's dead?" A vein bulged on his forehead, and his mouth gaped as he struggled for more words.

For several seconds, the only sound in the room was the rattling of a wall-mounted oscillating fan, situated on a perch in a high corner and trying in vain to stimulate the hot, humid air. Dub Jenkins pulled at his collar and tried to look anywhere except Alvin McIntyre's bloodshot eyes.

"Uh, Mr. McIntyre, I don't rightly know what happened, but they found his car rolled down an embankment over by Harmon Creek. I got a guy in the sheriff's office who told me. It happened sometime last night."

"Earl Swanger. My opponent. The opponent you were supposed to impugn with allegations of impropriety." McIntyre paced behind his desk waving his arms. "That *was* the plan, wasn't it?"

"It *can't* be connected," Jenkins said, but he could tell McIntyre didn't believe him. Jenkins didn't much believe it either, but pushed his speculations forward. "It's got to be some kind of mistake. A coincidence. That girl up in Trinity I corralled to do the job for us was just supposed to be seen with him *up there*. I'm sure this was just an accident, that's all."

"So remind me more about this woman."

"Betty Johnston. Prostitute.We went easy on her a while back."

"Ah, yes. So she wasn't in the car. I mean, she wasn't killed or injured or anything like that."

"No, sir. Swanger was alone."

McIntyre placed two fists on the desk and leaned forward. "I want you to find this woman and see if she knows anything. Not one word of this can be allowed to point back to you or me. Do I make myself clear?"

Jenkins stumbled to his feet and back-stepped, stammering, "Yes, sir," as he quickly exited the office.

McIntyre lowered himself to his chair and wiped sweat from his face with a bare palm. He looked at it momentarily, then opened a desk drawer and pulled out a fresh handkerchief to wipe his hand dry.

His thoughts took the form of a dialogue in his head. *Of course they're related. They have to be. This is all that idiot Jenkins' fault.*

McIntyre opened another desk drawer and pulled out a small hip flask and took a drink, coughing slightly against the biting aftertaste of the liquor. "The worst thing about prohibition is the shortage of good Scotch," he rasped. "My God, that tastes of wet hay."

He picked up the telephone receiver and, leaning forward toward the mouthpiece said, "Get me Sheriff Steele." He waited for a full minute before a new voice crackled on the line.

"Steele."

"Nathan, this is Alvin McIntyre. What's the latest on Earl Swanger?" He interrupted a period of short silence with, "Are you there? Did you hear me?"

Sheriff Steele cleared his throat. "How'd you find out about that? We're still piecing things together."

"I'm the district attorney. I make it my business to know what's going on around here."

"Well, we've towed his car in, and we're fixing to go over it with a fine-toothed comb in a little while. It was pretty beat up from rolling down an embankment."

"Where was it?"

"At the cutoff to the new bridge over Harmon Creek."

"Was he alone?"

"Yes, sir. Single car accident, one victim."

"I get that, but what I'm asking is, was there any evidence that someone else was possibly in the car prior to the accident?"

"Like I said, I was just getting ready to go for a follow up look. I wondered the same thing. Oh, and there *is* one interesting fact, Alvin."

"What's that?"

"Doc found three wounds. He said they were most likely stab wounds, probably from an ice pick."

"An ice pick?"

"That's right."

"Well, let me know when you plan to convene with the medical officer, the county attorney, and the magistrate."

"That's all standard procedure."

"I want this cleared up as soon as possible."

"I understand, Alvin. I do, too."

McIntyre replaced the phone receiver and sighed.

"Stabbed. He was stabbed." He sat and ran his fingers over the top of his scalp as if he still had a full head of hair. "What has Jenkins done to me?"

The mention of an ice pick spurred his memory, and he crossed the room to open a nearby file cabinet. He thumbed through a series of folders and quickly found what he was looking for.

"Betty Johnston," he muttered to himself.

He thumbed through the reports and made small grunting noises as he struggled to read the handwriting on the arrest reports until he found what he was looking for. He scanned the sheet of paper, a list of her logged personal property during one particular arrest.

He said it out loud. "I knew it. One ice pick. It's a common weapon for prostitutes." He took the file back to his desk and placed it in the drawer with his flask and locked it, pocketing the key. "It's best to keep this hidden. I don't want the Maceos to get wind of this."

Huntsville, Texas—11:00 a.m.

"Claude, you really need to eat some of this fatback and beans. You ain't had a bite since last night." Evie stood in the doorway, looking down at Claude's stooped shoulders as he sat on the back step

He shrugged and continued to watch the chickens scamper around the yard, saying nothing.

Evie sat next to him and took his hand in hers. "You is the goodliest man I know. There ain't nothing you could have done to help him."

"I should tell somebody what I seen. It ain't right."

"Even he told you what a fool thing that would be. You know these white folks. They ain't going to hang a murder on no white man as long as they think they can pin it on somebody like you." She squeezed his big hand as best as she could. "Ain't nobody knows you was out there, Claude. I think we should keep it that way."

Claude picked up a pebble and tossed it into the yard, startling one of the younger hens that ran away at a sprint. "Danged thing was a tiny chick just a short while back."

"That's life. Things stay to their nature. Look, I'm your wife and I love you. But I needs you here with me, not off in prison or worse, hanging from the limbs of some oak tree. You gotta know that's how it's going to end up. The worst thing you done is make a little 'shine. You did your time and Mister Buddie, he got you free. The last piece of advice he gave you was to leave him be to save yourself, and you did it. I knows it was hard, but it was for the best. Your best and *our* best."

"I still need to go find Miss Lily May, like he asked me to do."

"What you need to do is eat something. I gots to walk to town and pick up a few things, and I'll see if I can find out what's up. The gossip wagon is probably full to the top, so I'm sure I'll get the latest news. She likely still back home with her people, and there's no telling when she'll get back. And, Claude?"

"Yes'm?"

"You can't tell her a single solitary thing of what you know. Ever. You hear me?"

"Why not?"

"It will kill her. Lord knows, I understand your promise to a dying man, but you can look after her without hurting her with too much truth. Lordy, Claude, I can't even begin to imagine the pain I'd suffer if it was you that was killed. You understand me? We don't ever tell nobody nothing about what we know."

"But I finished with what Mister Buddie wanted me to do. I got no reason to go over there no more."

"She don't know that. You go over there and find something else to fix. You're the best handyman around here. Look at that still you built out of scraps and such. I hear tell it was the best 'shine in the county. I hated to hear anybody speak of it, but you want to know something else?"

"What?"

"I was just a little bit proud, too. Crazy talk, right?"

Claude rose, still clutching Evie's hand in his bear claw of a hand, almost dragging her up with him. "Maybe I'll have some of that fatback and beans."

Evie steadied herself and hugged the big man although she barely came up to his shoulder and her arms only reached halfway around him. "That's my man. Come on, now, you hear? Food is good for the soul. And I just thought of something else."

"What's that?"

"A death in the family means lots of folks will be paying their respects. I reckon we can be a couple of them, don't you?"

"It's a start," he said, and he followed her into the house.

Huntsville, Texas—2:30 p.m.

Fred Darby parked about a block from the café. He pulled out his watch and mumbled to himself, "Two-thirty. She should be getting to work soon."

As he approached the entrance, a woman exited the café and he almost did a doubletake when he realized it was the waitress he wanted to see. She was coming directly toward him.

"Hey, baby," he said. "I was just coming by to see you."

"Lucky me," she quipped as she quickened her step and walked past him. She abruptly stopped and spun around. "You're that guy from yesterday. Stiffed me on the tip. I never forget a cheapskate."

Fred swallowed hard. "Yeah, sorry about that. That's, uh, that's why I was coming to see you. I was skinned yesterday, but I'm flush today so I wanted to make things right." He reached into his pocket and pulled out a crisp twenty-dollar bill.

Sue glanced at his hand then smirked. "You kidding? A Jackson? What kind of girl do you think I am? I should smack you one!"

Fred stepped back. "Hey, no need to get sore about it. Why're you leaving now? I thought you'd just be getting to work."

"Oh, because I was here late yesterday? Other girl didn't show up so I had to work a double. Look, mister, I got places to be." She scoffed, "Forget about the tip. I'm used to it from the likes of you." She turned and resumed walking.

He followed and said, "I really wish you'd take it. This ain't entirely about yesterday's tip." His hand had dropped to his side, still holding the bill.

She stopped and spun around. She was tall, and her figure loomed over him. Her steely gaze lowered his body temperature by two degrees. "What do you want?"

Fred gulped. "I want you to not tell anybody you saw me."

The corner of her mouth raised. "So, you *were* following that woman, weren't you? I knew it."

Fred tried to conceal his shock. "I-I don't, I mean, uh, what woman? What are you talking about?"

"Don't play me for a sap. I've waited tables for years and have seen all types. I happen to know I read people pretty darned good, and I had you pegged from the start. You can keep your scratch. I already told one of the cops I saw you following that dame and that lawyer that got killed." She smiled. "Told them what your car looked like, too."

The twenty fluttered to the ground in Fred's wake as he ran down the sidewalk.

Sue stooped down and scooped it up and called back after him, "Bet you wish you'd left this yesterday!"

He glanced over his shoulder and could see she was holding the bill he had dropped.

He got in his car and slammed his foot on the starter. The engine groaned mightily but eventually coughed to life. He sped past the waitress, who laughingly waved the bill at him as he drove past.

"I've got to get back to Trinity," he said to himself. "Me and Betty need to dust out, toot sweet."

He slammed a palm on his forehead. "I should have left well enough alone. Now we're in for it."

He slowed while crossing the old bridge over Harmon Creek and glanced over to see if the Ford was still there. The car behind him honked, and he waved through the back window. "I'm moving, I'm moving, ya flat head."

He shook his head as the car passed him beyond the bridge, laying on its horn. "The wreck's gone, so that means the coppers are all over it by now. At least now we know they might be onto us."

He forced his foot harder on the accelerator, but the engine continued at the same pace, sputtering occasionally like it always did.

Huntsville, Texas—2:45 p.m.

The battered Ford had been towed from the accident site and now sat in a corner of Patterson's garage. Sheriff Steele joined Detective Bowman, who had conducted the initial assessment. They stood looking over several items that the detective had removed from the car and placed on a table.

Bowman picked up a brown briefcase. "Swanger's," he said. "At least that's what it looks like. It has papers relating to cases he was working on. Nothing out of the ordinary."

"Lipstick?" the sheriff asked, pointing.

"It could be something, it could be nothing. The guy is married, after all, so his wife could have dropped it."

"And these?" he said pointing at three long pointed objects.

"Those are nails. I assume they are from the bridge rail," Bowman said.

"These were inside the car?" The sheriff leaned forward for a better look. "Is that blood on one?"

"Yes, two on the floorboard, one on the seat. I'll have to go out and examine the railing at the scene to determine if they match the nails used in the construction."

The sheriff raised his head. "What do you think?"

"I'd say the nails were pulled out of the boards to make it easier for the car to go through it. These are slightly bent, as if they've been pulled out with the claw of a hammer. Look at the heads. Definitely looks like a claw has been used and the nails look fairly new. There's not a hint of rust."

The sheriff returned to look into the passenger compartment again. "Any conclusions?"

Bowman paced next to the evidence. "Looks like a setup to me. The doc says the guy was stabbed. And the car doesn't look like it was making speed when it went through, and these nails would indicate that someone tampered with the railing. Of course, he was thrown when the car rolled, so it's hard to say. Still, if it had been going fast, the wreck would have killed or seriously injured any passenger, too, but as far as we know he was alone. Then again, if he was alone, who pulled the nails?"

"Mmm-hmmm," the sheriff pondered. "Do you think the nails could have caused the injuries? If not these, maybe others on the bridge?"

"The doc would have to answer that one, Sheriff, but my gut instinct is no. But what do I know, I'm just a detective."

"Pretend you're on the stand in a murder trial, Bowman. *Could* they have caused the wounds?"

"Well..." Bowman fidgeted as his eyes darted around the garage. "I guess they could have caused it. Not likely, but I guess it's possible."

The sheriff sniffled and rubbed his nose. "Okay, good work. You said you're going back out to the bridge?"

"Yes, sir, I want to take another look around before the damage is repaired. I already told them to hold off until I gave them the okay."

Sheriff Steele left the garage and walked a block or so to Doctor Mendelson's office. The door was unlocked, and the darkened waiting room was empty. "Doc? You here?"

A voice emerged from behind a door. "In here."

The sheriff jiggled the doorknob until the latch bolt released from the strike plate. "The knob is loose on the spindle," the sheriff observed.

Doctor Mendelson looked up from his writing, peering over the top rim of his glasses. Paper files were strewn across the desk. "Yes, I've been meaning to have someone come take a look at that. What can I do for you, Nathan?"

"Swanger. We've been looking at the car. My detective found some nails in the passenger compartment. Do you think nails could have caused the injuries to the body? I mean as the car crashed through the railing?"

"I hardly think so, but it would depend on how long they were."

"I'd say they were probably 30 penny or 40 penny."

"The length is comparable, and they are of a similar nature, but the injuries were arranged in a way that would make any nails on a board to be an unlikely candidate. How could they be in a position to cause the wounds? And there's another thing."

"What's that?"

"Don't forget, the car would have been moving and any nails in a board wouldn't go straight in. They'd be at odd angles, and the forward motion would cause tearing. These were precise punctures. I've seen a variety of wounds in my time here, anything from bullets, knives, broken glass, and even ice picks. Inmates at the prison often fashion weapons from nails, and, used like that, they are essentially the same as ice picks. I've also seen injuries from quite a few automobile accidents. The closest match I have in my mind is an ice pick. I assume the nails you mention were bare?"

"They were just nails."

"Nails alone likely wouldn't suffice for these wounds."

"But—and I asked the detective the same question—*could* nails lodged in boards have done it?"

The doctor removed his spectacles and cleaned them as he answered. "It's possible, but highly unlikely."

"What makes you so certain?"

"Most of the bleeding was internal, but there was some blood in the car. I think he was stabbed first, then the wreck happened. Other injuries, at least the ones I could ascribe to him being knocked about in the wreck, did not look like the car was traveling at a high rate of speed. He likely tumbled around when the car rolled. He was apparently thrown out and the car rolled over on his legs. That alone shouldn't have killed him."

"I want to convene with the county attorney later today so the three of us can decide on a cause of death. I'll make sure I have my detective's report by then. I'd appreciate it if you have your report completed as well."

"Today? What is the hurry? I might have patients."

"Your waiting room is empty. He was a candidate for district attorney, and people are going to want to know what happened as soon as possible. I need it today." Steele leaned forward to add emphasis to what followed. "*Alvin* wants it today."

The doctor shuffled several papers on his desk, settling on one folder, which he opened. He began scribbling and without looking up, said, "I-I'll do my best."

Sheriff Steele returned to his office and, after closing the door, he stood at the open window staring blankly at the trees outside as cicadas crooned to him.

A knock at the door was followed by the appearance a young face. Deputy Mike Adams stuck his head in the door. "Sheriff?"

"Not now, Adams. I'm busy."

"Thought you'd want to know—I found out something."

"What?"

"I got a line on somebody Earl Swanger was talking to at the café."

The sheriff spun to face him. "What? How'd you manage that?"

"I almost messed up again. That waitress, Sue, she overheard us. Knew it was Mr. Swanger we were talking about. She told me she had been working there that night and that he came in. She said he talked with a lady and that they left together. She also said another man left right after they did, then followed them in his red two-door sedan."

"Did she have any idea who they were?"

"No, but I started asking around. Somebody remembered seeing a fellow named Fred Darby driving his red two-door about the same time."

"Why does that name sound familiar?"

"Two-bit hustler out of Trinity. He's got a rap sheet for a lot of petty crimes. We've arrested him down here a couple of times. No active warrants."

"And the woman?"

"Yeah, somebody else saw her parading around town earlier. Apparently, she's known to be a working girl. She's out of Trinity as well. Only got a first name, Betty, so I called up to Trinity and talked to somebody up there. They said it was most likely Betty Johnston. They know her pretty well up that way. They also said this Fred Darby is known to keep time with her, too."

"Why are you just telling me this now?"

"I was still on duty, Sheriff. I've been out on patrol."

Sheriff Steele smiled at the young deputy. "Good job, Adams. We might shape you into a law enforcement officer yet."

"Thank you, Sheriff."

He pointed toward the door. "Don't let it go to your head, now get on home to your mama."

Trinity, Texas—3:00 p.m.

Dub Jenkins approached the rundown bungalow, pausing as the same mangy, yellow mongrel he'd seen the last time he visited sauntered across his path. He winced at its stench of rotten eggs and skunk.

"Smells like something died," he said to himself before knocking.

A distraught Betty Johnston quickly answered his knock. Her eyes widened when she saw Jenkins, further highlighting her tear-stained makeup. She was obviously expecting someone else because she hurriedly tried to close the door. But Jenkins placed his foot firmly in the jamb to block it and said, "We need to talk," then he pushed his way past her.

"Hey, what are you doing?"

Jenkins stopped in front of a large suitcase open on the floor. He could see it contained a scattered array of clothes and feminine artifacts.

"Taking a trip? Looks like you're in some kind of hurry."

She turned away from him and faced the window. "My mother is sick. I'm going to see her."

"Sit down, Betty," he said, pointing to her settee. "Tell me about your meeting with Earl Swanger."

"He never showed up here," she said with her back still toward him.

"I'll tell you what I think. I think you went down to meet him in Huntsville."

"Why would I do that if he was coming here?"

Jenkins sighed. "I don't know, but he's dead, and we're trying to figure out what happened."

"He's dead?" She spun around but avoided looking at Jenkins by directing her gaze down at the carpet. "How could such a thing have happened?"

"You think I believe you don't know?"

"This is the first I heard of it, honest."

"Right. Well, I don't buy it, but it would appear our deal is off. McIntyre will want his money back."

"What if I don't have it? It ain't my fault the guy croaked."

"We'll return to that later." He kicked at the suitcase. "I hope your mother ain't too sick, because if I were you, I wouldn't go anywhere just yet. At least until after I get back up with you." Jenkins' scowl turned into a sneer. "We'd find you anyway, and you wouldn't like that, I assure you."

Jenkins turned and let himself out, leaving Betty to her own thoughts.

As he began to make a left at the end of the block, a Trinity County patrol car passed by, going the opposite way.

Huntsville, Texas—3:15 p.m.

A wall clock in the corner ticked ominously as Alvin McIntyre sweated in the hot confines of his office. He was due to meet with a reporter to talk about the election.

"Where is Jenkins?" he asked himself just before the phone rang. He picked up the receiver and leaned into the mouthpiece, "McIntyre."

"Alvin, this is Nathan Steele."

"Ah, Sheriff, what have you found out?"

"A couple of things, really. For one thing, we know Swanger left the café last night in the company of a woman. And they were followed by a man in a red car. The doctor is sticking with his opinion that Swanger died of one or more of his stab wounds and the wreck was secondary."

"Any idea who this mystery woman is?"

"Yes, indeed. We think her name is Betty Johnston. She lives in Trinity. I have the folks up in Trinity rounding her up as we speak."

"What about the meeting with Doc Mendelson, the county attorney, and the magistrate?"

"I need to speak with this woman first."

McIntyre tapped his right thumb nervously on the desktop. "Doesn't sound like Mr. Swanger was very discreet with this woman, does it."

"Based on what I know about the man, it would be completely out of character."

"Well, please let me know what you find out."

He had barely put the receiver down before the phone rang again.

"Alvin?" He recognized the voice of the county attorney. "Rob Burns here. The *Item* called and asked me to comment on the apparent death of Earl Swanger. I told them this was the first I had heard of it and asked them where they got their information. Turns out there is a rumor running around town—any truth to it?"

McIntyre closed his eyes and lowered his head, then took a deep breath and returned to face the mouthpiece. "Yes, Earl Swanger passed away last night. It is still under investigation. Sheriff Steele should be contacting you soon to get together with Mendelson and Randolph Custus to finalize a determination of his cause of death. It was a traffic accident of some type, so it should be a simple matter. We'll release a statement after that, so please say nothing more about this, not to the newspaper nor to anyone, until that time."

Trinity, Texas—4:35 p.m.

Betty Johnston's black-streaked face reminded Sheriff Steele of a picture he once saw of coal miners coming off their shift. Her demeanor was nothing new. He had seen his fair share of crying women during his tenure in law enforcement, so the smudgy streaks of bleeding mascara had little effect. During his career he had managed to identify three major causes of crying in his presence. Crocodile tears seemed to be the most common. To him it was fairly obvious when someone put on an act to cover their guilt, unless of course they were really good at it. Shock at hearing disturbing news was another cause and determining that required a bit more of a gut decision on his part. The third cause was plain and simple grief. As he talked to Betty Johnston, he knew it was up to him to figure out which of the three he was dealing with. He ruled out grief right away.

The Trinity deputies had picked her up and held her at his request. In the meantime, he dispatched two of his own men to retrieve her. They reported that she seemed fine at the start of the journey, but she began to break down when they got close to the Walker County Jail.

The windowless interview room was stark, lit by a single bulb. There was no fan to stir the hot air which only enhanced the dank mustiness that settled over a person like a cloak of regret. Sitting in this cauldron, Betty Johnston dabbed at her eyes and looked up at the sheriff, who stood over her like an irate schoolmaster.

"I just don't know what all this is about. Sure, I know who he is. Mr. Swanger's a lawyer, right? He's got a good reputation, but I don't know anything about all of this."

She sweated in the chair, and he could detect the odoriferous remains of the large quantity of alcohol she had recently consumed. Moonshine tended to ooze out of pores like slobber out of a hound dog.

Steele crossed his arms and glared down at her. "I'll lay my cards on the table. You were seen with him in his car. I have a witness."

She stifled her sobs by momentarily holding her breath, and the sheriff knew he had struck a nerve.

"Who?" she blurted out.

"It's a reputable witness. That's all you need to know. You were observed driving off with him and another man was seen following you. Tell me what happened."

"I-I don't know who thinks they saw me, but I rarely go down to Huntsville. I don't even have a car. Trinity is where I make my living."

"Some living." The sheriff picked up a paper and read out loud: "Prostitution, robbery, assault...on and on. It's a pretty long list for such a young woman. You must come down here often enough because at least two other witnesses recognized you walking around town earlier that afternoon, so we can easily place you in Huntsville that day. That's just one lie. If I have you in one lie, why would I expect that the rest of what you say isn't also a lie?"

Betty took in a deep breath and released it slowly. "The waitress saw me, correct?"

"I'll give you that one." He decided to hold the rest of his cards close to his chest.

Deputy Adams was in the corner scribbling on a sheet of paper.

She gulped. "Okay, I *was* in the car. My ride had taken a powder, and this Swanger fella said he was going to Trinity and offered to give me a lift. That's all."

"So, he just walked up to you and offered to give you a ride."

"It wasn't like that at all. He's a lawyer, right? Like you said, I have had a bit of trouble in my life, and maybe I was shopping around for a new mouthpiece. Lord knows the ones up in Trinity haven't been doing me much good."

"You're saying he agreed to represent you, is that correct?"

"For the most part."

"What does that mean?"

"Well, I hadn't paid him nothing yet. My dough was up in Trinity."

"He agreed to give you a ride so you could pay him his retainer?"

"You're putting words in my mouth, Sheriff, but that's the size of it."

The sheriff consulted the sheet of paper again, then placed his hands on the table and locked on Betty's eyes. "Most of your last charges were dropped, and you have no active warrants pending. Why did you need representation? Do you have other charges in another county? I can find out."

She turned her head to one side and feinted a cough, so Sheriff Steele knew she was thinking fast, trying to buy a few seconds of time. He knew he had her on the hook, now all he had to do was set that hook and reel her in. His mouth cracked into a sly smile.

She began to sob again. "Nothing like that. He was heading up to Trinity to do some campaign stuff, you know, for that election he's running in. I happened to see him in that café and talked to him a little about my past troubles and thought maybe he could help me out. Trouble follows me around like a bad debt, and of course, I figured maybe I could snag me a better lawyer, a good one, you know, like him. And what you said is right, he said he needed a retainer, that's the word he used, too. But I didn't have any money with me. I told him I was waiting for a ride that had never showed, so I says to him, if he gave me a ride to Trinity, where he was going anyway, I could pay him that retainer."

She was breathing hard, but the sheriff had to give her credit. She'd cooked up a plausible cover story in record time. He didn't believe a word of it.

"So you left together in his car and drove to Trinity? What about the man who followed?"

"I don't know nothing about a guy following." Then she hesitated as if she just remembered something. "But you know what?"

"What?"

"There *was* a car behind us on the road to Trinity. I remember now, I turned around and recognized the car. It was red, and I figured it was a friend of mine, the one who was supposed to give me a ride."

"In the dark, you could see that it was a red car."

She swallowed hard. "It wasn't dark yet...the sun was close to setting, but I could see it was my friend."

"What's his name?" the sheriff interrupted.

"I was getting to that. My friend Freddy, he was pulling up close, and I told Mr. Swanger that maybe I ought to get out and ride with Freddy, since he was following too close anyway, and I was probably concerned he'd be sore at me or something."

"And what about the retainer?"

"You know, he asked me the same thing. Shysters always go for the money, don't they?"

The sheriff didn't blink for several seconds as he stared at her. *She's quite the yarn spinner*, he thought to himself

She continued talking. "So I got him to stop. He was good about it. He's a nice guy, after all. I told him I figured I'd get up with him and pay him later. He told me that was fine, if that was how I wanted it. He pulled over to stop, and Freddy pulled up behind us on the side of the road and I got out and we both went our separate ways."

"Who is this Freddy fellow? Fred Darby?" Steele was reading from his paper again. He had already called Trinity to pick up and hold the man for questioning, but she didn't have to know that. Adams continued furiously scribbling.

Betty let out a deep breath, keeping her teeth clenched, and the air almost whistled as it slowly flowed between her closely set lips. "Yes. Me and Freddy got history."

The sheriff picked up another sheet of paper. "He has quite a record as well. I see he's done a couple of stretches in prison."

"So what? He done his time and they let him out. He's rehabilitated."

"Oh, is he?" the sheriff chuckled. "Have any idea where he is right now? I'd like to talk to him, too."

"I imagine he's around. Freddy don't stand still for long. He's always got something going on."

The sheriff reviewed the sheet again. "I'm sure of that."

"Look, I've told you what I know. Can I go?"

"I want you to go back over what you just told me so I can be sure we've got it right. Please indulge me and tell me everything one more time."

She took in a deep breath and huffed loudly before the words began to gush out. "Okay, sure. I met him in the café. We talked. I wanted him to represent me if I got into trouble again, which I don't plan on, but a girl can't be too careful, you know? But I told him my money was at my house up in Trinity, but I must have missed my ride, right? Then he says he's going to Trinity for his election anyway, so he'd be happy to give me a lift." She took in another deep breath and continued, "And I saw my ride, Freddy, following us, and I figured he might be sore and I'd rather ride with him anyways, so Mr. Swanger, he pulled over and let me out. I got in with Freddy and that was it."

Steele's neck popped when he turned to Deputy Adams. "You get all of that?"

"Yes, sheriff, word for word."

"Will I be able to read it?"

"My handwriting's always been good, Sheriff. It's one of my finer points."

The sheriff turned back to Betty. "I guess that's all we need for now. Do not leave Trinity. We may have some more questions later."

"How do I get back home?" she asked.

He looked over at Adams, but he didn't trust the young pup with this floozy of a woman. "Adams, get Henry Woolcraft to haul Miss Johnston back to Trinity." He did trust Woolcraft, the oldest hand on the force. He was tough and grizzled, and he did what he was told. She might try to talk to him, but he'd likely only respond with grunts.

When the door opened, Dub Jenkins was pacing just outside. "Sheriff Steele, I need to talk to you about..." he stopped in mid-sentence when he saw Betty Johnston emerge.

Steele noticed a flash of recognition on both of their faces, but that flicker faded, and they immediately began to ignore each other as if they were total strangers.

"Miss," he said, as if to tip the hat he wasn't wearing.

She walked past him, barely nodding an acknowledgement as she followed Deputy Adams. Sheriff Steele made a mental note of this as he said, "I don't have time for you right now, Mr. Jenkins."

"The district attorney will want an update. What did you speak to Miss Johnston about?"

"Oh, you *do* know her."

"I'm not sure what you mean."

"I thought I saw a brief recognition between you two, like you knew each other."

"She's been prosecuted a few times in the district court, so I know who she is. Is she a suspect in this Swanger case?"

"Well, we're looking at her. She was seen with Swanger the day he died. I need to check out the rest of her story."

"McIntyre wants this case tied up with all due haste."

"I always want cases tied up with due haste. But evidence and witnesses and facts all take time to process." Steele leaned forward. "Do you know more about this woman than you're letting on? Maybe we *do* need to have a little chat."

Jenkins backpedaled. "I-I-I...what are you insinuating?"

"Just a hunch. Don't you know about cops and their hunches?"

"Listen, I'm just asking for the district attorney. An opponent for office, for *his* office, has died right before the primary. We need to make sure this tragedy doesn't impact the voters more than necessary. I might remind you, Sheriff, you are running in the same primary."

"Unopposed," Steele reminded him. "I need to look for another witness who is mixed up in Miss Johnston's story so I can get more information. But at this point, it does appear that Swanger was alone when he died. Keep that quiet, but you can share it with McIntyre."

"Who are you looking for? Perhaps our office might have information helpful to you."

"Fellow by the name of Fred Darby. He's got a record longer than your arm. If I can get up with this Darby fellow, and his version tallies up with hers, I can convene the magistrate, the doc, and the county attorney, and we can likely tie this all up as neat as a pin."

"That's good news. I'll update McIntyre and see if we have anything current on Darby." Sweat had worked through Jenkins' shirt and was showing through the armpits of his coat. He hurried down the hall.

Adams approached. Phone call for you, Sheriff. It's Trinity. They found Fred Darby."

"Good," he said. He mumbled under his breath, "I'm glad that was fast. Now let me see if I can lure those two into a false enough sense of security and maybe they will spill something useful."

Trinity, Texas—5:45 p.m.

Darby knew one thing more than any other thing—he hated police stations. He had been picked up by the Trinity sheriff's office and brought in to be held for questioning by the Walker County sheriff. If he could have been afforded the chance to show emotion as he fidgeted on the weathered bench, he was sure he might curse loudly at his tardiness in confronting the waitress and as he sat, he silently resolved to be a better tipper from that moment forward. He'd always seen tipping as a kind of scam, but now he could see there was a certain usefulness to the practice. He remembered his old buddy Squint warning him during one of their long, late night prison gab-sessions. "It's them loose ends that'll always trip you up."

"Darby?"

"Th-that's me," he said, standing.

A uniformed man was holding out a telephone, but except for that, all Fred could see was a stern set of dark eyes fixed on him and a pair of sergeant's stripes on the sleeve. "Sheriff Steele in Walker is on the horn. He'll want to speak to us when he's through with you, so don't hang up."

He turned the mouthpiece toward his face and placed the receiver on his ear. "Yes?"

"Fred Darby?"

"Yes, my name is Fred Darby." The line protested with a crackle.

"We've been questioning a friend of yours, a Miss Johnston."

Fred thought to himself, *that waitress!* But he said out loud, "Maybe. Betty, you mean. Yeah, she's an acquaintance. Me and her, we go way back."

Fred chanced a sliver of truth, hoping to get a line on what she had said. "Yesterday, I gave her a ride to Huntsville." To him it was all part of the con.

"Anything more you can tell me about that?"

Fred thought fast and struggled to remember the details they had worked out. "Took her down there because we both had some business to attend to."

"What business?"

"A guy owed me some money and I went to collect. I'd sold him a car and he still owed me the last payment, okay?"

"What about Miss Johnston? What was her business?"

"I figure her business is her business, you know? If I was to guess, I'd say shopping. Them dames is always looking for something new and frilly, am I right?"

"And you gave her a ride back as well?"

"No. I ran late and couldn't find her so I headed back on my lonesome."

The sheriff continued, "She said she missed riding back with you and got a ride with someone else."

"That's what I figured. And there was this car ahead of me out on Nineteen. I seen its brake lights flash, and it pulled over. I slowed down, you know, in case somebody was having car trouble or something. It's what you do, right? And out pops Betty, waving at me and running to my car."

"So, she recognized your car following them and got out to continue her ride with you as she originally planned?"

Fred Darby was not a religious man, but he knew his prayers had been answered when the sheriff said this. It played right into his plan. "That's right. I thought to myself, she must have conned some yokel to give her a ride when she figured I'd scrammed out on her. She must have seen me behind them and got the yokel to stop, and then she got out and came back to ride the rest of the way with me. After that, we both went our merry ways."

"Who left first? The other car was in front of you, did it pull away first?"

Fred glanced at the clock, at the sergeant, and at the floor before he figured out what he hoped was the right answer. "I-I did. I pulled around that yokel and gave it all the gas I could. Truth be told, I was a little sore at her, but I took it out on the car."

"Is that all?" The line crackled again.

"Betty was yakking a blue streak like she always does. You know the routine, I was mostly ignoring what she was saying because she was mad at me for leaving her behind, so I didn't pay much attention to what was behind me. All I could figure was to get her home and out of my hair."

After some hesitation, the sheriff said, "That pretty much fits with what she said. Thank you, Mr. Darby. Now let me talk to the sergeant again."

He handed the receiver back to the officer, who quietly spoke some affirmative words and nodded at least once before hanging up. Fred had always marveled at how people would nod or shake their heads while talking on the phone, even though the other party couldn't see what they were doing.

"Okay, Darby, you're free to go. Uh, but Sheriff Steele wanted me to tell you this—don't leave town, just in case there are more questions. Thank you for coming in."

Outside, Darby spied his car on the street and seeing it reminded him of the entire escapade that had brought him to the sheriff's office. He had dropped by Betty's place, just as they had planned, but she wasn't there. After he drove off, a Trinity deputy flashed his lights at him and he pulled over. His heart skipped two beats as the officer got out of his car and came alongside. After a brief conversation, the cop insisted he follow him to the police station for some questioning.

Betty's absence concerned him because they had planned to take off together when he returned. He had a cousin in New Orleans and he knew they could flop there for a while. There was always plenty of work in New Orleans, if you knew the right people. He figured they both could pick up quite a bit of scratch while they cooled it out of state.

"I'm proud of that girl," he said to himself as he drove. He marveled at how easy it was to lay out the whole story. "I can't believe how much *they* spilled. Cops can be so stupid."

He parked down the street from Betty's to wait, and sure enough, after about fifteen minutes, a Walker County patrol car pulled up and she got out. She hurried up the walk, stumbling on cracks and kicking out at that yellow dog that had been lurking around her house the last day or so as she made her way to the door. The patrol car drove off and Fred pulled up and parked as soon as it was out of sight.

He saw her peek out the window when he closed the car door. As Fred reached up to knock, the door opened and he was immediately drenched with water. Betty stood in the doorway clutching an empty vase.

"Jeez, Betty! What'd you do that for?" Fred took off his hat and slapped it against his hip, adding moisture to the small puddle on the porch. He then shook droplets from his head like a wet dog.

"You boob!" she shrieked. "You said you were going to take care of the waitress. She must have dropped a dime."

"I got to her too late. How was I to know she'd be working the early shift, too? I guess the coppers like to chew there. It ain't my fault. Can I come in?"

Betty stepped aside and led Fred pass. "Of course the cops eat there. You should have found her first thing in the morning!" She spun around and put her arms around him and leaned her head on his shoulder. "I got hauled in," she said. "Spent a couple of hours in the clubhouse, but lucky for you I know how to think on my feet." She led him to the settee and they both sat. "I told it pretty much like we figured it in the car right after. I think I convinced those suckers that I got out of the car before anything happened. You was just my ride, see? And you was late so I hitched a ride with the shyster. Said I had talked to him about representing me. He wanted a retainer and so I told him all my dough was up here, but my ride, you, had disappeared on me. So he decided to give me a lift so I could pay him. I saw your car, so I said that maybe I'd rather ride with my friend after all."

"And they thought you was square? I mean, that's quite a yarn."

"They let me go, didn't they?"

Fred lit a cigarette. "They called me in too. I talked to that sheriff down there on the horn and I figured I'd play the same story. I tried to remember how all we had said it, played it just like you did. Even got them to lead me on a bit."

"You're a master of the con, Freddy."

"Heh, you ain't bad yourself, baby. We make a great team. I think he bought it too, must have been close enough to what you said to ring true."

"Help me pack," she said, nudging the suitcase.

"They told me to stick around," Fred said.

"They told me the same thing." She turned toward him. "When do we leave?"

Huntsville, Texas—6:45 p.m.

District Attorney Alvin McIntyre felt as if he had aged five years in the previous twenty-four hours and the persistent July heat only added to this sentiment.

"Third handkerchief today," he muttered to himself as he mopped his face. A knock at the door spurred him to quickly drop the damp rag to the floor under his desk.

"Come in," he said, wiping a clammy hand on his pants leg before the door opened, revealing Sheriff Steele. "Oh, Nathan. My man Jenkins told me you've interviewed that woman."

Steele nodded before sitting down. "Yes, I talked to the woman and I think she was most likely the last person to see Swanger before he died."

"Let's see," McIntyre feigned a moment of contemplation. "I believe her name was Betty Johnston, correct? My office has prosecuted her more than once."

"Yes, and Miss Johnston admits to being with Swanger before the accident. She claims she wanted him to represent her."

"Well, he's an attorney and, since she lives her life on the far side of the law, I would say it seems to be a reasonable explanation."

"Except she's got no pending charges or warrants, so it doesn't add up to me. Why would she need a lawyer if she had nothing pending?"

"That *is* odd. Still, if one is in the habit of breaking the law, I would suppose it does make at least some sense to be ready. You say she admitted to being in the car?"

"Basically, but her story is a little fishy. She said she came down from Trinity with a friend, but he was late and she decided to catch a ride back with Swanger to get the money to pay his retainer. Then she noticed her friend following them and convinced Swanger to stop and let her out."

"It seems to be a plausible story. So she got out and wasn't with him when he wrecked."

"That's the size of it," the sheriff said. "I talked to this friend of hers and he pretty much corroborated the story."

"Who is this friend?"

"Fellow by the name of Fred Darby. He's got quite a record."

"Ah, yes, Darby. He is no stranger to my office. Still, it isn't surprising these two are associated. They are both involved in crime and operate in and around Trinity. Well, I'm only the district attorney, but it sounds to me like you've got everything you need. A single vehicle car wreck and a victim. I think we can close this case today, don't you?"

The sheriff lowered his head. "I'm not too sure. The whole thing still seems a little odd to me. There's just something about both their stories..."

McIntyre leaned forward and said, "Sheriff, look me in the eye."

Steele looked up.

"I want this matter settled today. Do you understand me?"

Steele gulped. "But the facts..."

"I don't care about the facts. Listen, Nathan, you don't want to go against me on this. Swanger was a candidate—an opponent—and the primary is in a little more than two weeks. I don't want the election sullied by a prolonged investigation. Understand, there are others who will not like any additional attention drawn to this. They can make things very uncomfortable for both of us. Don't forget, they've got things they can hold over us."

Steele leaned forward. "Don't threaten me, Alvin. I've got the goods on you, and if need be, on them as well. Plenty of stuff."

McIntyre settled back in his chair. "Be that as it may, it's for the best all around if this thing is wrapped up as soon as possible."

"So, you just want to bury it, put it away all neat and tidy, right?"

"That's right, Nathan. Now you go along and convene your meeting and settle it once and for all."

After the sheriff left, McIntyre picked up the receiver and leaned in to the mouthpiece. "Please connect me with the Walker County Attorney."

Huntsville, Texas – 7:25 p.m.

The office of Justice of the Peace Randolph Custus had barely enough room for his desk and two chairs, but he had managed to squeeze in a third chair after Sheriff Steele had called him. Seated opposite from him were the sheriff, County Attorney Robert Bergen, and the County Health Officer, Doctor J. R. Mendelson.

"I see we are looking at the case of Earl R. Swanger, recently deceased. Mr. Swanger passed away..." Custus leaned forward, adjusted his glasses and squinted at the paper. He raised his eyebrows and asked, "He died...*yesterday*? Is that correct?"

"Yes, sir," Sheriff Steele answered. "Given the circumstances of the accident and his unique standing in the community, I felt the matter deserved haste."

"Highly unusual," Custus murmured under his breath. He glanced in turn at Burns and Mendelson, but they said nothing. He shifted his gaze to the sheriff. "Proceed."

"Mr. Swanger's death was the result of a one-vehicle accident. It went through a bridge railing and rolled down an embankment. There were no passengers at the time of the accident."

Mendelson broke his silence. "The cause of death was exsanguination, massive internal bleeding."

The magistrate interrupted, "And that is consistent with this type of accident?"

The doctor swallowed hard, glanced at Sheriff Steele and continued, "Not entirely. There were three st..." Steele abruptly turned his head toward the doctor. "...er...puncture wounds on the victim."

Custus shifted in his seat. "Puncture wounds?" He turned to the sheriff. "Is that true?"

Steele nodded.

The doctor mopped his brow. "Initially I thought perhaps they were some sort of stab wounds, but given that the victim was alone, I, er, well, the sheriff..."

Sheriff Steele interrupted him. "I believe they were caused by nails from the bridge, inflicted when the car broke through the railing." He produced some photographs of the nails, the car, and the bridge.

The magistrate pondered the photographs, then asked the doctor, "Could nails have caused the injuries?"

"I-I presume it is possible but, in my opinion..." he shot a glance back at the sheriff, "...the wounds could also possibly have been caused by something like an ice pick."

Custus turned back to Steele. "Was an ice pick found in the car or at the scene?"

The sheriff replied, "No, sir, only the nails."

"Earl Swanger was a candidate for district attorney in the upcoming election, is that correct?"

Rob Burns, the county attorney, broke his silence. "That's correct, Randolph, I agree that these facts do not warrant further investigation and with the election just two weeks away, it seems prudent to conclude this quickly. I concur with Sheriff Steele's determination that this was an accident."

The doctor shifted uncomfortably in his seat.

"You don't agree, Doctor?"

"I-I-I just don't see the need for us to hurry this along. He suffered injuries from the accident, yes, as anyone would in a rollover like this. But these stab wounds…"

Custus leaned forward. "*Could* they have been caused by the nails, Doctor?"

"Well, the nails were the right size and shape, but I don't see…"

Custus rustled the papers he was holding as he reexamined them. "Sorry for the interruption, but please answer my question. Could the nails have caused the injuries?"

Doctor Mendelson lowered his eyes. "Yes, it is possible."

Custus studied the police report, then the doctor's report, and reviewed the photographs.

He leaned back in his chair and closed his eyes in deep contemplation. Then he looked at Sheriff Steele. "I see from your report you interviewed a woman who was the last person to see Mr. Swanger alive. This woman was with him in that same car at some point prior to the accident." The judge read from the report, "Betty Johnston. I think we should keep her name private to protect her." He leaned forward again. "Are you sure her involvement was incidental, as you indicate?"

"Yes, I interviewed her myself, and I talked to her friend, the one who picked her up. Both accounts tell the same story. She exited the vehicle before the accident."

"Then I think I will tentatively rule this case an accident, but I will be willing to reconsider that decision if we receive additional evidence. I am always willing to change my mind if any new evidence surfaces." He scribbled on a paper and signed it. "I guess that is all, gentlemen. Adjourned."

When the door closed behind the last of them, County Attorney Burns tarried behind the other two men, and when they were out of his sight, he sighed in relief before exiting the building. He whispered to himself, "Hopefully this will keep Alvin McIntyre off my back."

Back in the courthouse, the magistrate's door cracked open and another face appeared.

Judge Custus set his mouth hard. "You're that reporter from the newspaper."

"Yes, Dan Coulter. Mr. Burns mentioned something to me about a meeting. Was it about Earl Swanger? Can you share anything with me about the Earl Swanger death?"

"I wish I had time to consolidate all of my notes."

"I have just enough time to file my story to make the next edition," Coulter said.

Custus gathered his thoughts and related the facts that had been presented to him.

After the reporter hurried away, Judge Custus muttered to himself, "Hopefully, this is just a local story, and that will be the end of it."

Eight

Thursday July 10, 1930

Huntsville, Texas—9:00 a.m.

"Where you going, Claude?" Evie asked.

"Going down to Mister Buddie's to water down my plantings."

"Seems a waste of time to me, being as the man's dead and all."

"Just seems fitting. I promised to look after Miss Lily May. She may be depending on this garden for food come fall."

"Mmmmm, hmmmm. You just be careful now, you hear me?"

"I will. The long walk will give me a chance to collect up my thoughts."

"You sure you is all right?"

"This will help me be all right."

Claude waved and continued his pace, first down the beaten path he and Evie always took on their way to town, then at some point he turned to use a shortcut he had found. He'd never shown it to Evie because she was afraid of snakes, and he knew there was always the chance of a cottonmouth along this trail.

A haunting chorus of cicadas followed him as he sauntered along the circuitous path. He crossed familiar dry creek beds and passed rotten fallen trees he remembered as full and green not long before. He'd wished he had remembered to bring his hat because the sun was a brutal hot iron on the top of his skull, but he pressed on, eventually making his way to Earl Swanger's smart little house.

He stretched the hose from the house and turned a broad stream of water down the rows he had tilled. He had noticed a slight decline where the garden was situated, and he had arranged the rows to follow that gentle slope. As he had planned, the water flowed down the rows. He repeated this with each row in turn, then placed his thumb over the end of the hose and the gush of water changed to a spray. He directed this up and down the hills, saturating the mounds and entire garden.

"I rightly should have done this much earlier in the morning," he said before completing his chore and returning to the house where he turned off the water.

A neighbor lady approached as he did this.

"I saw you out here working for the Swangers the last couple of days, so I reckon you hain't heard the news. Mr. Swanger was killed yesterday."

"Thank you kindly, ma'am. I did hear that, but I'd just planted this garden for him, and he done paid me for it, and I sure didn't want it going to waste none. I figure his missus is going to be needing these vegetables come fall and winter."

She smiled. "I'll tell her you dropped by. I imagine she'll be back soon."

"It's a powerful hard thing to lose one's husband. She going to need kindly neighbors like you to help her through it."

"What's your name, boy?"

"Name's Claude, ma'am."

"Claude, you're a good man. I'll make sure she knows you're doing right by Mr. Swanger."

Claude had methodically curled the hose in loops as they were talking. He placed it on the ground next to the house and responded, "I reckon I'll be back by here to do some more watering if it don't rain. Thank you kindly, ma'am."

He turned and headed back toward the hidden trail, and she crossed her arms and watched him walk away. He knew she was making sure he didn't hang around. When he was certain she couldn't hear him, he intoned, "Busy body neighbor ladies is better than a angry watch dog."

Huntsville, Texas—9:10 a.m.

Jenkins appeared at McIntyre's door, and said, "It's all over the newspaper."

"What? What do you mean?"

"The Swanger thing."

McIntyre could not contain his voice and shrieked, "What? Who released it?"

"Judge Custus. Right after the inquest meeting. Turns out Burns had alerted them."

"I had wanted to make the first statement, so I could control the information."

"Boss, the article mentions the stab wounds, but it also says the sheriff attributed them to nails."

"And the woman?"

"Betty Johnston was not named...the article only mentions a woman. It all sounded pretty innocent, it recounted her version of the story—that she got out of the car before the wreck happened."

"Can this get any worse?"

"Yes, I think it can. They put it out over the Associated Press wire."

McIntyre paced the office. "Get back up there and corral that woman, along with this Darby fellow she's consorting with. I want those two under wraps until we can play this thing in a way we can control."

"Will do, boss."

McIntyre rubbed his hands together nervously. "If the Maceos get wind of this, I'll be in for it."

The phone rang and a cold sweat broke out when he recognized the voice on the other end of the line, and he knew his previous statement had already come true.

"We need two things from you. You have to resolve this and get elected just as we planned. Who are these witnesses? Are they working for you?"

"Minor involvement, yes, nothing that should have resulted in the candidate's death."

"At a time like this, we can't be too careful. The frayed loose ends of an untied shoelace can cause a person a great measure of harm if you don't address them in time. We'll arrange for an associate from another organization to come help you out. As it happens, he's already in the area."

McIntyre hung up and started pacing his in his office.

"This is bad, really bad."

Marquez, Texas—10:15 a.m.

For a long time, Laura Carrington's large house in Marquez had served as a musical conservatory for young girls. She reflected on this fact as she welcomed yet two more visitors into her parlor. They were the latest in a steady stream of visitors, most of whom now crowded in the dining room. The latest arrival was Earl's mother, Eugenia Gindratt Swanger, accompanied by his stepsister Daisy. Laura led them to a quiet sitting room, away from the nearby chatter.

"I'm so sorry, Mother Swanger, Buddie was one of the..." Laura raised her hand and tried to stifle a sob.

Eugenia sighed. "Tut, tut, child, the good Lord knows I've suffered more than my fair share of loss, but He doesn't give us more burdens than He knows we can bear. Right now, I want to see Lily May." She and Daisy both settled onto a divan and their starched black dresses softly crackled as they sat. "Is Pearl here yet?"

"No, ma'am. She and Will are coming this afternoon on the train from Austin."

"Are Martha Pearl and Mary Margaret with them?"

"No, Martha Pearl is staying back to take care of her sister."

"That's too bad. Now, where is Lily May?"

"She's out on the sun porch. Poor thing hasn't eaten a bite all day. She's just been sitting and looking out the window. Do you want me to bring her in here?"

"No, my dear. Daisy, help me up. We'll go to her."

Lily May sat on the edge of a wicker chair and stared blankly out an adjacent window. Her black dress rustled when she rose to greet her mother-in-law with a kiss on each cheek. "I am so, so, very sorry."

"Hush, dear, it is you who we all feel sorry for. I've lost a husband, too. It is a trying time for anyone, but remember, the good Lord is there for us when we need His help."

"But your son..."

Eugenia was a handsome woman, even at sixty-five. She had been a striking beauty in her youth, and her most arresting feature was her bright blue eyes, which even now seemed to twinkle in her grief.

"I'm in shock, dear, just as you are, but we have to do our best to get through this awful tragedy together. Laura tells me you haven't eaten. I want you to come with me into the dining room for some lunch. It won't fill the emptiness in your heart, but it will give you strength to do everything you will need to do in the coming days."

Lily May nodded and rose. She crooked an arm through Eugenia's and walked alongside her while Daisy and Laura followed them into the dining room. Eugenia scanned the ample table. Neighbors had brought so many dishes of food it was overflowing. "I had no idea there were this many people in Marquez."

"People have been dropping by from all over," Laura said.

The four women nibbled at the offerings and retired to the drawing room where they received a steady stream of mourners throughout the afternoon. Many of them tarried a while on the porch and in the dining room, congregating with plates of food, each in turn approaching the grieving wife and mother to express their sorrow at the loss.

At one point Eugenia turned to Lily May and asked, "Have you read the papers?"

Lily May shook her head. "I don't think I can."

Eugenia patted her hand. "It's best you don't, dear. Your loss is enough to dwell upon. Newspapers always try to find the worst in any situation."

"What do you mean?"

Eugenia took her hand as Laura sat on Lily May's other side and put an arm around her. "Never you mind. Look at all these people here to support you. That is what is important. You can take solace in knowing Buddie was loved and admired by a great many people."

Lily May tried her best to embrace the strength displayed by Buddie's mother, but it continued to be an ordeal for her. She had been despondent from the instant she heard the news. Her life with Buddie always seemed promising, and to that end, she had done everything she could to further his political aspirations. Now, that part of her life had ended and instead of joining him in his campaign, she needed to plan his funeral.

She blurted out, "I'll need to go back home to Huntsville soon to see about poor Buddie's remains."

"You won't have to do that alone. I'm sure Pearl will go with you. We have plenty of other family ready to help you with all of that if you need us. But there's no hurry, dear, you just let us take care of *you* right now. Trust me, it is for the best."

Huntsville, Texas—10:15 a.m.

Alvin McIntyre straightened in his chair and smoothed what little hair he had on the top of his head before he leaned into the mouthpiece and raised his voice. "Governor! District Attorney McIntyre here. What an honor and a surprise it is to hear from you!"

His phone had been ringing constantly ever since the Associated Press had broken the story and had alerted the Maceos in Galveston, so he wasn't surprised it had attracted the governor's attention as well.

"I've read about the situation down there, and I want to see if I can help clear it up. Is there any chance the death of this candidate, Earl Swanger, is connected to the election? I shouldn't have to tell you that the ethics and sanctity of our electoral process is at the very core of our country's values."

"No, sir, you shouldn't. I totally concur. No, I don't believe it was connected. The sheriff, county health officer, and county attorney convened with the magistrate and, after deliberation, it was ruled to be an accident."

The governor coughed and said, "Just the same, I'm dispatching a Texas Ranger to look into it. It's not that I don't trust you people down there, but these things I'm reading in the newspaper seem to warrant a thorough investigation. I don't mean to interfere, but I'd feel much better going forward if we gave this matter additional scrutiny. I'm going to see if perhaps I can round up a reward of some kind as well."

"Of course, Governor. We appreciate the help. Really, we do."

McIntyre placed the receiver in the cradle and shook his head. "Just when things were beginning to look better..."

Sheriff Steele opened the door and entered without knocking. "My phone is ringing off the hook," he said.

"Mine is too. I just got off the phone with the governor."

"Governor Moody called here?" Sheriff Steele sat and stared at McIntyre.

"Yes. He's sending a Ranger down here to help with your investigation."

"But..."

"Yes, I know, you've declared it an accident and that should have been the end of it. I suspect he already talked to the magistrate or perhaps the doctor. I've already dispatched my assistant to intervene with the woman and her friend."

"Intervene?"

"At my request, he's going to sequester them to keep them away from prying eyes. I want their identities kept secret. Is that understood?"

"Listen, if a Ranger is working the case, I can't impede his investigation."

"No one is asking you to impede anything. Just stress to him the delicate nature of this thing. The reputations of a young lady and a rising young politician are both at risk here. That's the angle I want to project."

"I don't like any of this, Alvin. It's not what I was elected to do."

"Nor I, but our situations are both quite delicate. We have a stack of dominos standing behind us, and we can't afford to let any one of them to tip over or they will all fall *directly on us*! I assure you, Sheriff, if I go down, you go down as well."

Steele fixed a hard gaze at McIntyre. "It's the same with me, Alvin. It's the same with me."

Trinity, Texas—10:15 a.m.

Dub Jenkins parked outside the Trinity bungalow just in time to see Betty Johnston struggling to maneuver a large suitcase out the door, followed by Fred Darby carrying another smaller parcel. Jenkins had nudged his car behind a red two-seater on the street.

The two stopped three feet from the steps, and Betty dropped the suitcase with a dull thud as Jenkins approached.

"I am sure you were both told not to leave town. Where are you off to?"

"Dusting out, pal," Fred said. "Me and her. What's it to you?"

"He's McIntyre's man, Freddy," Dub said.

"Oh, the butter and egg man, huh? I figure we're due a ton more scratch."

Jenkins scoffed, "Oh, you do, do you?" Then he turned back to Betty. "Betty, the story is all over the news. We've kept your name out of the papers so far, but if the press ever gets wind of your identity," then to Fred, "or yours, there won't be anything we can do to protect you."

"That's why we need to breeze off." Fred reached down and picked up the suitcase. "Move, baby."

"Listen. You need to stay for a while…it'll probably be just for a few days. I know a travel court nearby where you can lay low. I'll pay. It's best for everyone if you keep out of sight and wait for things to blow over."

Betty looked at Fred. "He might have something there, Freddy. We can hide out for a couple of days, then go our merry way. If we blow town right now, it'll look like we done something wrong, and they'll try to find us."

Jenkins emphasized, "We *will* find you."

Fred tapped at the bottom edges of his mustache with the tip of his tongue. "A couple of days, tops. Then we drift, ya follow?"

"Now, please put your suitcases in my car and I'll take you over there. If McIntyre needs anything else from you, I'll get in contact."

"What about my car?"

"Park it in the alley behind Betty's place."

While moving his car, Fred contemplated taking off, then thought about how rough that would make things for Betty. "Naw, I can't do that to her, not now. She's a good kid, really." He parked and returned to Jenkins, who motioned Fred to the back seat with the bags.

When they arrived at the travel court, Fred remarked, "What a dump."

"Some friends of McIntyre own it. It's quiet, and we'll arrange for someone to bring you meals. We put witnesses here from time to time for safekeeping."

Fred pulled a cigarette from a stylish metal case and tapped the end of it on the lid. "I've heard it's used for other things, too."

Jenkins scowled at him and added, "Yes, hunters stay here quite often."

Fred laughed. "Yeah, they're hunting for something, all right."

"Never mind, you two stay put and you'll be all right. If you go wandering around and somebody sees you, well, we can't keep you safe."

"Safe from who?" Fred asked.

"The press, the law, vigilantes. With this thing in all the newspapers right now, there's no telling what might happen."

After taking care of arrangements and making sure Fred and Betty were settled into their respective cabins, Jenkins returned to Huntsville.

Somewhere in East Texas—10:15 a.m.

Special Ranger Timothy Homer Givens' lieutenant called him that morning and gave him a new assignment, one that had come on orders from the governor. His instructions were to investigate the case of a district attorney candidate's death near Huntsville. Givens' face was bathed by the toasted airstream from his car windows. He guessed the assignment fell into his lap because he was relatively close by. He'd just finished investigating a lynching in Lufkin. He reached over and made certain his Stetson was still in place on the seat beside him. There was nothing worse than a nice hat blowing to the floorboard and getting dirty, unless it just flew out of the car. Texas Rangers provided their own transportation, their own weapons, and their own clothes. He didn't mind because the budgets were tight and, as he read the news, he knew they were only going to get tighter. He loved being a Ranger, and it was just part of the job.

He'd read a small newspaper story about this case earlier that morning. As he drove, he tried to remember the details he'd seen in the paper. On the surface, it had the hallmarks of a routine case, and he figured he'd be done with it in a day or possibly two. Despite the fact that it was a political candidate, it, for the most part, sounded like a simple automobile accident. An awful tragedy, to be sure, but he'd been trained to keep an open mind, so he fixed his eyes on the road and pressed his foot on the pedal.

Givens pulled into Huntsville in the mid-afternoon on Thursday. The accident had occurred on Tuesday night. He'd been told the locals had already declared the death an accident, which to him seemed to be a hasty decision. He drove directly to the county jail and asked to see the sheriff. If a special ranger worked on a local case, the first stop was always the local sheriff. Givens knew he might not be particularly welcome, but he also knew he could expect to be given a fair amount of respect. Even a county sheriff was generally awed by the reputation of the Rangers.

"Sheriff Steele? I'm Tim Givens, from the Texas Rangers. The governor himself has asked us to look into one of your cases. I believe the victim's name was Earl Swanger?"

Sheriff Steele set his mouth hard. He respected the work of the Texas Rangers, but he was not appreciative of the governor deciding to step on his toes. "Of course," he said, extending a hand.

"Sorry, I never shake hands. Got out of the habit during the influenza outbreak and just never picked it up again."

Steele quickly withdrew the hand and instead indicated an empty chair. "Sit down."

Tim Givens was used to a certain lack of enthusiasm. The Rangers' authority extended over the entire state and it was only natural for local police to feel threatened by such an intrusion. He endeavored to get down to business with as little interference as possible.

"I'm sure it is all routine, Sheriff. Now I'd like to see the body first, then review your reports and the findings of your inquest. Then I'd like to go to the scene."

Steele leaned back in his chair. "We took pictures of the scene, but the construction crews have likely already started repairing the damage."

"So soon?"

"Well, we already determined a cause of death."

Givens sucked at his teeth. "Then perhaps I should alter what I just said. I had better go there first."

"Adams!" the sheriff called out.

The young deputy appeared and said, "Yes, sir?"

"This is Special Ranger Givens. Can you ride with him and show him where the Swanger accident happened?"

"Sure thing." He stuck out his hand. "Ranger Givens? I'm Deputy Adams."

Givens ignored the hand and motioned toward the door with his chin.

Adams rode in the passenger seat and proceeded to make small talk, generally pointing out places he found interesting on the short drive to Harmon Creek. Givens noted these were usually places where certain crimes had been committed, but he preferred to listen to the air rushing past his window.

Adams pointed forward. "Slow down. It's just up here, where the road breaks off to the new bridge they're building.

"So the victim pulled over here? Were there any skid marks?"

"I don't know that we noticed any. We had a thunderstorm sometime after the accident, so it might have washed them away."

Two men were nailing a thick plank in place on the side of the roadway a short distance up the cutoff.

Givens pointed. "So I suppose that's where he went off the embankment, after he broke through those rails?"

Adams nodded. "That's what we figured."

The two black men stopped their work as Givens approached, then stepped back as he squinted at the railing and the embankment beyond it.

"Did you build the original railing?"

"Yes, sir, we did." The speaker was the older of the two.

Givens saw his hands were a mass of calluses that spoke of many years' toil. He looked at the unbroken section of the railing adjacent to where they were working. "You do good work. It looks real solid."

"Thank you, sir. I trys my best and take pride in my work."

"Let me ask you something. Do you think it odd that the car was able to break through this railing like it did?" Givens kicked against the unbroken railing with a thud.

"I haven't given it much thought, but now that you mentions it, I don't rightly knows how he did it unless he was going mighty fast. But you know something?"

"What?"

"I've repaired a mess of wrecked rails in my life." He pointed at a cracked and splintered plank to the side. "I ain't seen one like that. It ain't busted up enough. And I builds 'em strong."

"What do you think?"

"I thinks maybe somebody done pulled most of the nails out. A rail likes this is only as strong as the nails what holds it in place. It's the only thing I can figure."

Givens eyed a pile of nails next to the work area. "Could I have one of those?"

"Sure thing. Grab all you wants. One thing we got plenty of around here is them nails."

Givens stooped and picked up one of the nails. "Thank you. I'll let you get back to your work now."

He put the nail in his pocket and returned to Adams. "And where did the car end up?"

Adams pointed and Givens returned to the railing, stepped over, and made his way down the embankment. Adams followed behind him like a cat expecting a handout.

At the base Givens pointed at a deep depression bordering an indentation in the soft floodplain. "Looks like the car pivoted on a wheel at this point, then rolled on its roof right here." He walked over to a spot peppered with shoe and boot prints.

Adams seemed astonished. "That's right where it was! How'd you figure that?"

"How long you been a deputy?"

"Not very long."

"Give any crime scene time, son, and the details will slowly tell you their stories."

Huntsville, Texas—11:55 a.m.

Alvin McIntyre sat motionless in his chair with his elbows on the desk and his fingertips touching. His thumbs converged at the base of his chin and both index fingers connected at the tip of his nose. He stared blankly, as if in prayer and didn't react when the door opened.

"I hope you have some good news for me," he said without looking up at Jenkins.

"I've got those two hidden away like you wanted."

McIntyre dropped his hands. "Any sign of Bill Thornton?"

"He's gone. Nobody's seen him."

McIntyre turned his chair so he could look out the window. "I was thinking this morning, what about Swanger's widow?"

Jenkins blinked back at the man behind the desk. "What about her?"

"I don't know her personally, but I've heard she is the type to speak her mind. School teachers usually are."

"Boss, she's a grieving widow. How much trouble do you think she could make?"

"I don't know." He sighed deeply before continuing, "It's something to think about. Do you have any clue how that Johnston woman managed to mess this up? All we wanted was to simply project the idea of a little hanky-panky into the minds of the voters."

"I think she and this Fred Darby fellow concocted a scheme they thought would work."

"How did he get involved anyway?"

"It wasn't my doing, boss, she brought him in. I was trying to keep our direct involvement out of it, so I left the details up to her. I think they've been cohorts for a while. I found them together when I went up there. They had packed their bags and were on their way out the door."

"Leaving? I thought we made it clear to them they needed to stay."

Jenkins smirked. "How often does *that* work? Anyway, I convinced them that they had to stick around for a couple of days or it would draw a lot more heat on them, and no matter where they went, we'd find them."

A curt knock on the door interrupted them, and McIntyre responded, "Yes?"

Sheriff Steele entered, followed by another man holding a Stetson in one hand.

"Alvin, this is Special Ranger Givens."

McIntyre extended a hand but retracted it when Givens failed to respond in kind.

"Ah, yes. The governor told me he was sending someone. You certainly wasted little time in getting here. I'm sure the sheriff has been giving you everything you need."

Givens got right to business. "I'm told there are two witnesses, a woman who was in the car and the man who picked her up some time before the accident."

McIntyre could feel a new layer of sweat forming under the glistening sheen of moisture that already covered his balding forehead. "Yes, we've taken steps to keep them isolated, to protect the reputation of the young lady involved, you understand."

"I don't care about that, but I need to interview them. I've examined the body, and I have questions that perhaps only they can shed a little light on. There isn't much to go on, a body, a railing, and a car. I mean no offense to the sheriff's investigation, but I'm not convinced it was simply an accident."

McIntyre glanced at Jenkins. "Jenkins here can put you in touch with them. He's the only one who knows where they are. We'd, of course, like to keep their location confidential."

Givens ran his tongue back and forth across his front teeth. With his lips closed it caused his jaw to jut out in a peculiar way. Finally, he broke his silence. "Whatever you think is best." He turned to Jenkins. "When can I talk to them?"

"I'll fetch them and bring them to the Trinity sheriff's office at six this evening."

"I know where that is. I'll be there," Givens said, then abruptly turned and left the three men alone.

"You had better get to it," McIntyre said to Jenkins. "The sooner he is satisfied, the sooner he leaves for good."

Jenkins nodded and made a swift exit.

As soon as the door closed again, Sheriff Steele said, "What made you put them under wraps?"

"We were worried they might take off, and I'm afraid our fears were well-founded. Jenkins got to them just in time. According to him, they had their bags packed and were on their way out the door."

"Might be easier all around if I could throw them in jail."

"On what charges?"

"Heh. I'd find something. Folks like them are always on the wrong side of the law. Doesn't have to stick, but we'd be able to keep an eye on them."

"We need them free and easy to manage, at least for now, Sheriff. Jenkins has things well in hand. He convinced them they'd be found if they tried to run, and running would make it look like they were guilty of something."

Steele sat heavily and asked, "Are they?"

"Are they what?"

"Guilty of anything. I came up with an alternate reason for those wounds, but seriously, Alvin, you haven't seen the body. The man was stabbed, pure and simple."

"We will never know what happened unless those two say anything that conflicts with what they've already said. Jenkins is more than capable of managing those idiots."

"I hope so. We're digging ourselves a mighty deep hole with this. I don't like it, but I don't rightly know why. Is it something to do with the election?"

"The less you know, the better for you. But, no, his death was not some plan on my part to stop his candidacy. I'm not a stupid man, Sheriff."

Before getting up, the sheriff stared long and hard at the district attorney. "I hope not, Alvin, because you want to know something? I'm not a stupid man either."

Trinity, Texas—5:00 p.m.

Jenkins arrived at the motor court in the late afternoon. He knocked several times to no avail, then tried the knob and discovered the door was unlocked. Inside, he found the room in disarray. On the far side, he could see that Betty Johnston was asleep sprawled diagonally across the bed, a wadded sheet partially covering her. She was dressed in a slip and one bare leg dangled over the side of the bed like a piece of wet laundry hanging on a line.

Fred Darby's chin was resting on his chest as he sat on the floor with a half-empty mason jar between his legs. A long trickle of drool oozed from his lower lip to his chest, where it ended in a wet spot on his undershirt.

Jenkins raised his voice. "What is going on here? You're both spiffed!"

Darby raised his head and squinted as he tried to focus on Jenkins. "Who wants ta know?"

At this point Betty stirred and lifted one eye open. "Oh, it's you..." She took a deep breath and lifted up on one elbow, revealing half a breast along the top edge of her slip. "What d'you want?"

"Cover yourself, woman. I'm here because a Texas Ranger is coming and he wants to talk to the both of you. Where'd you get the stuff?"

Darby laughed. "Imagine that coming from the likes of you. You guys have your fingers in almost all the booze in this area, so you gotta know it's not hard to find."

"What do you expect us to do?" Betty said. She sat up and straightened her robe. "You stuck us out here with nothing to do."

"This Ranger was sent by the governor to investigate the mess you've gotten us all into. The governor! He insisted on talking to the both of you, so I need you to get dressed and sober up. We're going to the sheriff's office for the interview."

Jenkins went outside and smoked a cigarette. He could hear the two of them bickering while they tried to get dressed.

A woman's voice pierced the silence. "Where's my other shoe?"

"How'm I supposed to know?"

"'Cause I threw it at you."

"There were probably two of me and ya must have thrown it at the wrong one."

The conversation then deteriorated into raucous laughter.

Jenkins looked at his watch and could see it was getting close to six, so he paced nervously and lit another cigarette.

He knocked at the door. "Come on, you two, we need to be there at six. We don't want to keep a Ranger waiting. You can trust me on that."

The door swung open and Fred stepped outside, blinking in the afternoon brightness as he tucked a remaining shirttail and lifted one suspender strap over his left shoulder before repeating with the right. His face was mottled with stubble. Betty followed, wearing the same dress she had worn the day before, but this time it was wrinkled from having spent the night wadded up on the floor. She was carrying a quarter-full mason jar.

"We'll have no more of that," Jenkins said, grabbing the container.

"Aww, just a little snifter for the road? I didn't even have time to put on my makeup."

"You can have it when we come back." Jenkins placed the open jar on the floor next to the jamb and closed the door.

Darby added, "You look all right, baby. Besides, what d'you want to do? Impress this Ranger fella?"

Jenkins interrupted, "Enough of that. You look fine, Betty." He herded them into his car.

He saw a small grocery along the way and stopped to buy each of them a bottle of Coca-Cola.

Betty quaffed about half the bottle in two gulps, and this served to perk her up. "Thanks, there's something about being hung-over that makes me crave a Coke. A Nehi just isn't the same, but this," she held the sweating bottle to her forehead, "does the trick."

Fred said nothing, but drained the rest of his drink and tossed the bottle out the window along the way. Jenkins glared at him but continued driving in silence.

At the police station, Jenkins stopped them before entering and adjusted collars and dusted shoulders like a doting grandmother.

"Now, stick to the same stories, just like you've been telling. Nothing more, nothing less."

"But Freddy has some new ideas we've been practicing. It'll cook that rube's goose something good."

Jenkins put his hands on her shoulders and locked her gaze on his. "Stick to the story you've already shared."

She brushed his hands aside and said, "All right, all right, get your hands off me." She winked at Fred as they turned to enter the station.

Givens talked to Betty first and spent about ten minutes alone with her. She emerged with a demure smile and sat next to Jenkins as Fred rose to follow Givens. Jenkins missed her second wink to Darby as he passed by.

When Darby reappeared at the door, Givens directed him to sit and summoned Jenkins.

"Close the door," Givens instructed, "and sit down."

"Yes?"

"Their stories don't match what they told Sheriff Steele earlier."

Jenkins blinked his eyes once, then again as thoughts spun around and slammed hard against the inside of his skull.

"They don't? Maybe they j-just remembered more details."

Givens frowned. "Not likely. The truth is the truth. And it's not only that, but I could swear they both have been drinking."

"I don't know how that could be the case."

"Mr. Jenkins, I've been a lawman for quite a number of years. I think I'm a pretty good judge of that. What is this? Are you keeping them hidden away with a supply of booze?"

"If they found something, they did it without my knowledge."

"Well, in my opinion, we're being told a bunch of lies. Oh, it has similarities to their previous story, but a person doesn't have to embellish the truth. And what they say sounds rehearsed. You been coaching them?"

Jenkins swallowed hard. "No, I've had no hand in anything they might have said. What now?"

"I'm returning to Huntsville. I'll think about it along the way, but from where I'm sitting, I have to tell you that I don't like it." He leaned in close. "And if you can't keep these people sober, maybe I should take charge of them."

Jenkins was quick with his answer as he backed away. "I'll make sure they don't drink anymore."

He hustled his two charges out of the station and into his car before commenting. "You changed your stories? I told you to say the exact same thing you said to Sheriff Steele."

"Yeah, but Freddy thought it would be better."

He glared at Fred Darby, who was smiling reservedly. "It wasn't that big a change, just adds a little to Betty's side of the story. He was mad, see? They both was mad, and they got to yelling to a point where she wanted to get herself out of the car."

Jenkins' face turned scarlet. "Yeah, great story, but he didn't buy it."

"What do you mean?" Betty asked. "I told it real convincing. I could have been an actress, you know."

"You tell him, Betty." The smugness in Darby's tone further irritated Jenkins.

He slowed and turned into the motor court's circular drive. "How can I put this so you'll understand? The Ranger said it himself, the truth doesn't change. It doesn't have to be embellished."

"It's all part of the con," Fred said. "Look, I know how to handle this kind of business...it's how I make my living. If you don't like it, just take us back to my car, and we'll be in the wind."

Jenkins grasped the steering wheel tightly and said, "I told you before. You won't be able to get anyplace we can't find you. Oh, and no more drinking out here. He's going to want to question you again, I'm sure of it, and you two smelling of booze doesn't help matters any."

153

"Okay, okay," Betty said as she sauntered back to the door, then she turned to Fred. "Let's send that boy out to get us some fried chicken this time."

Darby winked at Jenkins, then followed and under his breath he added, "Yeah, and another jar of that hooch."

"What a nightmare," Jenkins muttered as he drove south to Huntsville. "McIntyre will be livid."

Nine

Huntsville, Texas—8:30 a.m.

Jimmy Bryant spent two grief-stricken days sitting in his office staring blankly at the mess on his desk. The death of his friend and partner had hit him hard, and he still hadn't come to terms with the loss. But he also worried about the business end of their association, because he knew Earl had always been the better attorney.

"He carried me more than I ever carried him," he lamented out loud. "Financially, this firm is pretty much a bust."

He didn't flinch when the door opened and a wave of fresh summer warmth flooded the office like a momentary flash of heat from a bonfire. Jimmy raised his head and squinted at a tall figure in a prominent Stetson silhouetted in the bright light of the doorway.

"James Bryant? I'm Special Ranger Tim Givens. I was assigned by the governor to investigate the death of your partner."

Jimmy half-stood and stretched out his hand. "Please, Jimmy is fine. I wish I could say it was a pleasure to meet you."

Givens ignored the hand and settled his large frame into a chair opposite Jimmy. "Believe me, no one wants to be in this type of situation." He leaned forward and said, "I guess it's just best to ask you point blank, is there anyone in Earl Swanger's life who would want to see him dead?"

"I think you'll find that Earl was as good a man as you'll ever find anywhere. He never met a stranger, and even if he did slightly rub somebody the wrong way, he'd find some way of making things right. All that said, if there is anyone who had a bone to pick with Earl right now, I'd say District Attorney McIntyre would be my first thought. He was worried about Earl's candidacy, and the campaign was making headway."

"I hardly think a man like McIntyre would do anything so stupid."

"Maybe not, but if the rumors are true, he's associated with a lot of disreputable people."

"How about recent cases Swanger had in court?"

"The most recent one involving a crime was Claude Davidson. It was unusual in that it was being personally prosecuted by McIntyre, even though it was a routine bootlegging charge. It was even more surprising because I can't remember a time when McIntyre took a case against a colored man. He'd usually relegate that chore to one of the other prosecutors."

"Interesting, but there must be more to it than that."

"Earl thought McIntyre was singling out Davidson because of an association with outside parties interested in cornering the local market in illicit booze. They generally try to crush any competition and absorb their operation and, through McIntyre, use prosecution as a means to that end. At least that is what people say."

"That's quite an accusation. Understand, I'm not here to investigate anything more than Swanger's death. So he prosecuted this Davidson, and Swanger defended. Any chance this colored fellow would bear a grudge against his own lawyer?"

Jimmy Bryant filled his pipe and lit it, blowing a wide smoke ring after his first puff. "I doubt it. I only met him a couple of times, but he seemed a decent enough chap. He'd lost his job, and I think he was just trying to feed his family in these rough times."

"But he was bootlegging."

"Yes, he committed a crime and he spent several weeks in jail awaiting trial, but basically, Earl convinced the judge to convict Davidson with time served." He blew out another cloud of smoke. "If there are any grudges in this case, we'd have to go back to McIntyre and how he felt about Earl beating him in court."

"But it was a conviction. He won."

"You have to understand the way this man thinks. McIntyre wanted Davidson to go away for a long time." Jimmy blew another smoke ring. "He wanted to send a message to any others, and he also needs a steady stream of fresh labor for the chain gangs. He hires them out to the various counties in his jurisdiction, mostly for road work. State jobs too, you know, like the new bridge over Harmon Creek."

"Still, for a man in such a high profile position to kill someone, well, it defies rational judgment."

"McIntyre is dirty, and in my opinion, I'd say he's capable of just about anything, so nothing would surprise me. All you have to do is ask anybody around here about him, but I suggest you be discreet. It's a small town and, even though just about everybody knows what is going on, he has a lot of people indebted to him—or to those other interests."

"What about Swanger's wife? I heard she had gone to Leon County. Did they have any problems? I mean, it's odd to me that he happened to die when she was away."

Jimmy leaned forward. "You can forget that line of thought. Those two have been madly in love ever since they first met. She went down there to campaign for him, that's all. Leon County is where she grew up, and she knows everybody over there. She almost single-handedly got him elected county attorney.

Everybody loves her. I hate to think what this has done to the poor woman."

"I reckon I had better go interview her."

"She stays with an aunt in Marquez, Laura Carrington. I called down there yesterday to ask about her, and her aunt Laura told me Lily May is coming back on Friday to start making arrangements."

"Know anything about this woman who claims to have been in the car with Swanger?"

"I don't know any more than what's been in the papers and the rumors that have been whispered around town. Understand this, though—Earl Swanger was as straight as an arrow. The only thing I can figure is that she must have been a potential client. As far as I know, he was heading up to Trinity to campaign, nothing more."

"But you didn't know anything about a potential new case."

"No, sir. But people approach us all the time. Word of mouth is how we get most of our business and we've been struggling, so Earl would have been quick to snag a new paying client."

"Now, what about you? How long have you been partners?"

Jimmy had been expecting this from the start. "Earl Swanger was my best friend and he's the best lawyer I've ever seen. We've known each other since law school. Sure, our business has had a few ups and downs. The market drop hit both of us hard, really hard, but we were solid partners. Losing him is like losing a brother." Bryant began to tear. "So if you're asking me if I somehow wanted him dead, you couldn't be more wrong. Fact of the matter is, I *need* him here because the only way this practice worked was to have both of us here working."

Givens stood. "Well, thank you for the chat, Mr. Bryant."

"You're headed to Marquez?"

"I have a stop to make in Trinity first."

"You're really making the grand tour."

"Ranger work involves mostly miles and then more miles," Givens said, following with a chuckle.

Huntsville, Texas—9:00 a.m.

Sheriff Steele and District Attorney McIntyre stood on the courthouse steps surrounded by a throng of people.

"Sheriff, can you share any more about the Earl Swanger case?" The speaker was a reporter from a nearby town.

"Our initial determination is that it was simply a one-car accident."

"The county medical officer mentioned stab wounds."

The sheriff tried to conceal his disgust that this detail was known. "His injuries were most likely caused from building materials on the bridge railing and inflicted when the car crashed through."

"Mr. McIntyre, Earl Swanger was a strong contender for your office in the upcoming primary. Do you care to comment?"

McIntyre stepped forward. "My office is involved in the investigation as well. We are cooperating with Special Ranger Givens, who was dispatched by the governor to look into the case. I share the governor's concern that the death of any candidate for office should be thoroughly examined, but even more to the point, Earl Swanger was a worthy opponent who I highly respected."

"Sheriff, the report mentions a woman. Who was she, and did she have anything to do with Swanger's death?"

"There is no indication of impropriety, so we intend to protect her identity. All we know is that she accepted a ride from Swanger, possibly because they had some sort of legal arrangement, but she exited the car and got into another car before the accident. Apparently, she thought she had missed her ride and became aware this person was following and decided to go with him."

"There are rumors of an altercation between Swanger and the woman."

McIntyre spoke up. "We will have to reserve comments regarding the ongoing investigation at this time. I feel certain the sheriff's original assessment will stand true. This was simply a tragic accident. I want to extend my condolences to Mr. Swanger's widow and to all of his family. That's all for now. Thank you."

McIntyre and Steele abruptly turned and entered the courthouse. Once they had closed the door behind them, McIntyre turned to Steele. "How did they know about the wounds and about the woman?"

"I don't know, Alvin. There are a lot of loose lips in both of our departments, but my guess would be Givens or others listening in during his questioning."

"Put a lid on your people, Nathan, and I'll do my best to contain mine."

"And Givens?"

"We both need to see what we can do to guide his investigation so it can match our conclusions."

"I hope you're right, Alvin, but I've dealt with various Rangers in the past, and they pretty much go their own way."

McIntyre walked to his office and hurried in because his phone was ringing.

"Hello?"

"Mister McIntyre?"

"Yes. Who is this?"

"Hemmings LeBlanc. I work out of New Orleans for some mutual acquaintances. I am told you have some need for my services."

McIntyre had heard of LeBlanc. He gulped hard and set up a time and place to meet.

Trinity, Texas—9:15 AM

Fred Darby wiped his hands on a towel and took a sip from a mason jar. "This giggle juice ain't sitting too well with what's left of the fried chicken."

160

Betty Johnston reached over and grabbed the jar. "It's just fine, Freddy." She sniffled and wiped her forearm across her nose and mouth. "I'm just about going stir-crazy out here though."

Fred burped. "Jenkins said one more day, maybe two."

She pouted. "I know, but I hate it."

She crooked her head toward the front wall at the sound of a car door, then stumbled to the window and nudged the curtain to peek from a corner. "It's that Ranger fella!"

"What? Here? How'd he find us?"

"Jenkins must have told him where we were."

Darby screwed the lid on the jar. "Naw, he's a bloodhound. Coppers like him have a sixth sense. What's he doing now?"

"He went into the office. Should we get out of here?"

"He'd see us. We might as well talk to him. Tell him more of the story like we've been working on."

"Jenkins said we need to stick to the original story."

"All cops are morons. Trust me, we got to work the con here. We've set them up, now we give them what they really want. You tell it like I've been telling you. Now I'm going to slip out the back and go over to my cabin."

She pouted again. "Oh, you don't want to be seen cavorting with me, do you?"

Fred laughed. "Betty, we've cavorted for years. Why would I worry about that?"

"You think we'll really be able to start over in New Orleans, Freddy?"

"Sure we will. We'll get out of here and drive down there tomorrow. But I better hoof it before he gets here. It'll look better for your story."

Shortly after Fred made his exit, Betty answered the expected knock. "Yes?" she said through the closed door.

"Miss Johnston, this is Special Ranger Givens again. I have a few more questions for you."

She quickly placed the jar in a drawer and opened the door, gathering the top of her robe close to her neck. "I'm not dressed for visitors."

"I don't mean to intrude, but something's been bothering me about what you said the last time we spoke, and I want you to clarify it. You said you had a fight with Swanger. That was a change from your original account."

She took a deep breath and sighed. "This has been quite an ordeal for me. My mama always taught me to never say anything bad about the dead, so I kept some things to myself. But the fact of the matter is that Earl Swanger had been drinking. He practically forced me into his car and I seriously began to question his intentions. He said a lot of mean things and when he stopped the car, I was fearful he was going to beat me. That's when I got out and started walking down the highway. My friend Fred just happened to be coming along the road at the same time, and he saw me walking and, thankfully, he picked me up. That's the gospel truth. What happened to that awful man after that, I don't know."

Givens wrote everything down in a small note pad. "I appreciate your cooperation, Miss Johnston." He didn't mention any suspicions about her telling what amounted to three versions of her story. "I assume Fred Darby has his own room?"

"Of course he does," she said. "What kind of girl do you think I am?"

Givens had read her file and knew exactly what kind of girl she was, but he simply smiled. "Well, I'll leave you to it then. Thank you."

She had studied his face intently during their exchange, but Givens showed no reaction whatsoever. She stooped to the corner of the window to watch him as he slowly made his way to a sedan and drove off. She was surprised he hadn't visited Fred.

A minute after Givens was out of sight, Fred appeared at Betty's back door. "What did he want?"

"Just like you figured, Freddy. He wanted more information, so I fed him that new version of the story you cooked up."

"Did he buy it?"

"I think he did. He didn't seem to question it at all. I think we're going to be all right."

"I half expected him to come see me."

"Me too, but I guess I gave him everything he needed. I'll tell you one thing, though."

"What's that?"

She shook her head. "I sure wouldn't want to play poker with that guy. I couldn't read a thing on his face one way or the other."

"I wouldn't play poker with no copper anyway." Fred laughed and scooped Betty off her feet. He cradled her like a child and nuzzled her neck. "Now, let's keep talking about everything a guy needs."

Huntsville, Texas—10:00 a.m.

Claude returned to Buddie's house and proceeded to water the garden again. "That summer sun will dry out those seedlings if I don't keeps them wet," he said to himself.

He didn't know if he should be hanging around the house quite so much, but he had hoped Miss Lily May might have returned by then. He'd promised to keep her safe, and Mister Buddie's request had replayed in his head ever since that night down on Harmon Creek.

He looked to the far edge of the yard and saw the neighbor lady who had talked to him the day before. She was standing in a gap in the hedge and her long house dress billowed in the gentle summer breeze.

She called out to him, "Back at it, ain't you, boy?"

"Cain't let her garden burn up. Like I said before, I reckon Miss Lily May is going to need these vittles in the coming months."

She crossed the yard and stopped about twenty feet from him. "I called down there and talked to her. She told me she's coming back later today. I told her you were out here messing in the garden every day. She was fine with it."

"I figured she might be."

He removed his straw hat and used it to fan his face. "It's a powerful bad thing to be widowed."

"The Lord has His plan," she said, "And we can't do anything about it. I'm just sad that Mr. Swanger never got a chance to beat the pants off that district attorney."

Claude smiled broadly. "I know that's right."

"Well, I'll leave you to your watering. I'll tell her you've been doing a good job. I don't know that she'll be able to pay you."

"Oh, I owe Mister Buddie many times over, so there ain't no worries about that."

After she disappeared beyond the hedge, Claude shut off the water and coiled the hose into a neat pile next to the house.

"That old biddy trying to get all up in my business." He straightened his hat. "She better get used to the sight of me...old Claude and Evie are going to be regular visitors around here from now on."

As he made his way toward the woods, he realized someone was approaching from the street. He stopped, turned, and saw Jenkins, the man who had talked to him before.

"Does Mrs. Swanger know you're still working around her house? I doubt she'll be able to pay you."

"You know, I get tired of everybody telling me that like it's something I don't know. I owes the Swangers some work, so I aim to do it. She won't mind my help a bit and besides, it's the right thing to do, help her in her hour of need."

"Did you give any further thought to our discussion about your still?"

"Like I told you before. I ain't giving it up. In fact, it's gone. I already busted it up. I'm out of the business now."

Jenkins returned to his car and called back. "That's too bad. I would have paid you good money for it."

"I don't want your devil's money, Mr. Jenkins."

As the sedan sped down the road, Claude spit after it. "There's something mighty fishy about that man. I got a feeling maybe there's more to all this than it seems." He began walking again. "I hope Evie's got something good fixed up, 'cause I'm hungry."

Marquez, Texas—11:05 a.m.

Aunt Laura led a tall gentleman to the sun porch where he stood next to Lily May, who sat facing away from the two doorways so she could gaze out the window.

"Lily May, this is Timothy Givens," Laura said. "He's a Texas Ranger, sent by the governor to investigate the case."

She didn't react until he gently lowered himself to one knee next to her. She turned her head, revealing her reddened eyes to him. "Pleased to meet you, Ranger Givens."

"First of all, Mrs. Swanger, I want to tell you how sorry I am for your loss. Everyone I've spoken to about this case holds your late husband in the highest regard."

Lily May's eyes brightened a shade. "Thank you. Now, do you have news about his death? One thing everyone wonders is how this happened, or why? I would appreciate being able to tell our family and friends something."

Givens looked at the floor. "I am doing my best, but I am still investigating and that is why I'm here. I'm sorry to even ask, but, well, did your husband have any enemies?"

Lily May did not flinch at the question. "I suppose people will usually stammer and say no, not at all. In truth, in our hearts we all want to believe we don't have enemies, but I know my Earl has crossed horns with a few people over the years and as we all learn in life, some wounds run deeper than they appear on the surface."

"Can you be more specific?"

"Well, for one, he borrowed money to help start his business in Huntsville. After the crash, we lost quite a lot and he missed a payment. The finance company sued him along with his partner."

"Mr. Bryant."

"Yes, Jimmy Bryant."

"How was their relationship?"

"Jimmy was his best friend. There is no bad blood there, I assure you."

"And this finance company?"

"I believe that lawsuit was well on the way to being settled. They're suing everybody. If they killed everybody who owed them money, they'd never collect a cent."

"Anyone else?"

She dabbed at the corner of her eye with a handkerchief and Laura spoke up. "What about his opponent?"

"Yes, the district attorney. What can you tell me about their relationship?"

Lily May locked her gaze on Givens' and said, "McIntyre is as shady as they come. My Earl has always stood up for justice and for the people. McIntyre is just in it for whatever money he can squeeze out of everybody's wallets. This is one of the reasons Earl ran for the office."

"What about his clients?"

"Earl always did his best for the people who hired him, even if the case wasn't very good. He'd always say, 'Even guilty people need an attorney.'"

A petite woman opened the second door. "Lily May? I've finished packing our things. Are you all right out here?"

"I'm fine, Pearl. Mr. Givens, this is my sister-in-law, Pearl, Earl's sister." Then to Pearl, "This is Timothy Givens. He is a Texas Ranger."

Pearl closed the door quietly behind her. "Are you investigating Buddie's death?"

"I'm sorry...Buddie?"

"Yes, you have to pardon me. It's a family nickname. We've called him Buddie for as long as I can remember. What have you found out?"

"I'm afraid I can't say too much about that. I am not at liberty to discuss details. This is the Walker County Sheriff Department's case. I was just sent to follow up on some of the particulars to help them out."

"From what we heard, they already closed the case, called it an accident. Such foolishness. Why are you bothering a grieving widow?"

"Now, Pearl, he's asking me if Buddie had any enemies."

"Go after that crook he's running against, if you ask me. Motive? Best motive in the world. Buddie was going to beat the socks off him in that primary. I wish we still lived in the district so I could vote against him, too."

"Now, Pearl."

"Buddie was the best county attorney Leon County has ever had, and he was going to do the same thing as the district attorney. McIntyre stood to lose a lot more than an election when Buddie beat him."

Givens stood. "Well, like I said, this is just a routine visit to ask a few questions. It's always valuable for the next of kin to tell us anything they might know. I assure you I am looking at things with a fresh set of eyes, and even a small thing might shine new light on my investigation."

Lily May reached out and touched Pearl's arm. "Now, you go on back and I'll be along right after you."

Pearl cast a sidelong glance at Givens, then disappeared closing the door with a distinct click behind her.

"Don't mind Pearl. She and Buddie were quite close, and she's like a sister to me."

"Just the two of them, brother and sister?"

"Five other half-brothers and sisters. Their mama died and Buddie's father married another woman. Eugenia Swanger is Pearl and Buddie's mother."

"Big family. I see. Well, in my line of work I see a lot of grief and it seems to work in phases on people. For most, a period of anger is quite common."

"Oh, I have plenty of anger about this. I'm holding it in until I get back to Huntsville."

"You're returning to town?"

"I leave on the noon train. A wife has to bury her husband, and I plan on running my own little investigation. I assure you, Mr. Givens, this was no accident and I intend to find out who might be responsible."

"Mrs. Swanger, I am doing everything possible to figure that out. Please, leave it to the police."

"We'll see. Are you going to look at McIntyre?"

"I will look anywhere the evidence leads, you have my word. I'm heading to Huntsville. Do you want me to take you?"

"No, thank you, Mr. Givens. Pearl is coming with me and we both have our bags. We're used to taking the train and we can easily get a ride to the house."

Huntsville, Texas—11:45 p.m.

Standing in the sweltering heat of McIntyre's office, Sheriff Steele positioned himself as close to the fan as he could and tried not to sweat as he faced the district attorney from a corner of the desk. The scowl on McIntyre's face intimidated him somewhat, but then he remembered that this scowl was a practiced art, something he'd seen employed by the man dozens of times in court.

"Ranger Givens called me a little while ago from the Trinity sheriff's office. He managed to find that woman up there." The sheriff fanned his face with his Stetson, then lowered it and held it around the brim with both hands.

McIntyre stood and paced behind his desk. "How on earth did he find her? My man said he had hidden her well."

"The guy's good at what he does. Most Rangers are."

"Did he tell you what she said?"

The sheriff rotated his hat with his fingers. "According to him, she's telling a slightly different story."

"Again? That's the *third* time she's given us a different version. What is it this time?"

Sheriff Steele looked to one side and shook his head. "Said he was drunk and ornery and that's why she forced him to stop. That's when she got out and found another ride."

"Earl Swanger, drunk and unruly? Who's going to believe that? The man practically invented temperance. Still, that is the most useful version, to me at least."

"What do you mean?"

"Well, despite his good reputation, many people have a dark side, and this *could* cast a shadow on the reputation of the man. It makes him less of a sympathetic victim and adds credence to your conclusions about the cause of death. Drunkenness would lead to exactly that kind of accident."

"Except he wasn't drunk. The doc checked for that. When Givens told me this new information, I double-checked the report...there was no alcohol in Swanger's blood. Look, Alvin, I deal in facts and evidence. This woman is lying, pure and simple."

"Let it slip to a reporter anyway, like somebody did with her second version."

"You really want this to go away, don't you?"

"It's for the best," McIntyre said. He leaned forward to quietly add, "For *all* of us."

McIntyre looked at his watch. "Oh, I have a meeting later and I have some work to finish before then. Thank you for the information, Nathan. Uh, where is Ranger Givens now?"

"He went to Marquez to interview the widow. I imagine he'll be back presently."

After he closed the door, Sheriff Steele encountered the lurking figure of Jenkins in the hall.

As soon as the sheriff was out of sight, Jenkins opened the office door without knocking.

"Oh, wonderful, more bad news?"

"Why would you say that, boss?"

"Because whenever you burst in here without knocking, it's usually bad news. What is it this time?"

"I hear..."

McIntyre held up the palm of his hand. "Wait, are you sure Steele isn't listening?"

"I watched him walk away before I came in."

"All, right, go on." McIntyre sat and crossed his arms.

"I hear Swanger's widow is coming to town ready to raise a stink." Jenkins maneuvered in front of the fan. "And Davidson, that bootlegger Swanger represented, he's not cooperating. He claims he's out of the business, and he told me he destroyed his still."

McIntyre rubbed a hand across his mouth. "Jenkins, you've let this entire situation get out of hand. And now we have that Ranger sticking his nose into places he shouldn't. You've put everything in jeopardy."

"I just tried to set up Swanger the way you wanted. How was I to know the Johnston woman would mess it up?"

"The sheriff told me Givens managed to find her. I thought you said she was well-hidden?"

"Yes, sir, I didn't think even a coon hound could find her."

"A coon hound isn't a Texas Ranger," McIntyre replied as Jenkins left the room.

When he was alone again, McIntyre sat for a few minutes, contemplating his situation.

"The problem with leadership," he said to himself, "is that a leader has to put up with idiots who are incapable of doing anything right."

After working through a stack of case files most of the afternoon, he grabbed his hat and coat and walked swiftly to the main door. He glanced both ways as he exited the building, and then proceeded at a quick pace. He kept his head down wherever possible and meandered down a few side streets until he reached the hill leading up to the spires of Old Main, the prominent building of Sam Houston State Teacher's College. It was late on the warm summer afternoon, so there were few people on the campus. McIntyre ducked inside the imposing building and walked through the darkened corridors until he found an alcove behind the auditorium and waited. He checked his watch and, as he looked up, a short, swarthy figure approached.

"Right on time," the figure said.

"Hello, Mr. LeBlanc. I'm glad you were able to meet with me on such short notice." He was shorter than McIntyre expected.

"I was already in the area finishing up another assignment. What's this about? I was told our friends want two witnesses to disappear."

"Let's just say, we *all* need them out of the picture."

A sly smile spread across LeBlanc's lips, his gold front tooth almost glowing in the shadows. "Listen, I've been at this a long time and I know your type. How many others?"

McIntyre began to shudder as he took in a deep breath. "Probably three."

"Five in all? I might be able to retire after a weekend like this."

"Too many loose ends."

"Loose ends are the bread and butter of my business."

"That's good. I'd really like this all tied up quickly. The less interaction we have, the better."

"Okay. I assume you want them all to disappear, too?"

McIntyre looked down at his feet. "Yes."

"It'll be three large."

McIntyre nodded. "Three thousand is a lot of money."

"It's a lot of work. I assume you came ready to pay."

"Yes," McIntyre said as he extracted an envelope from his inside coat pocket and began counting out bills.

"Tell you what, two thousand now, and you can send the rest to me later. I might have me an idea about that. I'll contact you in a little while about the specifics of the jobs."

McIntyre gulped. "I hope I can trust that you'll do everything you say."

"Remember who I work for. I always do the job."

McIntyre's hand trembled as he handed LeBlanc the bills. He had added a small note on top of the stack, and LeBlanc scanned the words on the note and stuffed it into a pocket, then smacked his lips as he folded the bills before saying, "Now, give me a few minutes to duck out of here, then I don't care what you do. I'll be in touch."

McIntyre turned away as LeBlanc disappeared into the shadows. Then he made his way out of the huge building, descended the steep hill, and ambled toward downtown.

Pangs of guilt crept into the darkness of his heart, making it beat against his ribs like a jackhammer. Despite any doubts, McIntyre fully realized he was dealing with five threats to his future. He remembered LeBlanc mentioning another job and shivered slightly because he immediately thought of Bill Thornton. He knew Thornton had angered someone close to Maceo and had likely paid the price. McIntyre kept his head down and avoided people's eyes as he made his way to the safety of his office.

"I had better get my money's worth," he whispered under his breath as he slipped into the sanctuary of his office. Once inside, he pressed his back against the closed door and tried to calm the palpitations in his chest.

Huntsville, Texas—3:30 p.m.

Lily May stood on the top step of the passenger car and scanned the train station. An unsettling mood had fogged her brain the entire trip from Marquez, but now that she was back in

Huntsville, she resolved to put up a brave front and do what needed to be done.

"I guess I had better get to it," she said before she managed a deep breath and stepped down to the platform.

Pearl followed her and said, "Don't you worry about a thing, Lily May."

"Thank you for coming with me, Pearl."

Pearl patted the hair stylishly peeking along the borders of her hat. "No one should have to deal with all of this alone. Ma puts on a brave face, but I can tell you, she's devastated. We all are, but I can tell you there are more than a few questions I want answered." Pearl glanced around the platform. "Should we go see about poor Buddie, or should we head over to your house?"

"I'm not quite ready to face the undertaker. Let's go to the house first, and you can start airing it out while I go take care of business."

Pearl looked toward the street. "Do we need a taxi?"

"Buddie's office is close by. If Jimmy Bryant is there, I'm sure he'd be happy to drive us to the house. Then perhaps he'll take me on my errands."

"Of course. Where do you think you need to go?"

"I need to go see the sheriff, then the medical officer, oh, and I need to go by the bank as well."

They both lifted their suitcases and made their way down the street.

"Lily May, I can help you with all of those things, too," Pearl said. "You know that."

"Yes, I do, but I feel guilty taking you away from your own home for so long."

"You hush. Buddie was my brother, and I will help you in whatever way I can. But please don't worry about taking me away from anything. Will, Martha Pearl, and Mary Margaret will be fine. I'm here for *you* now."

Jimmy Bryant was hunched over an open law book when Lily May opened the door.

"Jimmy?"

He abruptly stood, knocking the book to the floor in the process. "Oh, Miss Lily May. You startled me. I wasn't expecting you so soon."

"You know Buddie's sister, Pearl."

"Oh, hello, Pearl, good to see you again. How's Austin?"

"Hot as the blazes."

Lily May said, "We were hoping for a ride to the house. I also wanted to inquire about Buddie's will."

"Oh, I've got a copy of his will right here. He had updated it right after we moved into these smaller offices. I knew you'd be needing it, so I already had it handy."

"Well, we can go over all of that after I have worked out the arrangements. Are you busy today? I mean to say, can you take me where I need to go?"

"Yes, ma'am. There is nothing here I can't put off. I mean, there's no court appearances or appointments or anything like that except for paperwork," he said. He grabbed his hat and pointed to the door. "Let's go." They had left their bags outside and when he saw them, he added, "I'll pull the car around."

At the house, Lily May and Pearl began opening windows while Jimmy brought in their suitcases.

"It's like an oven in here," Pearl said. "Where are the fans?"

"They're scattered about," Lily May answered and she started one in the front room. It rattled to life with jerky oscillations that barely managed to stir the sticky, thick-as-soup warm air to the far corners of the room.

Lily May surveyed the kitchen. "There are a few dishes to do, but dear Buddie kept the place pretty much as I left it." She stifled a sob. "He always tried to tidy up after himself. Never wanted to be a bother."

Pearl embraced her. "There, there, it's all right to miss him. I do, too."

Lily May looked past Pearl's head and realized Jimmy was standing in the front room holding his hat. "Jimmy, I'm sorry. I almost forgot about you. Pearl, can you make the house presentable? I expect folks will be dropping by as soon as word gets around that I'm back in town."

"Of course, dear. You go do what you need to do. Are you sure you don't want me to come with you?"

"I'll be fine. Besides, Jimmy will be with me." Then to Jimmy, "Is that all right?"

"Yes, whatever you need, Miss Lily May," he said.

Pearl began surveying the room, planning what she needed to do first. "You go on now, I'll make do."

As Jimmy and Lily May headed into town, she asked, "Do you know what is going on with the investigation? Are they still saying it was an accident?"

"There's a Texas Ranger going around asking questions."

"I know that. Ranger Givens came to Marquez to talk to me."

"He seems to know what he's doing. I hope he's making some headway with the case. I know the sheriff is still pushing the accident theory, but I heard that the doctor isn't satisfied with the idea that nails from the bridge railing caused Buddie's wounds." Jimmy shook his head.

"And what about that magistrate? What's his name? Custus?"

"Yes, he signed the order, but he said he'd reconsider if more evidence turned up. There's more as well. Something about a woman."

"My Aunt Laura told me about that rubbish in the newspapers. I never heard anything more outlandish. Our marriage was on solid ground, Jimmy."

"I know that."

"If Buddie had a woman in the car, there would have to be a reasonable explanation. Who was she?"

"Nobody knows. Someone from Trinity is what I heard. They're keeping her name private. I also heard her story has changed."

"There's our first clue. I've been married to an attorney long enough to know that a person doesn't have to change the truth. I'm sure that crook McIntyre says he is intent on protecting me from her allegations, but most likely he's protecting somebody else."

"Who?"

"Himself."

Jimmy laughed as he responded, "I can see that."

"If her identity is being hidden, then I have no doubt he's behind it. But I can't understand why Buddie had to end up dead. Surely even McIntyre wouldn't kill a man to save an election. What kind of monster would do that?"

"Do you really think Buddie could beat him?"

"People are afraid of the likes of McIntyre, but fear also makes them want to protect themselves. Yes, I'm sure Buddie would have won."

"Well, without a witness, we will never know the full story."

"Pull up here to the sheriff's office. I'll see what we can do to change all of that."

"Don't you want to go the funeral parlor? They took the body there yesterday."

"I want to talk to Sheriff Steele first."

Lily May strode into the sheriff's office unannounced. "Sheriff Steele, I want to know what you are doing to find out what happened to my husband."

The sheriff had been sipping a cup of coffee and jumped when she came in, spilling it across the front of his uniform. He set the cup down and brushed at the spreading stain. "Mrs. Swanger, I am so sorry..."

She pulled out a hanky and wiped at the spot as well and said, "We will have time for that later. I've heard the word sorry so many times in the last few days it has almost lost all meaning. I want to know about this woman mentioned in the papers. Who is she?"

Sheriff Steele sat and tapped his index finger nervously on the desk. "Her identity is being held for privacy reasons."

"Whose privacy?"

"Well, yours, for one, Mrs. Swanger. Such things can be quite delicate in nature."

"Mr. Swanger was not the type to step out on his wife. You knew him. He'd give a bum on the street his last dime if he thought the bum needed it more than him."

"I know, but, well, her story..."

"Has changed several times, from what I've heard. You think we don't get the papers out in Marquez? I read all about his supposed drunken outburst in the paper. Drunk? My Earl? Pure hogwash! I can tell you in the plainest of terms—*that* never happened."

Steele's face flushed. "Well, in the time I've known Mr. Swanger, it's true I never thought him the type to imbibe, but..."

"But, nothing! That was just a bold-faced lie and I won't stand for it! Was his blood checked for alcohol?"

Sheriff Steele looked down at his desk. "Yes. There was no evidence of alcohol."

"Hah, I thought so. Why wasn't *that* in the paper to clear my husband's good name? I was married to him when he was county attorney, so I have some inkling of the way these things work. The woman is obviously lying, but those lies must support some hidden agenda. Now, my question for you is, what are you going to do about it?"

"A Texas Ranger is on the case...perhaps he can turn up something new."

"I've talked to Ranger Givens. He came out to see if I knew of anyone who'd want to kill Earl."

"Do you?"

"Of course not. Earl Swanger was highly respected by everyone he met. And I'll tell you something else, *he* was going to win this election. That leaves one person who might have a bone to pick with him."

"You can't mean...that's preposterous."

"McIntyre? Has anyone investigated *him*?"

"There is no reason. I have to say, accusing a sitting district attorney of such gross impropriety is absurd."

"It is really the only answer. Isn't it?"

"Sometimes a fog can roll off Harmon Creek and blanket the road out there where it curves away from the new bridge cutoff. His car did crash through the railing and roll down the embankment."

Lily May's face bloomed almost rose red. "Do you really believe that nails from the bridge caused his fatal injury? *Nails?* I'm going to the funeral parlor right this minute to look at his body so I can see for myself."

Steele began to rise.

"No, don't get up. I'll let myself out. But please understand this—*Justice* was the centerpiece of Earl Swanger's life, and it's what I want to be the centerpiece of his death as well, and, frankly, I don't see it coming from you or anybody else officially involved in the legal system in this town."

Sheriff Steele looked as if he had just been kicked in the gut by a mule. She turned, loudly closed the door behind her, and breezed past a startled Jimmy Bryant. He double-stepped to follow Lily May down the hall.

Once outside, he caught up with her and said, "Miss Lily May, you aren't going to get the answers you want talking to the sheriff like that."

"Oh, Jimmy," she said, fighting back tears. "Can't you see? We aren't going to get the answers we want no matter what you or I do." She dabbed at the corner of her eyes with an index finger. "Now, I want to see Buddie."

The undertaker had apparently been alerted by the sheriff and was waiting outside when she arrived.

"Mrs. Swanger, I am so..."

"You can save that for later. I want to see my husband's body."

"Well, it's, well, we haven't prepared it yet."

"Not for a visitation, you mean. I demand to see it the way it is right now. We can commence with any arrangements after I've said goodbye to my husband."

"Of course, but understand..."

"I've lived through many rough times and I've seen death, sir. I've seen farmhands crushed by stacks of fallen hay and ripped apart by a thresher. I've even witnessed hangings. Show me my husband."

She was led past two viewing areas and into the back where she saw Earl laid out on a table. For all of her bluster, she was not quite ready for the reality of what she encountered.

"Oh, Buddie!" she sobbed. She touched his lips, then asked for more light and lowered the shroud that covered his chest to look closely at his wounds.

"Nails? Sheriff Steele says these were caused by nails?" She turned to the undertaker. "What do you think?"

He had been standing a few steps behind her. "It's not for me to say, Mrs. Swanger."

"You've seen more bodies in more poses of death than anyone. Do you think those wounds were caused by nails miraculously encountering a body *inside* a moving vehicle?"

"No, ma'am. They look like punctures. I've seen wounds like that from bodies that came from the prison. Smuggled ice picks, usually, or screwdrivers."

She took one last lingering look before she covered Earl's face again.

An hour later, Jimmy dropped Lily May off at her house. Pearl met her on the porch. They both went inside, arm in arm, to sit down and share a good cry.

Huntsville, Texas—5:30 p.m.

McIntyre parked his car on a lonely country lane just outside of town to collect his thoughts after Sheriff Steele called to tell him about his meeting with the Swanger widow.

"I knew she was going to be trouble," he muttered. He shook his head as he thought about the events he had put in motion, wondering to himself if he could somehow stop Hemmings LeBlanc, but he knew it was likely too late for that. In his despair he eyed the glove box where he kept a small thirty caliber revolver, then he shook the beginnings of *that* fool notion out of his head.

He started the car and exclaimed over the noise of the engine, "I'm not quite ready to give up, at least not yet. Things will settle down after tomorrow, I'm sure."

In town he stopped at the café and ate dinner. His wife and children were away for the month, visiting family in Galveston. That they were near the center of the Maceo organization had never been a concern to him until now. He sat near the fan but knew it was no substitute for the sea breeze. The waitress' name tag read 'Sue,' and he realized she was the person who had identified Betty Johnston.

Dark notions entered his mind. "Another loose end," he thought, and a vision of the Hemmings LeBlanc's prominent gold front tooth flickered through his brain like a flash of lightning.

She smiled and poured his coffee. It was a sweet smile, and he smiled back. "Thank you," he said.

He fought the impulse to echo his thoughts out loud, but inwardly he reminded himself, *I can't kill everybody.*

After returning home and retiring, he suddenly shot awake out of a fitful sleep. He didn't remember the dream, but whatever it had been, it left him shaken, so he decided to dress and take a walk. He retrieved the revolver from his car and fingered it in his pocket as he strolled. He checked his watch, squinting in the dim light of the moon. It was five o'clock.

Bullfrogs croaked their mating calls from a nearby pond, and crickets sang a lively chorus. It was still warm, and in the humidity of the dark morning, mists covered hidden depressions along the sides of the road, kindling thoughts of imaginary spirits lurking beneath their surface.

A sound of footsteps approached from ahead, drifting through the gossamer wisps of vapor. He quickened his step, encircling the pistol's grip with his fingers. A figure took shape and, for just a split second, he thought he saw the visage of Earl Swanger coming right at him. Just as he was about to pull out his weapon and drop the apparition in its tracks, the sound of a familiar voice reached his ears.

"Hey, Mr. McIntyre, you're out early."

It was a young neighbor who worked at the teacher's college. McIntyre took a deep breath. "So are you, young man."

"I work the early shift at the college's power plant. You'll catch me out here most days at this time, rain or shine. Have a good day."

The footsteps disappeared behind him, and McIntyre pulled out his handkerchief and wiped the sweat from his brow.

"Now I'm seeing dead men," he mumbled to himself as he returned to his house and sat in the dark where he brooded quietly.

He rarely visited his office on Saturdays but decided to continue brooding at his desk. With his family away, his home seemed almost alien and threatening. He felt much safer in his office, even though the darkened cavernous halls of the courthouse were eerie and foreboding without the hustle and bustle of everyday work.

McIntyre paced back and forth as he contemplated his situation. He felt a need to anticipate any possible fallback from the wheels of fate he had urged into motion. He had put his faith in Hemmings LeBlanc, and now he worried how much one might trust any hired killer.

"What is it criminals call someone like him?" he mused to himself, then answered his own question. "A Button Man."

He ran all the numbers through his head, and the five loose ends, as he had put it, were the biggest risks to his situation. With those two idiots in Trinity out of the way, the Ranger's investigation would stall and the county would be stuck with the sheriff's original determination that Earl Swanger had died in a tragic accident. With Swanger out of the way, the primary would be his and his operation would continue unabated.

"Things will get better after the primary," he blurted out.

He felt bad about the other three, who had nothing to do with this sordid affair or with the election. They were all simply thorns in his side he needed to pluck out to sooth his bruised ego, an irritation that needed a salve of redemption. The gold tooth of Hemmings LeBlanc haunted his thoughts.

Ten

Trinity, Texas—4:00 a.m.

As he waited alone in the darkness, Hemmings LeBlanc sat in quiet contemplation while gangs of crickets and tree frogs blanketed him with a wall of sound. He savored the huntsman aspect of his life's work, and even relished all of the tedious investigations and tracking. Then there was the drudgery, like now, as he stalked his prey. Still, he never minded when he already knew where they were going to be. It was easier, but just as tiresome.

Yet, the business was more than just a chore to him. He considered it to be a form of art. He knew that some droppers were just plain killers. To them, it *was* just a job, like dog catcher or soda jerk. For them, once they got a contract that was it. They went out, did the job, got the money, and went on to the next job. He shook his head as this thought rolled across his mind, thinking, *it's like they were sweeping floors or something.*

His early years growing up in the Atchafalaya basin had been a hard life. Well, for a kid it was full of adventure, but his father made life difficult. The old man had alienated himself from his

Cajun relatives early on by falling in love with a lovely Creole temptress, and they never let him forget their disgust and disappointment in his decision, and he spent the rest of his life taking his frustration with this tension out on the family. His mother was a strong woman, and she did her best to protect her children from the frequent drunken outbursts, yet she continued to love her husband through all of his misdeeds. In his mind, the old man felt as if he had lost his lot in life by marrying into mixed blood, and then the babies came, and supporting his family became tougher. His beautiful bride's beauty faded with the years until all he felt he had left was his anger and a houseful of mouths to keep fed. As a result, he worked himself into an early grave, but by then Hemmings endeavored to help his mother in any way he could. The one positive thing his dad bequeathed to him was the knowledge of a lot of things, especially in the realm of hunting and fishing. Using those skills, he was able to help his mother keep the family fed.

Growing up, any members of the LeBlanc side Hemmings happened to meet were cold and distant to him, acting as if they were better than he was. He judged that his father's troubles had more to do with the emotional baggage carried by all of his siblings than any hostility foisted upon him at his choice of a mixed-race spouse. Looking back, he could now see they were no different than anyone else, they were simply unhappy despite their professed and dedicated allegiance to the LeBlanc clan. There was a time he resented them for not helping when his mother became a widow, but he soon realized that every one of them carried personal burdens. They led their own hard lives, depending on game for sustenance, and getting what work they could, and so all of them trudged through life one miserable day at a time the same way his father had seemed to do.

His mother's side wasn't any better off, but they were happier. All of them reveled in life and had learned to take everything in stride. He fondly remembered his grandmother regaling him with stories of her own mother, a full-blooded Alabama Coushatta from eastern Texas. Those tales enraptured him for hours. His uncles liked him and taught him more skills in tracking and hunting than his father ever had. The basin was their livelihood, and they'd learned to make the most of it. He could hunt, kill, field dress, and butcher a deer or alligator in no time, not even thinking about where or how to cut next.

His current occupation had been an outgrowth of this upbringing. At first, he worked in the swampland and hired out to do whatever odd jobs he could find, whether that was working on road gangs, or lumberjacking, and he eventually put his field dressing skills to some use by apprenticing at a meat packing plant for a while. He grew to hate the tedium, but manhandling frigid beef and pork carcasses every day for months on end had given his muscles the strength to do just about anything he needed to do.

The plant manager, a purely mean SOB, was hated by everyone at the plant. But there was another fellow who hated him more. The manager had cuckolded this man by dallying with his wife. One day, this stranger approached Hemmings as he exited a small store, leading him to an alleyway. He tendered an offer to kill the manager.

"I'll give you a hundred dollars to do the job."

Truth be told, Hemmings had been on the verge of quitting, so the prospect of a hundred dollars in one lump sum was an attractive incentive. As he quickly contemplated the offer, he reasoned that he hated the guy anyway, so he agreed to do it. When the job was complete, there were no suspects because *everyone* was a suspect, and the local police were not too keen on continuing the investigation because even *they* hated the guy. It seemed like every family in the county had some beef with this man. The body was still hidden away, buried on a forgotten island in the swampland.

Hemmings left town soon after and found there was a ready market for someone willing to do the very same thing. He used the hundred dollars to meander around eastern Texas and western Louisiana, traveling the seamier sides of towns. Prospective customers kept any knowledge of his activities to themselves because his occupation struck a certain amount of fear into everyone who knew anything about him. It did not take long for his reputation to grow, and he soon attracted the attention of the Carollos in New Orleans. He wasn't a made man or anything like that, but they kept him busy and often lent him out to the Piranios in Dallas and the Maceos in Galveston. It made sense for these three families to outsource such operations to keep the local heat off.

Hemmings realized early on he *liked* all aspects of what he did. The physical act of killing a person didn't bother him, but to do it right took planning, and he lived by the old adage...the devil is in the details. Oh, he sometimes reckoned he might have been better off channeling his impulses into some sort of career, but when he really got down to the basics of life, he could not imagine himself in any other profession. There was no shortage of work, either. Prohibition and the Carollo family had seen to that. He was a prized commodity in a limited market. He knew how to get in, get the job done, and get out. The trick was to not leave any traces of his involvement, or anything that pointed back to, as a formal contract might say, the party of the first part. His mixed blood heritage helped him to do this by allowing him to pass for white when he needed to, while at the same time he could move comfortably among blacks. He bore no allegiance to any race, save the race for survival.

He broke his reminiscence and checked his watch. "Four-thirty," he said to himself. The watch was a fancy job attached to a chain. He'd acquired it on one of his recent business ventures. It was a rare token for him. He'd learned to never keep anything from a victim, but this job had been completed down in Mexico on an American who had been hiding out since the end of the last revolution. The bright red watch was the marker he'd been told to look for, and it had caught his eye as his prey checked the time just before ducking down a dark alley on some forgotten errand. After the deed was done, he'd snagged it for verification and, once the proof had been tendered, he was paid and the client wasn't interested in the watch anymore.

The tourist court was comprised of an inconspicuous array of small cabins, a bit off the beaten path, and he'd been watching it since early the previous evening. He parked his car up the road, just out of sight, and set up a vantage point beyond a tree line to one side, where he was well-hidden by thick underbrush.

The place was perfect for his purpose, secluded and quiet. He assumed it was busier during more temperate seasons and despite the hot night, he appreciated the tranquility. The man and woman had separate cabins but from what he could tell, they were the only guests, with the manager's cabin being the only other one that seemed occupied and it was at the far end of the compound. The man came to her cabin and left several times, but she didn't go to his. He seemed to spend most of his time in hers and he hadn't emerged since one o'clock. The only other being he had seen all evening was the dark shape of a dog in the underbrush not far away from him. Every time he looked at it, he imagined the mongrel staring at him. He looked at his watch.

"Good bet they're totally smoked by now," he mumbled as he emerged and looked around before trotting up the road to bring his car closer. He noted that the dog had disappeared.

He crept around the back to find a way inside. He'd nosed around one of the other cabins earlier and found out they all had both front and back doors, and he knew the best thing about these cheaper out-of-the-way cottages was their substandard locks. He snaked around the corner, keeping to the shadows, and saw an open window. It was high enough to prevent him from looking through it without making noise. He considered clambering through the window then negated the idea. He figured it was good for a backup plan, but he knew any noise would be risky. It would be quieter to simply force the lock on the back door.

He carried an array of tools on the inside of his suit coat. It was a custom job he'd had a seamstress up in Shreveport fix up for him. She'd sewn in various loops and pockets on both sides. With the tools he secreted there, he could jimmy a lock, hot wire a car, or crack a safe, if it was small enough. He picked a small flexible tool he'd had custom-made in Houston and worked the latch. He smiled as he felt it slide home, and the door was instantly ajar.

Two people at one time was a tricky business, but he was ready. He thanked his part-Coushatta blood for his good eyes. He scanned the darkened room and saw two motionless bodies. The man was sprawled on the floor in his undershorts. Hemmings sniffed and could smell the booze.

"Good," he whispered in an almost imperceptible hush.

The woman was slumped on a divan a few feet away. One breast had escaped the confines of her robe and he studied it for a moment, not to covet it but to observe, to give him a clear indication of how deeply she was breathing.

He reached into his right coat pocket and extracted a small metal container and a rag. He held it away from his face and opened the top, pouring a small quantity of liquid onto the cloth. He placed it against the woman's nose and mouth, thankful that ether was quicker when a person was already passed out and they weren't as likely to struggle. When he was sure of its effect, he repeated the process with the man, then he replaced and double-checked the cap and put the ether can back in his pocket. He pulled the woman off the divan and the back of her head hit the floor with a dull thud as he proceeded to drag her next to the man. He rolled them both onto their stomachs and bound them. This was just in case the ether wore off before he was finished with them. He was coldly methodical because that was the only assurance of success in his business.

He pulled a garrote out of his other coat pocket and proceeded to strangle them, first the woman, then the man. This was where the ether came in. Even someone dead drunk might stir while being strangled, but in this case, he took his time. It wasn't as easy to kill a person with your bare hands as most people thought. When he figured they were both taken care of, he made a final check and felt the spot along the neck a doctor in Dallas had once shown him. He was a good judge of life and he silently sighed as a pronouncement of death.

He stood and checked his watch again. "Five," he said. "Not much time."

Hemmings looked out the front window and saw nothing. It was exactly what he wanted to see. He returned to his charges, hoisted the woman over his shoulder and made his way out the back door, scanning and listening as he reached the corner, then crept to his car, where he placed her in a heap on the back floorboard.

He returned to the cabin and repeated the process with the man. Hemmings possessed almost brutish strength, another asset in his profession in that it generally allowed him to work alone. People were greedy, and associates could not be trusted for long. He made one last trip to the cabin to review the scene. He had managed everything with no disturbance and no blood. The place was a mess, but that was their doing, not his. He spied a suitcase in the corner and placed it on the divan, throwing random items of clothing from around the cabin into it, including the man's coat, shirt, and trousers along with the shoes he found close to both bodies. He found a small thirty-eight while searching the man's coat and secreted it in one of his own pockets.

"A bonus," he said. For him, it wasn't a token of the job, it was a new tool for his arsenal.

He filled the case and struggled to close it, finding and stuffing a remnant corner of a blouse intent on making its escape. Then he left through the back door, locking it behind him, and took the bag to his car.

"Makes it look like they flew the coop," he quipped as he tossed it on top of his passengers.

He wondered if he should perhaps check the man's cabin, but decided he had risked enough time on this part of the caper. He reasoned that if a man and a woman were in a hurry to leave, she'd take what she could, and he would just go.

"I gotta make my way east before sunrise," he said to himself.

He drove toward Louisiana, crossing the Sabine River just as the sun began to blind him, then turned down river and pulled into a small abandoned hunting camp he sometimes used. It was close enough to the river for fishing, and had thick woods to allow for good hunting. These woods also provided good cover, and the foliage along the river was thick enough to conceal any glimpse of the camp from the water, so he was hidden on all sides. His plan was to dismember the remains, then disperse portions at numerous spots along the river and in local swamps.

"Gators and turtles will take care of the rest," he assured himself.

He felt confident enough in the seclusion to build a good-sized fire, and he disposed of the suitcase and contents. "I'll come back later to sift out any buckles from the suitcase or things like shoes and whatnot. Them buckles will get you every time."

Hemmings worked quickly, in an efficient and practiced manner. He knew he still had a lot of work to do, followed by a long drive back into Texas for his next appointment.

Huntsville, Texas—10:00 a.m.

"Hurry along now, Evie," Claude called back. "We need to pay our respects."

"Land sakes alive, I'm coming. You got me all gussied up in my Sunday clothes and here it's only Saturday."

They made their way along a rough path through the woods and Claude helped Evie over a fallen log. "Preacher Davis will be waiting along the road up yonder."

"Nice of him to offer us a ride."

"I think he wants to pay his respects, too. He told me Mister Buddie helped him draw up some papers a while back."

"And don't forget, he's the one that got Mister Buddie to represent you."

"How could I forget that?" Claude said.

Evie spied a reflection of glass through the woods. "There he is. Not a minute too soon. It's too hot to be traipsing around dressed like this when it ain't even Sunday."

Preacher Davis stood next to his Model T. "I've left the top up in deference to Miss Evie's hair."

Claude nodded. "Much obliged, Preacher Davis."

Reverend Erasmus Davis stood straight and spread his shoulders back, almost popping his neck out of the starched clerical collar. "It's an honor to be of service. I owe the widow Swanger my respects as well. Her late husband is one of the only white lawyers around here who will offer services to our community."

"I know he done right by Claude," Evie said, as Claude helped her into the back seat of the small car.

"That's right. I'd be out on the road gang right this minute except for Mister Buddie," Claude said. His weight tipped the car slightly as he stepped up, with a resulting creak, then balanced as he settled next to his wife.

Preacher Davis reached near the steering wheel, set the spark lever, adjusted the throttle lever, and turned the ignition coil on. Claude winced because it clattered in a way that always seemed to make the car sound like it was a chicken fussing something awful.

"You know you could get a model with an electric starter."

The clergyman chuckled. "The good Lord will provide when He deems the time has come. Until then, this car will do just fine."

Then Preacher Davis hurried to set the crank dangling off the front of the engine and expertly jerked it to bring the car to life.

He hopped in, moved a handle on the left forward and started the car in motion. Claude held his hat tight to his head as the car lurched down the rough country road.

When they arrived at their destination, they could see two women sitting in the shade of the porch. Claude helped Evie out of the car, and the three of them cautiously approached.

"May I help you?" the smaller of the two women asked.

Claude stepped forward. "We looking for Mrs. Swanger."

Lily May stood. "I'm Mrs. Swanger."

"My name is Claude Davidson. This here is my wife, Evie, and that is Preacher Erasmus Davis, pastor of the Antioch Episcopal Methodist Church. We've come to offer our condolences on your loss. We're all powerful sorry."

Preacher Davis bowed his head slightly. "We never fathom the wisdom of the Lord's decisions, we simply bow to His will in the hope He does not give us ordeals we cannot survive."

Lily May held a hand to her mouth, and her eyes reddened before she responded. "Thank you for dropping by, Mr. Davidson, I'm pleased to meet all of you. I understand you've done a lot of work for my husband, on the porch and on our garden. We admired it yesterday. I know it must have taken you quite a while."

"Yes'm. The garden might could use a little more watering today, which I'll be happy to do before we leave."

"I'm not sure I can pay you anything, Mr. Davidson."

"Please, ma'am, you can call me Claude. Me and Mister Buddie was on first names. No pay needed. I'm still paying off what I owe him for his help. I couldn't pay him in money, so I was obliged to work it off."

"I won't hold you to your debt. You've done plenty, more than plenty by my accounting."

"Not by my reckoning. And I got to at least see your seedlings through to middle age." Claude smiled. "And you got any other chores you need me to do, you just give me a list. I can fix most anything."

"And I want to give you what help I can, too," Evie said. "I can take your mind off house chores for a few days. I remember when my daddy died, my mama was fit to be tied trying to do everything all by herself even with us kids helping. The good Lord says we must help them in need, so I'm offering, for as long as you need me. I do some paid work for the Lieberman family, but it won't get in my way of helping you out here. If you want, that is."

Lily May smiled, then looked toward Preacher Davis.

"I'm just a taxi service today, but I do want to offer my sincere sorrow at your immense loss. Mr. Swanger was known far and wide as a good and just man and he had only recently done some work for me and my congregation. It is a terrible loss for us all and I will most certainly be offering up prayers on his behalf during tomorrow's service."

Claude took a step back. "I guess we best be leaving now, Mrs. Swanger."

"Please, Claude, call me Lily May. Oh, and this is Buddie's sister Pearl, visiting me from Austin."

Claude's eyes widened. "Austin? No fooling?"

"No fooling," Pearl said. "I'm originally from closer by, Normangee, but I agree, Austin always sounds so far away, but really, it is not as distant and exotic as it sounds."

Claude paused and pointed to the back of the house. "I almost forgot, I need to run some water down those rows. Won't take but a few minutes. They need a little every day it don't rain." He looked up at the sky. "Don't seem too likely today. Come on you two, help me with the hose."

Evie called back, "I'll be along with Claude the next time he drops by."

The three of them pulled the hose from the house to the garden, and Claude watered it as he promised.

Near the Sabine River, Louisiana—3:30 p.m.

Hemmings LeBlanc had spent the better part of the day dealing with the remnants of his night's work. The skills he had learned in the meat packing plant served him well, and the spoils of his work now filled several large pails. He'd placed them on top of a large oilcloth he spread over the floorboard of his car alongside two burlap parcels the size of bowling balls.

He filled a large washtub with water and lye soap and meticulously washed several knives, and the two saws he had used. He stashed them in a secret alcove under the floorboards of the small shed. He planned stops at several locations he knew up and down the Sabine River and a few of its tributaries.

"I know where most of the biggest gators live. They're gonna be my partners for a spell, them and the snapping turtles."

At his first stop, he found the small path off a beaten dirt road. He grabbed two buckets and carried them down the path to the river. Each bucket had a slag of lead in the bottom he had picked up from somewhere he didn't quite remember.

He'd said at the time, "A guy can always use a couple of hundred pounds of lead."

He had knocked several holes in each bucket with a hammer and a big screwdriver and, although he had drained off as much blood as he could, some crimson seepage continued to ooze out. "Good thing I spread that oilcloth over the back."

When he got to the bank, he scanned for any interlopers, both on shore and off. Then he spotted a snout and two eyes poking out of the water not too far from where he stood.

"I see you," he jibed. "Hope you're hungry!"

He swung and tossed a bucket out as far as he could. It landed with a splash, floated briefly, and then bubbled under the water. The gator had momentarily disappeared at the disturbance but returned a second later and was now gliding toward what had moments earlier been the center point of the rings of ripples. He tossed a second bucket just as he saw two more denizens of the river approaching. He watched for a moment, spread some dirt over the small scarlet patches left behind by the buckets, and trotted back to his car.

He scanned the trees surrounding the path along his way and found a spot he reckoned wouldn't have many tree roots underneath. When he got to the car, he retrieved a shovel and one of the two parcels, then returned to the spot. He dug a narrow hole as deep as he could and dropped the bag. It hit the bottom with a dull thump. He shoveled loose dirt back into the hole, stomping it down with his full weight before adding more soil. He kicked the remaining loose dirt around and pulled handfuls of loose grass and spread those on top. He looked at the sky.

"Now I just need some rain. I expect some will come before too long."

He repeated this process at other spots up and down the river, until only one bucket remained, along with the oilskin fabric covering the floorboard. It was splotched with small pools of burgundy. The bucket was empty except for a brown glass bottle of Clorox. He drove to one more spot on a tributary of the Sabine, and carefully folded the fabric before carrying it and the bucket down to the water's edge. He spread the oil cloth close to the bank and sprinkled Clorox over the reddened spots He dipped the bucket in the river and returned to douse the fabric. He did this again and again until he had used all the bleach and the oilcloth was shiny and clean. He shook out the cloth and folded it, placing it in the bucket, and threw the empty bottle into the river.

"That'll about do it for those two," he said to himself as he drove back.

He dropped his wares at another small shack he sometimes used and headed back to Huntsville for his next job. "Three bodies in one day is quite a chore," he whispered to himself as he drove, "but I'll manage."

He stopped at a small place where he occasionally ate when traveling through the area and walked around the side of the building. He stooped to run some water over his hands from a faucet sticking out of the ground. He inspected his clothes and shoes for any telltale ruby spots or splotches. "Looks good," he said under his breath.

Inside, a combination of smoke from cigarettes, cigars, and the smell of hickory wafting in from the back almost made him gag. He coughed into his hand momentarily, but quickly recovered and adjusted his lungs to the tainted air the same way one got used to the perfume on a prostitute.

A large black woman approached. "What y'all want, honey?"

"Ribs," Hemmings said, "and some beans."

"You ain't been through here in forever. Where you been?"

"Here and there."

"Working?"

"Keeping busy."

She eyed him up and down. "How a skinny boy like you keeping a job? Most ever body around here's been cut loose."

He grinned, showing his gold tooth. "So far, so good."

"Praise God," she said.

He was famished and savored the tender pork, sucking away the last remnants of meat the way he remembered his father doing, leaving a plate full of bones that looked like they were ready to bleach in the sun.

The woman came back by. "Honey, you sure you were hungry?" she asked, eyeing the scant remains of his meal.

Hemmings laughed. "It was good. You're right, I haven't been here in a while, but it's still good as ever. How much I owe you."

"I ought to charge you extra 'cause they's nothing left on them bones for me to feed my dog. Twenty-five for the ribs, fifteen for the beans."

He left a dollar bill. "Keep the change."

Huntsville, Texas—3:30 p.m.

McIntyre stared at the stoic figure seated across from him and asked, "Can you repeat that?"

Ranger Givens replied, "The governor wants to offer a reward for information. He also might send another ranger to help speed the investigation."

"I'm not sure that's necessary. Have you turned up anything that substantially differs from the sheriff's account? I've read the reports and I have to tell you, I think the evidence for it having been nothing more than a tragic accident is quite strong."

"I'm not so sure about that. The Johnston woman's story has changed three times." Givens sneezed. "Must be something in the air," he said, then continued. "A person doesn't change the truth."

"Sometimes people remember details they might have inadvertently omitted the first time around. At any rate, the background picture she's painting now seems to put Mr. Swanger in an unsavory light. I don't think I want to put his widow and family through the ringer of that doubt and revulsion, do you?"

"What a load of hogwash. Except for the implications in Betty Johnston's last version of her story, every single person I've talked to says Swanger was a saint. Look, it took her two tries to come up with that latest line of garbage. Plus, she'd been drinking the last two times anybody talked to her. I talked to her, you didn't. I don't believe a word that comes out of her mouth, be it the first version, the second version or the third."

"And you think she was somehow involved?"

"I do indeed. She and that other man, Fred Darby. I want to bring them in for additional questioning. I can't sign off on this until I'm certain we're getting the truth from those two."

"And the other Ranger?"

"I agree it is probably unnecessary, but I don't have the final say on that. The thing is, we're spread pretty thin, so I'll believe it when I see it. Now about those two up in Trinity."

McIntyre leaned into the phone. "Get me the Trinity sheriff's office." A moment later he said, "Go out to the Westerhaus Travel Court and take Fred Darby and Betty Johnston into custody and hold them as material witnesses for Special Ranger Timothy Givens. He's on his way." McIntyre looked back at Givens. "That is the best I can do. I hope you know what you're doing."

McIntyre sat back in his chair and smirked after Givens left and again imagined a vision of Hemmings LeBlanc's gold tooth.

He picked up the phone and made a call.

"I know it's Saturday, but I need you to pick up an envelope from my desk and deliver it for me this evening." He said, "The time and location will be on the envelope."

Trinity, Texas—4:25 p.m.

Ranger Givens was disappointed when he arrived at the Trinity sheriff's office. Johnston and Darby were not there, but he was told to proceed to the Westerhaus Travel Court. When he arrived, he observed several patrol cars parked nearby and the door to Betty Johnston's cabin was open, as was the door to an adjacent cabin.

A sergeant approached. "You Ranger Givens?"

Givens answered, "Yes, I am. We have a crime scene here?"

"Well, we're not too sure. Maybe yes, maybe no. They're both gone. *Vamoosed.*"

Givens stepped into Betty's cabin and scanned the interior. "Any personal belongings?"

"A few, but the manager said he knows she had a suitcase, and we didn't find one. I'd say she packed in a hurry."

Givens eyed some makeup strewn about the small bathroom. "You married, Sergeant?"

The officer was somewhat taken aback. "Yes, sir, almost twenty-five years. Why?"

"If your missus needed to go someplace in a hurry, do you think she'd take her makeup?" he asked, pointing toward the bathroom.

"Say, now that you mention it that way, by golly I think that would be the first thing she'd grab."

"I agree." Givens walked around the room and nudged a half-full mason jar on the floor. He tested the lid; it was screwed tight. "I've met these two before. I don't see them leaving this either. What about the man's room?"

"It's not as much a mess as this one, but there's a suitcase. I figure maybe they were in too big a hurry, she managed to grab her clothes, but maybe he didn't have enough time to grab his."

"It just doesn't add up that way. Not the way I see it."

"Well, the makeup, that's an angle I hadn't thought of. So I can see where you're headed."

"Do you? Have you checked for any evidence of forced entry? Or found anything like blood or bloody objects?"

"The doors were both locked...we had the manager let us in."

Givens inspected the latch on the front door. It was worn but otherwise looked normal. "You said doors, there's a back door, too?"

"Yes, sir. I reckon it's a holdover from before them having indoor plumbing."

Givens inspected the back latch. He squinted and drew his eyes closer, then put on his reading spectacles and got even closer. "There it is," he whispered.

The sergeant looked over his shoulder. "What, I don't see anything."

"Tiny scratches. This door was forced open."

The sergeant got a closer look. "Hey, you're right. But how do we know that wasn't done a while back?"

Givens sighed. "We don't know, not for sure at least, but these scratches are shiny, so they look fresh. Beyond that, we need more evidence. Have your men scour both of these rooms for anything out of the ordinary."

"But what does this mean? Didn't they just take off?"

"Possibly, but more likely I think they've been removed by someone else, taken away in the night."

"You mean like kidnapped?"

"Probably more than that," Givens said, dropping his head. "Somebody doesn't want them talking."

"Oh," the sergeant said, swallowing hard.

Huntsville, Texas—5:00 p.m.

A Saturday phone call from Sheriff Steele urgently requested a meeting and Alvin McIntyre hurried over, wondering what prompted the request. Steele hadn't wanted to give more details over the phone, and it infuriated him.

He burst into Steele's office. "What's this about, Nathan?"

"You better sit down, Alvin," Sheriff Steele said, pointing to an empty chair.

"I hope this is important," he said.

"Well, I'll let you be the judge of that. Ranger Givens just called from up in Trinity. It seems your two birds, as the crooks like to say, have made a clean sneak."

McIntyre feigned surprise. "What?"

Steele glared at him. "You said your man had them under control."

McIntyre had done a bit of acting in school, and it was an experience that had served him well in years of arguing before the bench. He mustered some of that skill now.

"I haven't seen Jenkins since yesterday, but the last I heard, they were secure. Givens is up there now?"

"He had a few more questions for them."

"I knew that. I asked Trinity to go out there and bring them in and hold them so he could question them."

"He told me he was suspicious of her changing story. I wondered about that, too."

McIntyre watched a fan churning away at the thick air. "Why do you care?"

"Come on, Alvin, a veteran prosecutor like you should know she was lying through her teeth. Where is Jenkins anyway?"

McIntyre thought fast. "It's the weekend. With the election coming, we'll be quite busy so I don't begrudge him a little time off."

"Election seems pretty much a sure thing now, don't you think?"

"Are you insinuating..."

"Don't get your dander up," Steele said, then hesitated as he realized McIntyre might take offense. "Sorry," he said.

Sweat beaded on McIntyre's head, but he was so consumed with the thought of concealing his own lies, he paid no notice to the comment. "Although you're running unopposed, I had a strong opponent before this tragedy."

"Well, Givens wants to talk to Jenkins as soon as possible. Come to think of it, so do I."

"This changes nothing. Swanger's death was an accident, Sheriff, pure and simple."

Steele's hand rested on the desktop, but he fingered the center drawer pull of his desk with his index finger as he sat back in his chair. "It might have been an accident, but there's nothing simple about it. I might call foul on the word 'pure' as well."

McIntyre rose. "If that's all, I have places I need to be. If I talk to Jenkins, I'll tell him you want to speak to him."

"See that you do," Steele said.

McIntyre hesitated in the doorway and spun around. He focused a cold stare at the sheriff. "Nothing has changed concerning our past arrangements, Nathan. Nothing." He turned, opened the door, and quickened his pace down the hallway.

He managed to drive a couple of blocks before the enormity of his situation became too much for his nerves and he pulled over. Some children were playing baseball in a nearby field and he blankly watched them for a minute while he tried to keep his brain from doing cartwheels.

"Hemmings LeBlanc!" he said, banging the steering wheel with one hand. "How stupid of me. I should have pushed back on the Maceos."

He assumed Betty Johnston and Fred Darby had already been swept away by the predicament they had gotten them all into. He prayed the killer had left no clues that might link their disappearance to him or worse, to his bosses. He knew that would swing back at him as well. Worry flooded his eyes, and the combination of sweat and tears made them burn. He swiped at the moisture with his already damp handkerchief. "One of the hottest days of the year," he mumbled.

He rubbed his face trying to fathom a way he could contact LeBlanc and stop the continuation of his impulsive fiasco. He sobbed quietly as he realized there was no way to stop the man from fulfilling his contract. Then he wondered if perhaps he should warn the intended victims. Then another thought entered his mind: *That's the kind of loose end that might unravel this whole affair.*

He inhaled deeply and slowly through his nose, throwing his head back and closing his eyes in the process, and lowered his face with a slow exhale through pursed lips before starting his car again.

"May God have mercy on my soul," he intoned, but deep inside he knew it was likely too late for anything like that.

Somewhere in East Texas—5:30 p.m.

Hemmings LeBlanc hummed as he drove. "I've heard they're going to figure out a way to put radios in cars. When they do, I'm getting me one." Hot wind whipped at his face through the window.

He was tired. It had already been a long day. He had been up most of the night, but he still had three more jobs to complete. He had concocted a plan for the first one and he ran the steps of his scheme through his mind as he drove.

"It's trickier," he said to himself, "taking down a guy face to face. But he's not expecting it, so I'm sure to have an easy time of it."

He'd told McIntyre the time and place to deliver the final payment. LeBlanc had chosen a quiet place that would almost certainly provide no witnesses. It was a spot he knew out in the pine forests to the east of Huntsville. "It's way too hot for many folks to be out. If it was hunting weather, it'd be different." Talking to himself on these long drives helped him sort out the details.

The idea was to meet down a lonely logging road at a spot he knew where local folks sometimes came to be alone. He knew it was chancy, but it was more likely to be occupied late into the night than it might be in the late afternoon on a hot July Saturday. His plan was to arrive early, because he had work to do before they met.

When he arrived and parked his car, he reached into the back. When he'd dropped off the bucket and oilskin, he had retained the pick and shovel. He had also stopped at a small store along the way and bought a coil of rope. He took these items with him as he marched off a couple of hundred paces into the forest. The pines swayed above him in a warm breeze as he scanned the ground looking for a likely spot. A layer of pine straw covered one area more than others. He knew from experience this was a slight depression. He used the flat surface of the pick to rake the overburden from the bare earth in a huge swath, then began digging, alternating with the pick and the shovel. The forest floor here, covered by the thick layer of natural mulch, was loam rich, just as he had hoped. The roots he encountered were easily chopped with the shovel and he worked steadily, always checking his watch for the time because Jenkins was due at dusk and the afternoon was already waning. At one point, he attached the rope to the closest sturdy tree and stretched the end of the coil into the hole.

As he dug deeper, he said, "My granddaddy always said 'ten-dollar hole for a two-dollar tree.'" Soon, the top of his head was at ground level.

He used the rope to clamber out and stood back to examine his handiwork.

"It looks plenty big enough." He knew the one thing that could prematurely ruin a situation like this was animals finding a way into a shallow grave. Once there were bones scattered about, some nosy human might spot them.

He leaned the shovel on the far side of a large pine, dusted off his shirt and pants and hoped any dirt caked on his boots would walk off as he headed back to the logging road. The shadows were lengthening, and he expected Jenkins would be along soon. He put the pick and rope in the back and leaned against the car to roll a cigarette. He spotted the dark outline of a stray dog or coyote watching him from down the road. He said to himself, "Some dang hound always hanging around," as he took his last drag. He contemplated the glowing remnants a half inch from his fingers when he heard a car and saw headlights approaching. The car passed the spot where the dog had been. He casually dropped the butt and ground it into the graded roadbed with the tip of his boot. The car stopped and Dub Jenkins got out.

LeBlanc smiled, revealing his gold tooth, and said, "You're right on time. I appreciate it."

"McIntyre sent me," Jenkins said, reaching into his coat pocket. "Who are you?"

"Trust me, you don't want to know. I did a favor for your boss. Do you have something for me?"

Jenkins extracted an envelope. "You mean this?"

"Yeah, that." LeBlanc smiled and approached. "But I need to show you something first."

"What?"

"It's for your boss."

"I'd rather just give you this and leave." Jenkins was still clasping the envelope in his hand.

LeBlanc pulled out a pistol and pointed it at Jenkins, who raised his hands, still holding the envelope.

Jenkins blurted out, "What is this?"

"I insist. Your boss will want you to see what I need to show you. Hold onto that and I'll show you, it's out yonder," LeBlanc said, motioning with the gun. "It's not far."

"Listen, there's no need for this. I believe you. Go ahead, take it." He waved the envelope.

"Naw, I *have* to show you something." LeBlanc motioned with the gun again. "Get moving."

They silently marched through the darkening forest until they approached an ominous mound. "Stop right over there, you'll soon see," LeBlanc said, waving the gun.

Jenkins slowly walked in the direction LeBlanc had indicated and stopped at a large, dark hole in the forest floor. He squinted and gazed into it, recognized it for what it was, and he whirled around, screaming, "What the h..."

A red speck appeared on his forehead before he could complete his statement. He fell back into the depression just as the sound of the gun echoed through the woods. The envelope fluttered to the ground next to the edge of the hole.

"So, you see, you were just a loose end and this is over, except for me covering you up." He stooped down to pick up the envelope. "Just so you know, you were paying me for a job, so this here is rightfully mine."

He returned to the cars and fashioned the rope into a makeshift tow, using a piece he cut off to stabilize the steering wheel. "Don't need to get it too far, just maybe a mile away from here."

He drove to another wide spot in the logging road and slowed to a gradual stop. Jenkins' car gently bumped into his, then he pulled forward a few feet and stopped again. He untethered the tow rope and pushed the second car further to the side, then got into his car and turned around. He still had two more steps in his plan.

When he returned to the hole, he could see Jenkins still patiently waiting for him. Hemmings LeBlanc bowed his head. "There's no hard feelings. I don't even know you, but, you know, in my business, a job's a job."

He resumed humming while he worked, shoveling rapidly, and when he was done, he packed it by jumping on it a number of times. Then he covered the bare area again with the pine needles he had previously scattered away. He spread them around and checked his progress with the light from a match.

"Should be good. Nobody will likely be nosing around too much way out here." He scanned the surrounding trees. "These won't be harvested for another two or three years."

LeBlanc stumbled back to his car and returned to Jenkins' vehicle.

"Hope he's got plenty of gas," he mumbled, as he inserted a length of hose into the rear filler. He sucked and gagged when a stream of cold, foul liquid reached his mouth. He had brought a mason jar and he filled it again and again, letting the gas trickle under the car as he threw jar after jar of the stuff over the interior of the car. The stench of fresh gasoline filled the air. Finally, he let the hose dangle and more gas pooled underneath the vehicle. He stepped to the side and wiped his hands as best as he could against the forest underbrush.

"I sure hope this ain't poison ivy," he said, then stood to light a match. He tossed it toward the pool of gas under the car. A sudden rush of sound broke the silence as the gasoline exploded in a momentary flash. A brief wave of intense heat baked Hemmings' face, then the fire cooked down to a steady blaze and he returned to his own car. He didn't look back but knew the charred metallic carcass would continue to smolder behind him for quite a while.

He had other things on his mind and continued to his next appointment. He knew nothing about the man, but a single individual didn't seem like much of a challenge. After a short rest he knew he'd scout his prey and complete the job as quickly as he could. He anticipated no problem at all with the last job. Afterward, he anticipated a high time in New Orleans because working for the Carollos had its perks. As he cruised along a maze of forest roads, he recounted the day's events then gulped when he remembered one small detail he had forgotten.

"Damn," he said. "The plates."

He thought about turning back, but knew they'd be too hot to handle for a while and there was always the chance someone had seen the fire. It was the reason he'd buried the body before starting the fire in the first place. "What's done is done," he muttered. "Heading back now would be an even bigger mistake."

He absentmindedly draped a hand over the top of the steering wheel. "The devil's in the details," he mumbled.

Eleven

Sunday, July 13, 1930

Trinity County, Texas—10:15 a.m.

The investigation into the disappearance of Betty Johnston and Fred Darby extended from the travel court to Miss Johnston's bungalow where Givens found Darby's red sedan secreted in an alley. He canvassed local stores and service stations in a broad area, asking about the car. At one stop, a helpful citizen overheard and shared what he knew.

"I saw a car like that the other day. I noticed it because it was going down to an old played-out fishing hole. Not too many people go there these days, but up to a few years ago there'd been good fishing. That's why this car caught my notice. Not much reason for anyone to go down there."

The witness continued, describing a secluded oxbow lake near the Trinity River. The path of the Trinity was dotted with such lakes as it meandered its way to the coast, and each one marked a spot where the river had changed its course during some ancient flood.

"How do I find it?" Givens asked.

"There's a small turnoff to the west from the main road just across the river from here, close to Riverside."

Givens followed the directions and found a muddied path that led through a dense line of trees. He drove slowly until he reached a dead end next to a quiet body of water and parked near a scorched spot close to the bank. He got down close to the blackened bits and sniffed the remains.

"Recent fire," he said.

He squinted at the residue, intrigued by a certain thickness in one area of the otherwise fine ashes, so he stirred at this with a stick and spied flashes of color. He crouched and looked closer, nudging at the scraps with the tip of his finger.

"Cloth. Somebody burned clothes out here."

He returned to his car and retrieved several manila envelopes and a pair of tweezers. He painstakingly picked up the larger scorched remnants and placed them in one envelope. The fabric scraps were all small, ranging from a scant quarter of an inch to an inch in size. A couple appeared to be discolored with a rusty stain of some sort. Then as he stirred around in the ashes, he hit something hard. He used the tweezers to poke around and then pulled a small object from its hiding place.

"Shoe buckle," he mumbled. He knew ladies' shoes often sported such a buckle. He poked around and found another and placed both of them in another envelope. "So, somebody came out here to burn clothes, but lucky for me, they always forget about the shoe buckles."

He stood and scanned the small clearing, then walked in a series of concentric circles around the spot, looking for anything out of the ordinary. When he got to the bank, he stopped when he saw something bobbing in the water just off the shoreline. Givens squinted in the bright sun and could see it was small, barely poking in and out of the water like a long lost fisherman's float.

He looked up and down the shoreline but could see no one fishing. It was only about a yard away from the bank, so he got on his hands and knees and reached out, deftly plucking it from its soggy home. He stood and examined the object in his hands.

"Ice pick." Givens smiled. "Now why would somebody throw a perfectly good ice pick out into a lake?"

He examined it, but the exhumation from its watery grave left no telltale marks. He took it back to his car and placed it into another envelope.

"I may have to come back here with help, to see if there are any other secrets we can find."

He returned to the Trinity Sheriff's office and inquired about the rest of the investigation, choosing to keep his recent discoveries to himself for the time being. For one thing, he wasn't sure if the lake was in Trinity County or in Walker County.

A deputy told him, "We went over the place she rented, it was pretty clean, cleaner than the travel court. Looks like she hadn't been there in several days. Landlord says the weekly rent was due. We towed the car you found to the lot in back."

"What about the man?"

"We found a room he was renting locally and went through it. There was nothing much there. Spare suit in the closet, a few things in drawers. Basic toiletries. But we did find some of those things in his cabin at the travel court, too."

"So these two have apparently just cleared out *without* most of their belongings."

The deputy nodded, then asked, "What about you?"

He changed his mind about keeping all of his secrets. "I'm still working on it, but found a spot south of here, on one of the oxbow lakes. There was evidence of a recent fire. It looked like somebody had torched a pile of clothes."

"Was that in Trinity County?"

"To be truthful, I'm not sure."

The deputy led him to a large wall map. Givens studied it for a few seconds and tapped on a particular feature. "There it is."

"Just inside Walker," the deputy said. "Find anything identifiable?"

"Just scraps of clothing."

"Anything else?"

Givens decided to withhold mention of the ice pick. "No," he said.

Huntsville, Texas—10:20 a.m.

Sheriff Steele allowed a moment of weariness to overtake him, and he slumped behind his desk. After so many years in law enforcement, the last several as sheriff, he should be used to working seven days a week, but the constant grind wore on him like an old pair of ill-fitting shoes. But he knew that some weeks this was just how things ran. For one thing, the heat had a tendency to fray people's nerves and, although they always managed to let off some steam on the Fourth of July, as the summer weeks went by and the temperature continued at a slow simmer, folks settled back down to the regular indiscretions that always kept a sheriff's office busy. But this Swanger deal added a fancy bit of rancid icing on the moldy cake of summer drudgery.

Deputy Adams leaned into the doorway. "Sheriff?"

"What is it, Adams?"

"San Jacinto County called. They found a burned-out car in a pine forest, registered to someone from Huntsville."

"Do they have a name?"

"That's what they wanted me to look up."

The sheriff stared at Adams for a few seconds, before adding, "And did you?"

"Oh," Adams blinked rapidly, "yes, sir! I did. It came back to a Percival Jenkins."

Sheriff Steele closed his eyes momentarily and his shoulders drooped.

"Sheriff? You okay?"

His eyelids fluttered open. "Yes, I'm fine. You and I are taking a trip out to San Jacinto County. Find out exactly where that car is and tell them we're coming to look at it."

By the time Sheriff Steele and Deputy Adams got to the car, the local boys were almost ready to tow it out.

Steele approached the only deputy on the scene.

"Nathan Steele. Sheriff of Walker County."

"Oh, yes, Sheriff, we have this well in hand. I figure somebody probably burned it for the insurance money. We've been seeing a lot of that lately."

"That's your theory? An insurance fraud?"

"A lot of people lost all their money in that stock market thing. Did you find the owner?"

"Not yet. I know him, though."

Adams shot Steele a questioning look.

"He's the district attorney's assistant."

Now Sheriff Steele had two shocked deputies staring at him for several long seconds before the San Jacinto officer finally broke the silence. "I-I, uh, we, we had no idea."

"Puts a little different light on it, doesn't it? Now, listen, I don't want to step on your investigation here, it's out of my jurisdiction, but have you combed the surrounding area for any additional evidence?"

"No, sir. I made the original discovery, then checked to be sure there wasn't nothing like a body inside, then drove back to the station with the plate. I figured out it was from your neck of the woods and called you, then came back out here to supervise the tow."

Steele poked his head into the charred remnants of the vehicle. "I reckon there ain't too much left in here." As he said this, he noticed what looked like shards of glass from a broken jar on the floorboard. He immediately looked on the ground behind the vehicle. "What's this?" he asked, pointing to an elongated cinder stretching underneath the wreck.

"I figured it was probably a stick. You know, from one of these trees," the deputy said, sweeping his arm.

"A stick. Well, Deputy, if you were in my department, I'd suggest you bag it. Given the location, and the fact that it looks as much melted as it looks burned, I'd guess it was a piece of hose. Somebody must have syphoned gas out of this car to light it up. Did you notice the broken jar on the floorboard? They probably used a jar to splash some of the gas from the syphon into the car and tossed it in there with the last batch. I would imagine the glass broke in the heat of the flames."

"Well, I'll be," the deputy said. "You figure I should save those pieces of glass, too?"

Sheriff Steele smirked and said, "What do you think? Have your boss call me when he finalizes this investigation. I'll try to find Percival Jenkins. Maybe his car was stolen."

On their way back to Huntsville, Steele and Adams sat in stony silence except for one comment the sheriff made as they reentered Walker County.

"I hope you learned a little something about how *not* to work a crime scene."

Huntsville, Texas—10:30 a.m.

Alvin McIntyre sat alone in his darkened office contemplating the events of the past week. All he had wanted to do was add a little smear to the reputation of his opponent. Now, four people were dead, possibly five. When he first started in this office, he had entertained high ideals, wanting to pursue justice, but now he wished he'd never debased himself with the lure of easy money. Somehow along the way, a single offered financial incentive from the Maceos proved to be a temptress that embraced his soul and, as he found, once you dip your hat into that well and taste that sweet elixir, you find yourself returning to it again and again. It is what gave him a nice car and afforded him the luxury of giving his family a summer in Galveston.

He stood and contemplated the pecan tree right outside his window. Several green sheaths surrounded nuts that were growing almost an arm's length away. He dropped his head and faintly said, "What's done is done."

He worked the fingers on his left hand to fight a lingering numbness he'd been experiencing all morning. "Must have hit my funny bone," he guessed.

A flash of lightning and sudden crack of thunder startled him, then he heard a knock on the outer door. He didn't expect anyone here on a Sunday, and in fact he had come to the office so he wouldn't be disturbed. He opened the door a crack and saw the sullen face of Special Ranger Givens.

"Do you know it's Sunday?" McIntyre asked.

"I didn't find you at your house, so I took a chance on finding you here. We have to talk."

"Did you find Betty Johnston and Fred Darby?"

"No, they were gone by the time I got there."

"Left?"

"Apparently. Looks like they were in a hurry, too. Funny thing, though, Fred Darby's car was at Miss Johnston's bungalow. Near as I can tell, they had no car with them up at that travel court."

"That's odd. Perhaps they had a confidante helping them."

"Well, that's certainly one theory, but we found a few things that were very peculiar. Like, it looks like she left all her makeup."

McIntyre shook his head. "Women can always buy more makeup. In fact, my wife has makeup she hasn't used in years because there's always some newfangled thing they want to buy."

"It's still odd. Another thing, I followed up on Darby's car. A witness saw it heading to one of the little oxbow lakes dotting the

Trinity around Riverside. I took a look and found the charred remnants of clothing out there."

"Unless we can tie the clothing to them, or perhaps to Swanger, that's nothing in the way of solid evidence of...well, of anything."

"I wonder. Have either of those two ever been associated with an ice pick?"

McIntyre's heart began to race. "Ice pick? That's an odd thing to ask."

"Well, the doc speculated early on that the wounds on Swanger's body were made by an ice pick."

"But the sheriff insists they were made by nails from the bridge, when the car broke through the rails."

"Mr. McIntyre, I've seen the nails they use on those rails, and I've seen the wounds."

"Just what are you getting at?"

"I found an ice pick floating in that lake. Right up close to the shoreline."

"Floating?"

"Bobbing like a tiny apple."

"Do you have it with you?"

"I have it out in my car, along with what charred remnants I could salvage out of the ashes. I was going to turn them over to Sheriff Steele when he returns. He's apparently out on some kind of call. The deputy said it was a vehicle fire."

"*Another* fire? All right. I'll discuss it with him after he's reviewed what you found. Unless you want to leave that evidence with me."

"I'd feel better if he saw it first. I'm going to drop by my hotel on the way over there and perhaps grab a bite to eat."

"You've been very busy these past few days. It's Sunday, you should relax."

"Relax?" Givens gravely said. "Texas Rangers are rarely given an opportunity to relax."

McIntyre locked the door as soon as Givens left and returned to his desk. His head felt as if it were about to explode, and he massaged his temples. His gaze fell on the desk drawer where he had hidden Betty Johnston's file. His thoughts then turned to his conversation with Hemmings LeBlanc and for a moment, he wished he had pushed harder on the subject of Givens. Then the Ranger might have been nudged out of the way.

He began to sob. "I've become the same kind of monster I'm expected to prosecute."

A slight twinge in his chest accompanied his headache and the numbness in his hand extended up his forearm. He flexed his fingers several times, then decided what he needed to do was go home and try to get some sleep.

Huntsville, Texas—11:10 a.m.

The hotel clerk waved at the Ranger as he walked through the lobby. "Mr. Givens? There's a telegram for you, sir."

As he lowered his head and read it, Givens' eyes widened, then he folded the paper and stowed it in a pocket inside his coat.

"Trouble, sir?"

"Just business. Can I check out right away?"

"Sir? Of course. But I have to charge you for today."

"Listen, I am working on official business for the State of Texas. I've hardly even slept in that room. Even slept in my car up in Trinity last night while working my investigation. Look, I'll pay you through last night. If you want any more, you take it up with my captain."

The clerk swallowed hard. "I'll make up your bill right away."

Givens packed quickly, paid his bill, and threw his bag into the back of his car. He drove to the sheriff's office and carried his manila envelopes inside. Sheriff Steele was still gone, so Givens wrote hasty notes on the outside of the envelopes and left them with a deputy. They explained where he found the items and under what circumstances.

He said to the deputy, "You tell the sheriff that Betty Johnston and Fred Darby are missing, and he should pursue finding them." He pointed to the envelopes. "I think these are related to those two, or perhaps to their disappearance. I'll try to come back, but I have no idea when. I've been called away to a situation up in Shamrock."

"Oh, I heard there was some sort of Negro trouble up there. Must be worse than I thought if they're sending a Ranger up there."

"Four of us," Givens said. "It most likely means the trouble is being caused by white folks intent on lynching."

The deputy whistled under his breath.

Huntsville, Texas—1:15 p.m.

Sheriff Steele knocked hard and kept knocking until Alvin McIntyre finally appeared, somewhat disheveled as if he'd been asleep.

"Nathan? It's Sunday!" McIntyre's bloodshot eyes further enhanced a sour milk pallor painted across his face.

"Sorry if you're feeling poorly, Alvin, but I assumed you'd want to know what's going on."

"What now?"

"Your man Jenkins' car was found this morning in San Jacinto County, burned to a crisp.

"Where is Jenkins?"

"Nobody's seen him. I'm going to the office now to coordinate a search for him locally, and I'll follow-up with their sheriff and suggest they take a look in the forest around that spot. I said as much on the scene to the deputy working it, but he seemed a bit wet behind the ears.

"Perhaps the engine caught fire."

"No chance of that. I found a charred siphon hose right outside the gas filler. That usually indicates a case of arson."

"I see."

"So, you don't know why he might be out in a remote area like that?"

"It's the weekend, Nathan. What my man does on his own time is of no concern to me."

The sheriff began to walk to his car, then turned and said, "Well, I just thought you'd want to know."

"I appreciate it. Thank you. Now, if you don't mind, I will continue my nap," he said, closing the door with an abrupt thump.

Steele returned to his car where Deputy Adams had been waiting for him. "Has he heard from Mr. Jenkins?"

"No," Steele said as he put the car in gear, gravely adding, "and he didn't act very surprised either."

"What do you mean, Sheriff?"

"Adams, when you've worked in law enforcement for a bit longer, you'll acquire a sort of extra sense — sometimes you just know when people are lying. It's up to you to realize it at the time, but not acknowledge it. You have to give your suspicion an opportunity to develop, but once you've picked up on that notion, it is a good place to start."

"But, well, I mean, Mr. McIntyre—he's the District Attorney."

Sheriff Steele made his way to his office. "I know. I can't quite figure it out," he lied. "It's why we need to bide our time. Keep this conversation under your hat, you hear me? Tell no one."

"I will, I promise." Adams slouched down in his seat and looked straight ahead.

A black sedan pulled behind the sheriff's car as he parked, followed by two quick beeps of the horn. He turned and squinted to see who was inside and recognized Ranger Givens. He got out and walked to the open window.

Givens said, "Glad I caught you, Sheriff. I found some interesting items up at an oxbow lake on this side of Trinity.

"Were they in Walker County?"

"We checked on the map and they looked to be just inside your county line. I suspect they are related to Darby and Miss Johnston. It's your case, so I left them inside. I hope to be back in a few days to discuss them with you."

"Not now?"

"No, I'm afraid I'm headed up to Shamrock. Seems some of the locals are causing trouble up there with the Negro populace."

"Shamrock?" Steele shook his head. "I read something about that in the paper. A white woman was killed across the state line in Erick, Oklahoma. That's a long way from here. What's going on, another Tulsa?"

"It's smaller than Tulsa. Shamrock is just a bump in the road, so I'd just say it is pure foolishness. Those poor Negroes have nothing to do with the case; the whites are just looking for revenge."

"But if this Negro…"

"Sheriff, I've seen situations like this before. Most likely that boy didn't kill anybody. It's not my case, but the first place I'd look is at the danged husband. Easiest thing to do is kill somebody you don't like and point the blame at some poor Negro. Case closed in most people's minds. They believe what they want to believe."

Sheriff Steele scratched his chin. "Well, you may have something there, but popular opinion is a hard thing to fight. Now about these things you found."

"Burned remnants of clothing, a couple of charred shoe buckles, and an ice pick. A car like Fred Darby's was seen heading to an abandoned fishing spot a few days ago, and that's where I found them. I left a note that should be able to lead you to the spot."

"And you think…"

Givens looked straight ahead. "I don't know what to think. Darby and Miss Johnston are both missing."

"Missing? They left?"

"That's for the Trinity County sheriff to figure out." Givens sighed. "Which means we'll probably never know. I have to tell you I don't have a lot of faith in his department. I wish I could stay on this case, but I have a long way to go, and we're burning daylight already. Good day, Sheriff."

Steele rubbed the sweat from his eyes. "I guess I had better tell McIntyre. I was just up at his place, too."

"He already knows about them."

"He does?"

"I told him. Why were you there?"

"To tell him about his assistant's car. It was found in San Jacinto County. Somebody torched it. Odd he didn't mention what you found."

Givens shook his head and inhaled through his teeth so hard he almost whistled. "It is, but he didn't look well."

"Yeah, I think I woke him up. Probably just slipped his mind."

"I really hate to leave you in the middle of my investigation, Sheriff, but the governor doesn't want another lynching, so I had better get a move on.

"Be careful up there."

"I will, good luck with the rest of this," he said, before gunning his engine and driving off.

Inside the station, Sheriff Steele asked, "Did that Texas Ranger drop something off for me?"

"The envelopes are on your desk, Sheriff. He told me to tell..."

The sheriff interrupted, "I just spoke to him. Thank you. Did anyone look through them?"

"No, sir, he said they were for you."

Steele closed the office door and opened the three manila envelopes. He carefully extracted the bulkiest item.

"Ice pick," he whispered.

He remembered the doctor first mentioning an ice pick as the likely weapon used on Swanger. McIntyre's insistence on a quick closure of the case had spurred him to seize on the nails as the cause of death. He put the pick back into the envelope and looked in another envelope.

His throat was parched and his voice cracked, but he managed to croak out, "Buckles from a lady's shoe." He peeked in the third and saw the splashes of color amidst the scorched remnants. "Nobody burns clothes unless they have something to hide," he muttered.

A newspaper was also sitting on his desk. He scanned the headlines and found a new article about Earl Swanger. Someone had leaked the woman's latest outlandish story. It differed a great deal from what she said the first time he interviewed her. This account cast Earl Swanger in a bad light and Steele could feel internal sinews tying themselves into taut knots in the pit of his stomach.

He stood deep in thought at the open window, trying to figure a way out of this mess. He went back to his desk and looked through the items in the envelopes again.

"I think I'll just file these away unless McIntyre mentions them," he said.

Givens had scribbled some notes on the outside. He remembered he had a supply of those same types of envelopes in his desk drawer and pulled one out. He emptied all the items into one fresh envelope, then folded up the originals tightly and dropped them in the trash. He placed the new, unmarked envelope in the back of his least-used filing cabinet. He never wanted to be accused of destroying evidence, but he wanted those things hidden so no one could ever tie them to any of his cases.

"I'll let it stand as an accident," he murmured. "It's best all around." *After all,* he mused, *I have my own election to think about.* Even unopposed, a bad outcome in a case like this never looked good.

Inwardly, he hoped the Ranger was gone for good. "They are shorthanded and overworked. After that mess up in Shamrock, he'll likely be pushed onto something else before he ever thinks about this case again."

He swallowed hard. "I hope so, anyway."

Huntsville, Texas—1:25 p.m.

Claude made his way through the woods to the Swanger residence. He was bound by his word and, although he'd say he was there to water the garden, his true intention was to look in on Miss Lily May. Evie had another one of her odd dreams the night before, and she woke up with a deep sense of dread and shook him to tell him about it. He shivered after she told him, as if he expected something evil to pop out of the shadows and accost him.

When he arrived at the house, he began to stretch the hose to the garden. Seedlings from a stand of radishes he'd planted had appeared. He always marveled at how quickly they grew and matured. Most garden crops took months, but radishes gave quick rewards. He used his thumb over the end of the hose to direct the spray over them, before running the flow down each row.

"You've done mighty fine work with that garden, Claude."

Startled, he spun to see Miss Lily May, still clad in black. Then he relaxed his shoulders and answered with a meek, "Yes'm."

"I didn't mean to scare you. But I did want to tell you that I'm sure Mr. Swanger would say you've repaid him many times over."

"I'm not rightly sure about that."

"Well, I am. What I want to say is that this may no longer be necessary. I'll be burying Mr. Swanger later this week in Marquez, and I mean to move back there. With him gone, there's no reason for me to stay here. I appreciate you helping with the garden and porch. And I am quite grateful for Miss Evie's offer of help."

"She's planning on coming by later today after she finishes at the Lieberman's. She always goes over there after church to cook them a Sunday dinner. Moving can be quite a chore, don't you need help with that?"

"Well, now that you mention it, I probably could use a little help cleaning. I won't move out of a house and leave it a mess. But I'm not sure I can pay you."

"Miss Lily May, I can't explain to you how I feel about things right now, but Mister Buddie, he was one of the kindest souls I ever met. I feel like he would want me to give you whatever help I could, and I aim to do that very thing. Evie too."

"You're a good man, Claude."

"I tries, ma'am, I really tries. Well, I had better turn off the water, that garden's got enough now to last two days. I'll fetch Evie over this afternoon and we'll get to work."

Lily May smiled at Claude, who turned his attention back to the garden. She had disappeared into the house by the time he had coiled the hose and deposited it by the faucet. He went back into the woods to find the back path to the Lieberman's. He found his usual spot, a downed tree, where he sometimes sat and waited for Evie to finish her work. He didn't like her walking through these woods by herself and joined her whenever he could. He lowered his head in thought as he waited, until he softly snored.

A hand gently shook his shoulder and a voice penetrated the mist, "Claude?"

He opened his eyes and at first thought he saw an angel's face framed by the glare of the sun.

"Evie?"

"Of course, it's Evie, fool. Who else you expecting out here?"

"Must have dozed off. Come on, let's go. Miss Lily May's expecting us."

Claude held her hand as they walked.

"Might be more work for us over there than we first thought—she's fixing to move."

"Move? Where she moving to."

223

"Marquez. I think she's got people there." Claude squeezed Evie's hand a little tighter. "Might change some stuff for us, too."

"What you mean?"

"I promised Mister Buddie that I'd look after her. I figure that don't change if she moves."

Evie stopped and turned to Claude. "You mean to tell me you want me to move to Marquez? What are we going to do there?"

"We'll find us something. We always do. Living in one place is pretty near the same thing as living in any other place."

"Claude Davidson, I think you're crazy, but I love you." She tilted her head up and kissed him. "And far be it from me to keep anybody from going back on a promise to a dying man. That's about as sacred a oath as any. Sacreder than most, I expect."

When they arrived at the Swanger house, they saw Lily May and Pearl struggling to drag a rolled-up carpet to the wash line. Claude stepped in and hoisted it to his shoulder. He and Evie unrolled it and folded it over the line.

Pearl appeared with two carpet beaters.

"If you moving, why you cleaning this carpet?" Claude asked.

Evie spoke up, "Whether you're leaving it or moving it with you, you want it clean." She shook her head as she exchanged a look with the other two women. "These men," she said.

Pearl stifled a laugh, then added, "Yes, it's staying but we want to leave the house spotless."

Claude took the beaters and handed one to Evie, saying, "Miss Pearl, you go on back in the house. We going to beat the living daylights out of this thing."

In a moment, clouds of dust were billowing across the yard, momentarily obscuring the almost hidden outline of a figure crouched in the underbrush.

Huntsville, Texas—1:25 p.m.

When Hemmings LeBlanc returned to Huntsville, he discreetly asked around until he found out that his next victim's wife worked as a maid for one of the local families. He spent the morning watching the house and followed her when she left. As he had hoped, she led him directly to Claude Davidson. He planned to continue his stalking until he could get Claude alone, so he crept through the underbrush at a distance while they made their way back toward town. Their route confused him, because he had been told their home was some distance in another direction, but when they reached another house and began to work, he surmised they had a side job. He settled in and watched. He was exhausted, but he kept his vigil. He caught himself falling asleep a couple of times, but he'd wake and realize it had just been a few moments at most. The afternoon wore on, and he knew they'd soon head back home. As soon as he knew where the house was, he hoped he could allow himself a nap before setting up his ambush.

He could tell that Claude was large, but Hemmings had faith in his own strength combined with his experience. He simply needed to wait for the proper time to catch the big man alone and unaware, then he'd make his move. He daydreamed about his planned festivities in New Orleans as he watched and waited.

Huntsville, Texas—5:45 p.m.

What had been intended as a short visit turned into a long afternoon of household tasks. He and Evie made good on their offer to help Miss Lily May prepare for her move and, by the time the sun hung low in the sky, the two women shooed them away, insisting they go home and rest. Claude and Evie wearily made their way back to their house, meandering down the familiar footpaths. At one point, Claude stopped.

"You hear something?" He looked all around, eyes and ears at the ready like a cat's.

"There's always something scratching around out in these woods. Probably just a skunk."

"You might be right," he said, as he resumed walking with Evie close behind.

They emerged into a clearing beyond their house, and she stood admiring the warm shadows of dusk that cast the small frame building in a mix of muted shadows.

She caught up to Claude and looked up at him. "I'm gonna miss this place. I like it here, but if you're dead set on us moving, I expect we'll need to start packing."

"Yeah, we got a lot of work to do, but I got something else to take care of first."

She had reached the porch and turned to meet Claude face-to-face. "What you talking about?"

"With all that trouble with Mister Buddie and all, I never finished busting up my still. I promised him. It's sitting out there in pieces."

"Leave it be, it'll rust to nothing in no time. We've got a mess of work to do. Besides, it's getting on to dark."

"It won't take me too long and I almost always go out there in the dark anyway. I promised him, Evie."

"Land sakes, you and your promises. Don't forget, you promised to be a good husband to me, too."

Claude looked sheepishly down at his feet. "Ain't I been?" He reached out and took her hand in his. "I've tried. But this is important, you got to understand."

Evie squeezed the big fingers. "Okay, go on, but be careful. You be sure to get back here in one piece."

Claude nodded and kissed her, but she broke it off and pointed. "You see that?"

He turned and saw what looked like a dirty, yellow dog watching them from the edge of the trees. He looked down and saw his dog sound asleep on the porch.

"Ain't ours, I'm going to shoo it away," he said. He started toward it, but Evie put a hand on his shoulder.

"Leave it be."

"Why?" Then he looked again and it was gone.

"Ghost dog," she said. "Most likely means something bad is coming our way. Don't forget that last dream of mine."

"Oh, it was likely just some stray," he said before heading down the path to Harmon Creek.

Evie called back to him. "I mean it, Claude. It's an omen. You be careful!"

"You know me," he said. "I'll be extra careful."

He had walked through these woods at night hundreds of times, but as he made his way down the trail, he sensed something different. He was a big man and he made a certain amount of noise as he pushed through the brush, even when he tried not to. But his ears were used to the sounds of this thicket and they detected the hint of something slightly different.

He stopped and listened, but could only hear crickets and the distinctive 'who cooks for you, who cooks for you all' hoot of a barred owl from some unseen perch hundreds of feet away. He resumed walking, treading more slowly, and began to imagine he could hear echoes of his footsteps. His heart thumped harder the farther he went. He knew he was getting close to the still and slowed to better see where the trail broke off to the left.

Claude stopped cold when he heard a distinct *snap* close-by. He slowly twisted his head back and forth, listening intently while he stealthily pulled his daddy's four-inch pocket knife out and opened it. He couldn't even touch it without thinking back to his childhood when he had cherished the weathered ivory handle with undecipherable scrimshaw carvings. He held it so the blade rested on the inside of his wrist and took one more step.

A voice with a peculiar hint of Louisiana broke the silence. "That's far enough."

Claude felt something hard poke at his back through his overalls.

"What you want?"

"Turn around."

He slowly rotated his body, crooking his head around to get a first glimpse of the interloper. He faced a man a full head shorter than he was. He tried hard to make out the features, but the voice created a chill like a piece of hard ice, and the darkened face spoke again from its shadow existence. "You Davidson?"

Claude stared down and said nothing.

"Well, no matter, I *know* you are Claude Davidson."

Claude had played enough poker in his life to know when to hold his cards close. He gingerly fingered the handle of his knife like he was palming a hidden ace of spades.

"Where you going out here all alone in the dark? You got a lady friend? Naw, I seen you kiss your woman. I've followed enough cheaters in my life to know a man rarely kisses his wife good-bye like that if he is traipsing off to another's arms."

Claude continued his blank stare. "That what this about? You after my woman?"

A shrill laugh cackled through the dark. "No, this is much worse than that. I do think I heard something about a still. You got a still up here, boy?"

The word did what it was designed to do, it cut a hole in his soul, and rage began to seep through the cut.

"That what you want? My still?"

The face laughed. "No, I don't need no still. Seems somebody wants you dead. Maybe that's why. Maybe *they* want your still."

Now Claude was the one who laughed. "Who'd want me dead? I ain't never done nothing to nobody, ever."

"I never ask too many questions when someone pays me to do a job. Ain't my place to make any judgment. Then again, I don't usually talk to the people I kill, but you've been a hard man for me to nail down, so I expect it don't matter much if I tell you, since you aren't going to be in any condition to repeat it. Besides, it feels good to talk openly once in a while. Fella by the name of McIntyre hired me. I don't know much of what it's about, it's not really any of my business, but he hired me to take care of five people around here. You're the last one on my list. Well, except maybe for some lawyer's widow."

The small gun was still pointed at Claude's chest, and he could tell the man's shoulders were tightening. Claude moved fast for a big man. He always had. Evie would sometimes be amazed if he accidentally knocked a glass off a table and he'd snatch it in mid-air. Seven out of ten times he managed to catch it, but the other three times he'd usually get a good piece of it. At the mention of McIntyre's name, he knew he had only one chance to continue living. But the mention of someone who could only be Lily May was too much for him and he snapped.

He struck out at the gun with a broad forearm, knocking it up and away. The gun was airborne by the time the inevitable shot echoed through the trees.

Claude could almost feel wrath seeping out of the man's pores as flailing arms grabbed at him and Claude shoved him back. The man was strong for his size, with steel spring fingers that clutched at Claude's neck, but after they had grappled for a few seconds, the bigger man could tell he had the edge in strength. He hated the thought of using his daddy's knife against a man, but he knew he might have little choice in the matter and the implied danger to Lily May had sealed the stranger's fate. He seized the interloper by the throat and lifted him off the ground with his left hand. As he gripped tight, he heard tiny cracks as the man struggled against his grip. He looked the smaller man in the eyes, then thrust upwards with his knife hand, hitting him at a spot just below where he knew the two sides of the rib cage protected his assailant's heart.

He dropped his foe and the man backpedaled, clutching at the wound. The look of shock and horror on his face unnerved Claude, but this was quickly replaced by a new wave of anger as he again lurched forward and bloody hands reached for the bigger man's neck. Claude brought his knife up, dead center into the base of the man's throat in one quick thrust, and the man dropped at his feet like a sack of seed corn.

It had taken a few seconds for the pain in his shoulder to register, but a searing sting made him realize the shot must have hit him. He was still holding the knife in front of him as he watched the man clutching at his neck, gagging and coughing. Claude was thankful he didn't see the gun, so he assumed it was lost in the dense foliage surrounding them. He felt around his shoulder but there was no hole, just a pain, and he assumed he'd been grazed.

"Guess you got paid for nothing. Who the hell are you anyway?"

The man writhed back and forth at his feet, and managed a blood sputtered, "Hemmings Le..." before dissolving into unconsciousness. Unsettling gagging and gurgling sounds continued for a few minutes, then the body stopped twitching. Claude lowered his head and said a silent prayer.

He reoriented himself with his trail and began dragging the body the rest of the way toward his still. After taking three steps, he felt something hard under his shoe and reached down. It was the gun, so he picked it up and put it in his pocket.

He found his work site just as he had left it that other fateful night and proceeded to examine the body of his attacker. Claude reckoned it would just fit into the boiler if he folded it up enough.

"Can't leave him out here, that's for sure. What kind of name is Hemmings anyway?"

He turned the boiler on its side, removed the top, and shoved the body in head first. He twisted, turned, and folded the limbs and torso to maneuver it into the confined space.

"Good thing this fellow's small," he said, as he grunted from the exertion.

He heard several bones crack in response to his efforts, but finally he reattached the top as best as he could.

"Would have been tough if he'd already stiffened up."

He used a hammer and a rusty screwdriver to poke several holes on all sides of the drum. Claude's mind raced as he worked. The moment he had heard the man mention Lily May it was like he'd become a rabid dog inside. He knew that if this hired killer threatened him and Buddie's wife, Evie was likely also in danger, and he couldn't live with anything like that. Then it all seemed to fit together as cleanly as a dovetail joint. He reasoned that the people who had killed Buddie likely had some connection to that district attorney, as did this Hemmings fellow. He'd heard the rumors about local connections to the Galveston bosses and beyond and had himself been arrested and pressured due to those same connections, so it was simple enough to grasp the truth— McIntyre and the people he was tied to were capable of anything.

"I know one thing, there ain't no more question about it, we moving for sure," he said to himself as he began rolling the boiler down toward the creek. Lightning flashed upstream and, as the thunder boomed over him, he remarked, "Storm's coming. I hopes it's a real big one."

There had been summer thunderstorms almost every day, so the creek was up. He pushed the boiler ahead of him toward what he remembered was a deep hole.

"Caught me some big fish there," he reminisced.

The boiler lingered for a few minutes and then bubbled below the surface, thanks to the holes Claude had knocked into it.

The interval between flashes and thunder was shorter now. Claude studied the sky and walked about forty yards farther upstream and threw the gun and knife into another deep hole. "I'm using up all my best spots," he said and lowered his head. "Sorry, Daddy, that knife is the last thing I have that was yours, but it's for the best."

He walked back to the clearing and gathered up the final remnants of his operation and returned to the creek. He threw every piece into the water. A bright flash quickly followed by a loud crack of thunder hurried him on his way.

The rain came down in thick sheets, drenching him as he returned the way he had come. It managed to wash away all traces of the struggle from his body and clothes. All that remained was a lingering stain of guilt.

Evie was standing on the porch looking for him as he approached the house.

"Claude, you is soaked to the bone. Did you at least take care of it for good this time?"

"I took care of everything," he said.

She smirked from her protected spot. "You could have saved yourself the trouble, this rain's gonna flood that creek. Everything around it is going to wash on down to the river."

He blinked the rain from his eyes and decided this was one secret he'd take to his grave. "Good, I want everything up there long gone from my life," he said.

She moved toward the door. "You get out of them wet things, and I'll get you some dry clothes."

He stripped and followed her into the lighted warmth of their home.

Twelve

Monday, July 14, 1930

Huntsville, Texas—8:30 a.m.

Early Monday morning, Sheriff Steele cornered McIntyre at the courthouse. "Any word from your man Jenkins?"

"No, and I must say I am very worried. He's an industrious young man, and I depend on him to handle many of the things I don't have time for. What have you found out?"

"Well, San Jacinto County hasn't come up with anything new. They checked the area for about a half mile around the car and found nothing. We took a look around his room, but all was in order there. He hadn't packed or anything. It looked like he planned to return."

"Well, keep me informed. I'll see if I can contact his family and see if they've heard anything."

"We've already done that. They have no idea where he is."

As he talked, Nathan Steele tried to discern a hint of anything telling in McIntyre's composure.

McIntyre continued, "It's totally out of character, though, I'll tell you that. I wonder if those two up in Trinity have any connection to this—you don't think they took him with them, do you? I know he had to lean on them pretty hard to get them to stay put, maybe they kidnapped him to get him out of the way."

"Well, I checked around for stolen cars, and came up empty.

"What do stolen cars have to do with this?"

"They clearly didn't take Fred Darby's car, and Jenkins' car is burned. If they left and took him with them, they'd need transportation. At this point, I guess anything is possible." The sheriff turned to leave. "I'll let you know if we find something."

Once outside the courthouse, Steele replaced his hat and walked around downtown, greeting people he passed. He was cordial, but inwardly he was troubled. There was something fundamentally wrong with this entire situation, and it had soured him on his job. McIntyre had dirt on him, so he knew he had to play along. But he had plenty on McIntyre as well. He was also confused why McIntyre hadn't mentioned the Ranger's evidence and decided to keep the items hidden. He thought about Jenkins again, then Betty Johnston and Fred Darby, then he came to a stark realization as a final image of Earl Swanger entered his mind. His inner cop instinct told him that everything was related and the last three would likely never be found. The thought gave him a deep chill and he shivered despite the hot July sun.

Sheriff Nathan Steele returned to his office and closed the door, then reached far back into the bottom drawer of his desk and extracted a bottle of Canadian whiskey he had confiscated from a raid a year earlier. He opened it and took a long, lingering drink, then sealed it up tight and put it away. He leaned back in his chair, put his feet on his desk, and wished he were a beat cop in Houston or Dallas. "Anything would be better than this," he said to himself.

Thirteen

Friday, July 18, 1930

Marquez, Texas—10:00 a.m.

A lingering weak tropical storm had resulted in a persistent rain. Will Hollis removed his hat and looked at the overcast sky as he said, "Dreary day to put someone to rest."

Pearl clutched her husband's arm and added, "Most every funeral I've ever been to has been dreary, but at least it's a bit cooler than it has been."

The crowd was immense by Marquez standards, and many folks had come from surrounding areas to pay their respects.

"That brother of yours was certainly well-liked."

Pearl's eyes watered. "By all who knew him."

"Surprised to see some coloreds watching. Should I tell them to move on?"

Lily May had been quiet up to this point as she sat next to them, still staring at the coffin, but she looked up when she heard this. "Don't you dare. Buddie proudly served *everyone* in his community, black and white. Those folks are friends. That's Claude and his wife Evie. And that's their preacher next to them, along with some of his congregation. Buddie's helped them all in one way or another. They are welcome guests."

"Oh, of course, Pearl said they've been helping you get ready to move back down here."

"That's right. Claude thought the world of Buddie and back in Huntsville, he seemed intent on making my wellbeing his special project."

After the services concluded, everyone retired to Laura's big house for a reception. Claude and Evie lingered outside with Preacher Davis and several others, whispering together. Claude intermittently glanced up at the house with a soulful expression on his face. The rain had stopped but the humidity remained.

Pearl looked out the window and remarked, "I don't feel right that Claude and the others are standing out there. We have plenty of food, more than we'll ever be able to eat. I'm going to ask them in." A few guests showed mild shock at this suggestion so she added, "It's what Buddie would have wanted."

Lily May spoke up. "It's exactly what he would have wanted."

She stood and made her way outside and down the steps and called out, "Claude and Evie?"

He looked up and saw Lily May beckoning to them, and they timidly approached. "Yes'm?"

She could see that his face was wet with tears. "Claude, y'all come in and get yourselves a bite to eat." She took him by the hand. "You stood by me and Buddie and I think he'd want all of you to feel welcome here." Lily May led him up the steps.

He stopped. "I don't much think those folks would want us in there, Miss Lily May." Evie lingered in Claude's shadow.

"Nonsense. There's plenty of food. You should eat before you go back to Huntsville. You've been such a help, I will surely miss you."

"Ma'am?"

"You're going back to Huntsville tonight, aren't you?"

Evie and Claude looked at each other before he responded. "Well, yes, we going tonight, but soon we'll be moving just over yonder." He pointed. "Next to them woods."

"That old place? It's been empty since Silas Fremont died ten years ago."

"It's still sturdy, it has a good solid backbone. I reckon I can fix it up." He felt the railing next to the steps. A wobble was slight but noticeable. "I can fix up things around here, too."

"Now, really. You don't need to leave your life back there for me."

"Our life back there isn't much good nor bad. It's just living. We can do that here just as well as back there. I've been asking around...folks hereabouts need a hard worker who's handy at fixing things, and I think I can make a living at it. And folks always need help with their housework and cooking, and Evie here is the best there is."

Lily May smiled. "Well, come in and eat. You must be famished."

They stepped into the big room and conversation momentarily stopped. The stares were obvious, as the entourage, led by Lily May, made their way to the food table.

"Everyone, Claude and Evie were special friends of Buddie's and I'm beholden to them myself." She pointed at the rest of the group that followed. "This is Preacher Davis and some other members of his congregation. Buddie did some legal work for their church as well. Now you all go back to your talking."

Claude leaned in and whispered, "If it's the same to you, we'll grab ourselves a few tidbits and mosey out to the steps and eat out there. It's powerful warm in here anyway."

She took his arm. "Try some of this ham a neighbor brought. It's quite good. And those biscuits Buddie's sister made are heavenly."

Fourteen

Wednesday, July 30, 1930

Huntsville, Texas—8:05 a.m.

McIntyre gulped hard when he recognized the voice on the other end of the phone line.

"Our friends in New Orleans say their man is missing. Did he do what you paid him to do?"

"I can only assume so."

There was a pause, then another question. "Did you give him any side jobs?"

McIntyre gulped again and lied. "No, just the one you requested."

"We've got people looking for him. So does New Orleans and Dallas. Call us immediately if he shows up for any reason. Oh, and congratulations on your reelection."

"Uh, er, thank you," he said.

The voice responded curtly. "We need to lay low until we figure out what happened to him. We'll be in touch."

McIntyre replaced the earpiece and sat back. He knew three of the intended victims were taken care of, but not the last two. "LeBlanc probably skipped town and kept the money. Good riddance. I heard the other two are leaving the area for good anyway."

238

Fifteen

Tuesday, August 5, 1930

Huntsville, Texas—8:05 a.m.

McIntyre sat down across from Sheriff Steele at the café. "I thought I saw you come in here. I haven't seen you in a few weeks."

"Between the primary and everyday general law enforcement, I've been busy, Alvin."

"Have you turned up anything more about Earl Swanger's death?"

Steele put his fork down as he slowly chewed his potatoes. He stared at McIntyre during this mastication before he swallowed. "If I had, you'd have been the first to know." He narrowed his eyes. "I would have thought that you'd be more interested in your assistant, Jenkins."

"Of course, how is that case coming?"

"He's disappeared without a trace except for his car. Same with that man and woman who claimed to be mixed up with Swanger right before his death. Vamoosed. Really odd, too, since those two were the last ones to see Swanger alive."

"That *is* odd."

"Even stranger, your man Jenkins was the one who was supposed to be keeping them safe. He was the one who put them in that travel court. It's just a gut feeling, but I think those three disappearances are related."

"The Johnston woman and Fred Darby were known criminals. They probably fled to Mexico."

Steele motioned with his cup for more coffee. "Maybe, and maybe they decided to do Jenkins in before they left."

"Do you think that is possible?"

"If he threatened them, it is. Or maybe those three had some other angle they were working when they got mixed up in this, and they all left together."

"And Jenkins' car?"

"It could be a ruse to throw us off. Anyway, there's been nothing new and, unless any one of those three pops up somewhere, we are stuck with the original determination that Swanger's death was an accident." Steele raised one side of his mouth in a sneer. "Anyway, you won your primary by default, although he got a surprising number of votes for a dead man. I guess the word didn't quite get out."

McIntyre's face flushed. "At least the news stories about the case have died away. Well, as far as the election goes, I'm sure I would have prevailed in any case."

Steele rubbed his tongue across the front of his teeth, making a slight sucking sound as he did this. "I'm not so sure."

"I hope you're not insinuating..."

"I'm not insinuating anything, Alvin. Suppositions don't mean a thing in my line of work. But you need to understand this—from here on out, I won't have anything to do with your extracurricular activities."

McIntyre's face approached a new shade of scarlet. "Why, you, I'll..."

"What, get me thrown out of office? I'm elected, just like you. Sure, I can be removed, and you could engineer that, but for all the dirt you have on me you need to remember one little thing—I have just as much dirt on you, maybe more, and you can be removed from office as well." Steele leaned forward and continued in a hushed tone. "I don't really know what happened to Swanger, and nobody knows what happened to those three, but I think you were behind all of it. I have no proof, and likely never will, but I will not be a party to your shenanigans anymore. We have to see each other professionally, so I will be civil in public, but in private, I want nothing more to do with you. If *anybody* in my county breaks the law, I'll arrest them."

McIntyre stood and stomped out of the café without another word.

Steele cracked a sly smile, sipped at his coffee and flagged the waitress. "Check, please."

Sixteen

Saturday, August 9, 1930

Marquez, Texas–2:30 p.m.

Preacher Davis waved down at Evie from the cab of a small truck. Claude jumped out of the back as it squealed to a halt in front of the ramshackle house.

"This here is where you're going live now?"

Claude laughed. "It ain't much to look at now, but I'll fix it up all nice and proper. It's cheap, and we'll be able to keep an eye on Miss Lily May from here. She lives just yonder," he pointed, "through that copse of trees."

Evie stepped forward and grabbed an armful of belongings. "Thank you kindly, Preacher Davis, for helping line up Mr. Jameson and his truck."

Jameson waved from the truck bed. "Happy to help."

Preacher Davis stepped forward. "I hate to lose a God-fearing woman with such a good choir voice, but you've always been so obliging, I had to return in kind."

Jameson stood, shaded his eyes, and pointed. "Who's this coming?"

Evie looked up. "Why, it's Miss Lily May and Mister Buddie's sister, Pearl."

The two women approached, one carrying a basket and the other a huge jar with liquid sloshing against the sides.

Claude stepped off the porch. "Miss Lily May, what y'all doing walking way out here in this heat?"

"Now Claude, we heard your truck and thought you would surely like a little something to eat. These are Pearl's famous biscuits, and there's fresh butter and honey, and I made a jar of lemonade."

Preacher Davis stepped forward, taking the jar from Pearl's hands. "It's cold!"

Evie called out to Claude from the porch, "Where did you put my kitchen things?"

"Already in the kitchen waiting to be unpacked."

Evie ran into the house and emerged with a small stack of plates and some glasses. "Will y'all be joining us?"

Pearl responded, "We'll leave you to it, Miss Evie, but thank you kindly."

"We the ones be needing to thank you. This is very good of you."

Preacher Davis sniffed at the basket. "These biscuits smell really good."

Pearl said, "There's some slices of ham in the basket, too. You are all working so hard, you deserve a little break." She turned to Lily May. "We should leave these folks to their chores."

She and Lily May turned to leave and Claude called out, "Thank you kindly. I'll bring back your basket and such later."

"There's no hurry, Claude," Lily May said. "I'm sure I'll be seeing you soon enough."

Epilogue

Claude Davidson stood by as friend and protector to Lily May Swanger for the next thirty years, until he was too feeble to continue and he went to live with a daughter in San Antonio.

Lily May Swanger lived in the big house in Marquez for the rest of her life, finally passing away in 1972. She never remarried.

Nathan Steele served two more years as sheriff, but did not run for reelection. He applied to work for the Texas Rangers, but his application stalled when Governor "Ma" Fergusson disbanded the Rangers in a case of political revenge against the Ranger hierarchy, who supported her opponent in the 1932 election. He eventually moved to Houston where he became a police officer, just as he had once fantasized.

Alvin McIntyre's fortunes suffered as the Depression weakened the economy and certain mob associates became disenchanted with his fading influence with local police. His health declined over the next year, but his eventual death came not due to ill health, but through what was thought to be a mysterious accident. He was apparently electrocuted by a damaged cord when he plugged in a lamp in his office.

Timothy H. Givens was wounded during the incident in Shamrock, Texas when he was hit in the head by a brick thrown out of the white crowd that threatened the black segment of the town. He convalesced for over a year and returned to service only to be fired along with all the other Rangers by Governor Ma Fergusson. He died a few months later. The injury had affected some of his more recent memories. He never completed his report and never mentioned the case again.

Jimmy Bryant had depended on Earl Swanger to keep their law practice together. He fell onto hard times as the Depression grew. He never got over his best friend's death and died less than two years later. His was one of several local deaths tied to improperly distilled illegal spirits.

Earl "Buddie" Swanger was a real person, the great-uncle of the author's wife. He was a candidate for DA and died in July, 1930 in a one car accident adjacent to Harmon Creek. It was just over two weeks until the primary. The family was always suspicious of the death, which was officially ruled an accident, *less than two days* after his death. Their contention was that the incumbent was dirty, which was a major reason Earl was running against him. They felt strongly that his opponent was behind the death. Stab wounds were mentioned in early reports, but they were indeed "officially" attributed to nails from the bridge construction site.

Newspaper accounts from the time were quite active with various details of the incident in the days after the accident. After about two weeks, nothing more was ever mentioned in the papers, at least from what the author could find. Given how easily the earlier reports were to find, it seemed quite suspicious that the story abruptly dropped from sight. The mysterious woman's story did indeed change three times. She and her 'friend' were never named. Her final version implied philandering and drunkenness, but by all family accounts, these allegations were completely out of character for Earl Swanger.

This story is fiction, painted over the backdrop of these few details. The direct relatives are mentioned by name. The rest of the characters have been renamed. The author tried, through this fictional tale, to explain all of the questionable aspects found in the news stories and reconcile them with the family lore.

In the case of Claude, he was a real person as well. The author's wife remembers him as a handyman and a constant presence at her great-aunt Lily May's house in Marquez. She remembers his role, not as an employee in any regard, but as a trusted friend. In his memory, he was placed at the center of the events to help explain his long loyalty to Miss Lily May, a relationship that extended well over thirty years. Again, this fiction has been painted over the backdrop of reality.

Earl R. (Buddie) Swanger, 1894-1930

Meet Thomas Fenske

Thomas Fenske currently lives in North Carolina but he was born and raised in Texas, and his native Texan roots run deep.

He's braved long stretches of endless Texas highways in search of the best chicken-fried steak, chili, Texas BBQ, and Tex-Mex food. He's hiked west Texas mountains, canoed rapids on the Guadalupe River, suffered through waves of mosquitoes in The Big Thicket, and rafted the Rio Grande. He's blistered in the heat of the long Texas summers, endured hurricanes, ice storms, hail, wind, and floods. He has even ridden across ranchland looking for a lost "little doggie"...how many Texans can say they did that?

Why did he leave the Lone Star State? Well, one must do many strange things to better provide for a family.

He and his lovely wife of thirty-plus years currently share their home with a dog and nine cats. Somehow, he still manages to write amidst the chaos.

Works from the Pen of
Thomas Fenske

The Fever

In the late 1800s, Ben Sublett was already known for his secret gold mine in the far reaches of west Texas. When Ben died in 1892, it was thought his secret died with him. Eighty years later in a central Texas jail, a dying, homeless wino named "Slim" Longo whispered a long-held family secret to twenty year old Sam Milton.

A Curse That Bites Deep

After years of frustration and sacrifice, Sam Milton's life seems to be on track. In The Fever he got the girl, he found the mine, and he hopes he'll soon have the gold, but he forgot one minor detail: the curse and its ripples are affecting almost everyone around him.

Lucky Strike

A bitter, decades-old grudge surfaces with a vengeance in a small west Texas town.

Penumbra –

Reluctant treasure hunter Sam Milton and his girlfriend Smidgeon Toll find themselves immersed in the search for a missing man they have never met and end up on the trail of a cache of ancient gold in the desert southwest.

The Hag Rider

This Civil War memoir explores a fifteen-year-old cavalryman's transition to manhood, complicated by the spectral manipulations of a hoodoo witch sworn to protect him.

Harmon Creek –

When political candidate Earl Swanger ended up stabbed and dead next to a bridge in rural Texas it looked like a case of homicide, right? Then why was it ruled an accident within two days? This fictional account revisits the 1930 cold case and the possible skullduggery behind the coverup.